The Secret Keeper

Also by Susan Lewis

Fiction

A Class Apart
Dance While You Can
Stolen Beginnings
Darkest Longings
Obsession
Vengeance
Summer Madness
Last Resort
Wildfire
Cruel Venus
Strange Allure
The Mill House
A French Affair
Missing
Out of the Shadows
Lost Innocence
The Choice
Forgotten
Stolen
No Turning Back
Losing You
The Truth About You
Never Say Goodbye
Too Close to Home

No Place to Hide

Books that run in sequence
Chasing Dreams
Taking Chances

No Child of Mine
Don't Let Me Go
You Said Forever

*Series featuring Detective
Andee Lawrence*
Behind Closed Doors
The Girl Who Came Back
The Moment She Left
Hiding in Plain Sight
Believe In Me

*Series featuring Laurie Forbes
and Elliott Russell*
Silent Truths
Wicked Beauty
Intimate Strangers
The Hornbeam Tree

Memoirs
Just One More Day
One Day at a Time

Susan Lewis

The Secret Keeper

CENTURY

1 3 5 7 9 10 8 6 4 2

Century
20 Vauxhall Bridge Road
London SW1V 2SA

Century is part of the Penguin Random House group of companies whose
addresses can be found at global.penguinrandomhouse.com.

Penguin
Random House
UK

First published in Great Britain by Century in 2018

www.penguin.co.uk

A CIP catalogue record for this book is available from the British Library.

ISBN 9781780896106 (Hardback)
ISBN 9781780896113 (Trade Paperback)
ISBN 9781473537699 (ebook)

Typeset in 13/16.5 pt Palatino LT Std
by Integra Software Services Pvt. Ltd, Pondicherry

Printed and bound in Great Britain by Clays Ltd, Elcograf S.p.A.

Penguin Random House is committed to a sustainable future for our
business, our readers and our planet. This book is made from
Forest Stewardship Council® certified paper.

Chapter One

OLIVIA. I was sixteen when Sean Kenyon came into my life; he was twenty-two. I suppose it seemed quite a big age difference to some, but not to us. We knew right away that something special was happening between us, and even my parents were soon drawn into the magic of it.

The first time I saw him, my friend Andrea – we call her Andee – and I were walking along one of the jetties at the marina here in Kesterly. We'd just finished school for the summer and were due for our first sailing lesson with the new instructor everyone was talking about. We were excited, apprehensive, all the things you'd imagine of girls our age embarking on a new adventure. I'm sure I saw him first, but Andee says she did. It doesn't matter; what I can tell you for certain is that suddenly there he was, leaping from the deck of a sailboat to land in front of us, all six foot two of him with the kind of aura, or presence, or just drop-dead good looks, that halted us in our tracks. His fair hair was thick, wind-mussed, and tangled around his neck; he was hard-muscled and tanned, and his face looked as though it had been carved by someone who adored him. I could give you all the usual clichés, such as he took my breath away, made my knees go weak, set my pulses racing, because I'm sure they all happened. Andee summed it up well when she whispered to me, 'Wow, a real-life dreamboat.'

We found that funny of course, thought the play on words was clever, the way you do when you're young and barely know the difference between corny and comedy.

Sean was from London, he told us, but he and his family travelled a lot, so it could be said that he was from everywhere. As he spoke his eyes were mainly on me. I could feel myself blushing, and was aware of how much Andee was enjoying the build-up of chemistry; I think she might have been even more aware of it than I was in those moments. She already had a boyfriend, Martin, who was in the same year as us, but I'd never been serious with anyone. I'd just had a couple of dates that had never led anywhere, mainly because I'd never met anyone who really interested me.

Sean went beyond that; he completely fascinated me, and every time I looked at him I felt myself lighting up inside. It wasn't just the way he looked back at me, although that was something else, his deep, navy eyes seeming to speak in a way that made me blush and laugh and feel so reckless I could have done anything in the world, even fly. He had a way with him that seemed to draw everyone in. He wasn't the least bit arrogant, which he could have been given how worldly he was, far more than the rest of us, that's for sure. Nothing ever seemed to faze him, or if it did he found a way to get over it. His passion was sailing, so of course it soon became mine too.

We were inseparable that summer. As well as teaching me how to handle a boat, he showed me how to surf the way he did, and he got me waterskiing like a professional. He was learning to fly so Andee, her boyfriend Martin, and I went out to the airfield to watch him take off, loop the loop and land. We paraglided with him, dived from rocks, barbecued on the beach and sang songs together, with him and Martin playing their guitars. He turned me from a naïve, silly schoolgirl into a confident, determined young woman who couldn't get enough of him or the world he told us so much about.

When the summer was over Andee, Martin and I took our places at the local sixth-form college, while Sean returned to London. His uni days behind him, he was now working his way up through his family's business. I didn't know much about it then, only that they were into large-scale construction projects from hotels to shopping malls, leisure centres, even marinas. Sean's degree was in business management, and he was also studying company law, but I know he found being hands-on with his father and the managing partners far more exciting and educational. Even then he was as confident in his instincts as he was in his ability to land a deal. He thrived on the adrenalin of it all, and somehow made more friends than enemies, which seemed unusual for someone involved in big business, and of his age.

I was terrified he'd forget me as soon as he returned to London, but that's not what happened. We were in touch every day, unless he was out of the country when he'd send postcards to make me smile – and of course to make me wish I was there. We hadn't really got going with texts and emails at the time, all that came later.

He returned to Kesterly at Christmas and again at Easter, and again the following summer – actually there were two more summers – and the closer we became the more certain we were that we were made for each other. When I finished my studies there was no question of me going to uni then – I already had a place at St Martins, but I deferred for a year to go travelling with Sean. His father was all for it; he didn't want Sean to become enslaved to the business the way he had been as a young man. He believed very strongly that Sean's world experiences were going to count as much in his future as his academic accomplishments, and even his knowledge of the company. It was important, Philip always said, to know as much as you could about other cultures, to see them in action and understand them on a level that was both respectful and informative. His wife had felt the same way, he once told me, and after she'd died when Sean was only fourteen, Philip's beliefs were reinforced.

It was as if she was speaking to him passionately, he explained, wanting to make sure that no matter how successful he was, he didn't forget to be human. She was a woman of much beauty and many qualities, he said, as well as a philanthropist and effective campaigner, for she recognised talents in people that others didn't always see. It was his belief that Sean had the same innate gift for connecting with others and using it to everyone's advantage.

I'm making him sound like a saint, aren't I? He wasn't, believe me, in fact he was far from it, but in spite of his many faults I always believed in the spirit that drove him.

So during the year after I left college we went travelling. We experienced so many places, some I'd barely even heard of before. We sailed and swam, climbed mountains, flew over deserts, camped in beach huts, and I came to see and understand the world in a way I never could have without him. On several occasions my parents flew to wherever we were to spend time with us – I remember how they loved Vietnam and Bora Bora, and how much they missed me, and loved Sean. I suppose you could say that they were already seeing him as the son they'd never had.

My memories of that time are all happy, and I know my dreams for the future were completely centred around him.

Then it came time for me to take up my place at St Martins.

Sean didn't want me to go. He said I was having a far more valuable education getting to know the world with him. In many ways I couldn't deny it; my horizons had expanded so much in the space of a year that I could hardly remember who I'd been before, or even what I really wanted from life. My home town seemed embarrassingly parochial and even London no longer appealed to me in the way it had before I'd started my gap year. But at the same time I felt I needed some grounding, to get a sense of perspective on who I was and what I wanted from life. It was around the same time that Sean's father and the company partners decided to move into Australasia. It was going to provide, Philip said, the perfect opportunity for Sean to start proving himself, and Sean was all for it. There were so many opportunities Down Under, he insisted when he told me, and if I was still set on going to uni then why not in Sydney, or Melbourne, or Auckland? It didn't have to be London.

I was tempted, of course; more than tempted, I even got excited enough to look into it, but I knew I could never settle anywhere that was so far from my parents. Travelling was one thing; not speaking to them for weeks on end was just about bearable since we'd already experienced that, but setting up a permanent home in a place that seemed so inaccessible back then, especially to them, was another altogether. I'm an only child, you see, and we've always been close. I'm sure they wouldn't have stopped me; in fact I know they wouldn't have, and maybe that was what made it so difficult. It would have broken their hearts to think of me starting a new life on the other side of the world, and they'd never have told me.

In the end Sean gave me an ultimatum. It was him or them – what he actually said was 'London or Sydney' – and because I was so furious with myself for not being able to choose I ended up telling him he should go without me.

So he did.

That shocked me I have to admit, although it shouldn't have, because I knew him well enough by then to accept that he could be as stubborn as I could.

So he went to Sydney, I went to St Martins to study art and design and I ...

Deep breath here to get us from that horrible parting to what happened next ...

I'd been in London for about three months when I met Richmond. I wasn't looking for anyone, it was the last thing on my mind, but then along he came and ... Well, he was different to Sean in just about every way: looks, character, view of the world. He wasn't quite as tall or as handsome, but he was definitely attractive in a physical sense. I guess in the early days it was my anger with Sean that drove me into a relationship with Richmond, a kind of rebound situation, if you like. Maybe I wanted to punish Sean for leaving me. I didn't know if he had already met someone else, but even if he hadn't I knew he would sooner or later, so why shouldn't I?

One of the first things I noticed about Richmond was his sense of entitlement. He had an air of superiority about him that I detested, and I knew Sean would too, but at the same time it was strangely appealing. It's odd, isn't it, the things your psyche does to you for reasons you never understand.

Anyway, Richmond had already graduated by the time we were introduced by friends at a party. He was working at a brokerage firm in the City and was, as everyone kept telling me, the next big thing in high finance. Did that mean anything to me? Of course not. Did I even care? No, not really. I just liked being with him, partly because it helped me to stop thinking about Sean, and partly because we had a great social life together. I didn't analyse our relationship much more than that, there was no reason to, and anyway, you don't at that age, do you?

Richmond's reasons for being with me? Well, I shouldn't try to speak for him, because I've no idea what was going on his mind back then, and I certainly didn't know what was going on in the background of his world. All I can tell you is that I believed he was falling for me, just as I was falling for him. Actually, I still have no reason to doubt that. We were good together, and so when I discovered I was pregnant around eight months into our relationship and he said he wanted to get married, I saw no reason not to.

Did I think about Sean during that time? Of course, I thought about him often, but I'd already heard through the grapevine that he'd found someone else and so I asked myself, what was the point of holding on to dreams that were never going to come true? I had new dreams now that perhaps weren't as bold or exciting, but they had a sense of rightness and attainability about them that were as compelling as the baby kicks that were drawing me deeply into my new life.

Richmond hired a nanny who would help with the baby while I continued my studies. His family was quite well off – I guess you already know that – and I thought, at first, that his parents were fully supportive of our marriage. His father was, I never doubted that, but his mother... Well, she's another story altogether.

Now would be the time to tell you that I'd never heard of Richmond's previous girlfriend, Ana Petrov, before we got married. Neither he nor anyone else had ever mentioned her. When I did find out about her (at a party for Richmond's father's birthday, which she wasn't at) I was shocked, and I admit intimidated. My predecessor was the daughter of a Russian billionaire who owned half of London. OK, that's an exaggeration, but the man was seriously rich and seriously powerful in a way that made me uncomfortable just to look at him. And she, Ana, I saw from the photos Richmond's mother showed me, was seriously beautiful. She was also insanely spoiled and weird, but of course I didn't know that then. Her mother was Malayan, I think, which would account for her and Ana's exotic looks. Richmond's mother, who laid claim to some Slavic roots going back a few generations, was in total awe of the Petrov family, I discovered, and adored their only daughter.

Anyway, the first time I actually came across Ana was just after I had my son, Luke. My parents were coming to stay as often as they could at that time, but they had their own businesses to run back in Kesterly so it was never as often as they'd have liked. It was always a relief to have them there, because Richmond's mother was so critical and dismissive of me. She adored the baby, I'll give her that, but I could tell that she was never going to warm to me.

Luke was a few months old and we were living in an apartment in Holland Park when Ana's crazy insinuation into our lives began. Apparently she'd been in New York since she and Richmond had broken up. She'd worked for her uncle, her father's brother, but I've no idea what he did. I'm not entirely sure what any of them did apart from make enormous amounts of money. If she and Richmond had stayed in touch while she was gone I had no knowledge of it, but it wouldn't surprise me now to learn that they had. At the time it would have upset me a lot to discover that he'd maintained contact with an old girlfriend and kept it a secret, especially when I was no longer in touch with Sean, but there was much more to come ...

I didn't think of Ana Petrov as a stalker at first, but after a while there was no other way to see it. You'd have thought someone in her position, with all her wealth and opportunities, would have found better things to do with her life, but no. She started turning up in places she had no reason to be, and she'd somehow make sure I saw her, but from a distance. There would be this creepy, supercilious sort of smile on her face as if she wanted me to think that she knew something I didn't. It was the scariest time, especially when she started to leave things in our mailbox. At first they were letters addressed to me telling me I shouldn't trust Richmond, that he was cheating on me, and that he intended to take the baby away from me. Richmond contacted her parents, asking them to step in and control her, but if they did speak to her, and I somehow doubt it, all it did was seem to make her worse. I can't remember exactly when she began threatening to harm me, but I guess it was before the day she walked up to me in a café and in front of every-one slapped me in the face. 'There's more to come,' she told me, hissing like a cat, and I'll always remember the way she looked down at my son in his pushchair before she left.

I was already carrying our second child by then, and this really freaked me out. I was having a difficult preg-nancy, too difficult for me to complete my final year at St Martins, and in a way I didn't mind. I was so unnerved by Ana's behaviour that I never wanted to let my son out of my sight. I was terrified she was going to try to snatch him, and of what she might do if she succeeded.

In the end things got so bad that her parents shipped her out of the country. It was either that, or a restraining order, and they weren't going to tolerate anything so ignominious for their precious princess. I think they settled her somewhere in the Far East for a while, but I honestly don't know for certain. Richmond's mother stayed in touch with her, because she'd often drop her name into the conversation saying how well she was doing, or that she sent her love. Can you believe that? Richmond's mother used to tell us that our stalker sent her love? That will give you some idea of the kind of woman she was – and still is.

Luke was nine years old, and his sister Sasha seven, when my father had a stroke and was unable to carry on running his business. He got better over time, you'd hardly know now that anything had happened, but back then everyone was beside themselves with worry. Richmond didn't hesitate. His own father had passed away by then and his cousin whom he'd never got along with was running the Benting family law firm, so Richmond felt no obligation there. Besides, he'd started having difficulties with a couple of new partners at the brokerage firm he was managing, so it made perfect sense for us to leave London. He could help my father with his financial planning services, he said, and work on bringing in new business, while my father retained his oldest clients and moved his life into a slower lane.

Richmond found us our house in Kesterly's Garden District, a few streets back from the seafront, and his mother followed us to the area so she could stay close to Richmond and her grandchildren, although she kept her house in London.

I should probably mention here that I saw Sean just after Sasha was born. He was in London and got in touch to ask if I wanted to meet. I could see no reason not to – what was the harm in catching up with an old friend?

I was shocked by the way my heart turned over when I first saw him. I hadn't expected to feel so thrown, or so drawn to him. It was like small, hidden parts of me were suddenly finding the sun again. I realised it was the younger me reacting, the girl who'd been swept away by a teenage romance that had never really stood a chance of surviving. It had been a wonderful time, however, and we enjoyed laughing at our memories as they bloomed and faded and bloomed again, sometimes more brightly than ever. He didn't tell me much about his life in Sydney, nor did I talk about mine with Richmond, but before I left he asked me if I was happy.

I assured him I was, and he said he was glad, but if I ever needed to get hold of him I knew how to find him. I thought it was an odd thing to say, but typical of his generous nature.

When I got home I dug out some old photos from our travels, and I was so absorbed in them that I didn't hear Richmond come in. To my astonishment he was furious. He grabbed the photos and threatened to destroy them. I tried to get them back, but he pushed me out of the way.

I fell against a chair, knocking my head, but he didn't notice. He was already leaving the flat. I never saw the photos again, and I didn't speak to him for a week, maybe longer. In the end he apologised and said he'd been wrong to do what he had, but he loved me so much that he couldn't bear the idea of me even thinking about another man.

I forgave him, because I had to. We had two children who were already sensing the tension between us and where was I going to go with it? Nowhere that would improve our marriage that was for sure. We were battling a bit of a rough patch due to Richmond's long hours and frequent spells away from home, and I could only remind myself that he was a wonderful father when he put his mind to it. And there was no doubt the children adored him.

There were plenty of moments, days, weeks, months, when I adored him too. He could be very charming, lots of fun and always generous, especially when he knew he'd been difficult, or overly critical, or even neglectful. He worked hard, and as I mentioned just now, things weren't going well at the brokerage firm, so he was under a lot of stress. When we moved to Kesterly he threw himself completely into Penn Financial, determined to make an even bigger success of it than my father had. Within a year he'd opened a small office in London, and it wasn't unusual for him to spend two or three days a week there.

So, fast-forwarding over all the usual challenges of an eighteen-year marriage, and there were plenty, believe me, we get to a few weeks ago when I first discovered that Sean Kenyon was in Kesterly. He hadn't been in touch to say he was coming; in fact I hadn't heard from him since the time we'd met just after Sasha was born, and she's now sixteen. I will admit that there had been times when I'd felt like contacting him, usually after a row with Richmond, but he was an entire world away with a doubtless full and demanding life of his own. Besides, I was hardly his problem, and I certainly didn't want to create any more for myself. Richmond was never physically violent, but his temper had grown increasingly unpredictable over the years and I usually – not always – went out of my way to avoid provoking it.

The coincidence of Ana Petrov also coming back into our lives at that time was ... surprising? Curious? I'm more inclined to say unsettling. Yes, it was definitely unsettling, because anything to do with that woman set me on edge. It was only later that I discovered there was a connection to her and Sean turning up at the same time.

As she finished speaking Olivia's eyes drifted to the clouds gathering outside the window, noting the darkness of their centre, the belligerence of their intent – and the brilliant borders of sunlight encompassing them in a steely grip. It seemed symbolic in a way that made her restless and uneasy.

After a while she sighed gently and turned back to the two people who were there to interview, inter- rogate, her: a casually dressed woman in her early thirties, and a solemn-faced man of around the same age. They didn't look judgemental; there was noth- ing in either of their expressions to tell her what they might be thinking, but she could see they were hop- ing to capture more for the recording device on the table between them.

Of course they were interested to know more. So far she'd only given them a brief background on the main players in the events that had brought them here. They couldn't do their jobs without a full account of what had happened during the two years since Sean Kenyon and Ana Petrov had emerged from the shadows of the past to change everything.

It wasn't only Olivia's story to tell, others would have their say as well, but it was right that she should start it. Maybe she'd have the final words too, but that would depend on the two people sitting across from her now, patiently waiting for her to continue.

She could see no point in holding anything back, so she wouldn't; she just wished that while tell- ing the story she could alter the truth in a way that would avoid the terrible, life-shattering outcome it led to.

Chapter Two

Two Years Earlier

The house should have been deserted. It wasn't time for anyone to be at home yet, but as Olivia Benting pushed open the front door of the Folly – a quirky, stone and red-brick town house designed by an eighteenth-century eccentric who'd wanted his own creation to stand out amongst the traditional Georgian facades either side of it – a sixth sense seemed to be telling her that she wasn't alone. She checked her watch. Ten past four. Sasha, her sixteen-year-old tornado, had said she'd be back around six at the latest; Luke, her eighteen-year-old superhero was – well, she wasn't entirely sure where he was, but with any luck an email was waiting to enlighten her – and Richmond, her husband, was at the London office today.

Deciding it had to be Sasha, back early, she allowed a heavy bag to slide from her shoulder and land with a thump on the marble floor. Making a quick check of the mail piled on the hall table, she called out, 'Sasha! Are you home already?'

Her voice echoed around the smooth white walls of the double-storey entrance hall and up over the welcoming central staircase, whose black wrought-iron banisters and low-rise steps fishtailed on the upper level to surround the mezzanine landing. Above the front door was a circular stained-glass window currently turning the rays of a warm July sun into a cascade of rainbow blades in the mote-specked air.

She glanced up, while thumbing open an official-looking envelope. No sounds coming from the first-floor bedrooms – the master, Luke's den and a guest suite, all of which opened off the mezzanine, while Sasha's personal space was on the top floor, next to Olivia's studio. If Sasha was at home her shoes would have been discarded inside the door, and music would be blaring, or she'd be banging about the kitchen …

Olivia started towards the three partially open doors to the left of the hall. The first led into the TV room. It was empty, untidy and presumably half dusted, since Mrs Kelly's stepladder, with a can of Mr Sheen and a yellow rag on the top, had apparently been abandoned mid-task. Since Mrs Kelly often took off at the ping of a text from a disabled husband Olivia wasn't surprised by the clutter, and thinking no more of it she moved on to the second door.

'Are you in here, darling?' she said, stepping into Richmond's study. She called him darling when she wanted to be friendly, and it usually worked. Friendly was a sensible place to start when they hadn't seen each other for a couple of days, much better than kicking off with fractiousness or suspicion or downright disappointment. It wasn't often she felt the latter, but it happened, for both of them, more now than it used to and she knew she was as much to blame as he was. However, they could just as easily be pleased to see one another and eager to share some news, fall into an embrace, or get ready for a social event. What could dismay, or even depress her instantly, was the appearance of a deep line etched between his brows, a warning that something had gone wrong at the office, that his day was disappearing fast up the creek, and his temper was close behind. No point trying to connect with him then; best to wait it out and hope that whatever was causing the stress would somehow right itself and set the reasonable, easy-going him free to relax, or at least stop worrying.

The computer was off in his study, the desk was tidy, and there was definitely no one there, so she returned to the hall and looked at the third door. Behind it was the staircase to the cellar and wine store.

Certain no one would be down there, she stood quietly listening, trying to catch the sound of someone moving, or speaking, or girlish shrieks muffled by Sasha's closed bedroom door.

Everything was silent and still, apart from the muted beat of her heart and the faint sound of a car passing outside. She looked at the answerphone and saw, to her surprise, that there was a message. Almost no one called the landline these days.

She pushed the playback button, and waited. It was the roofer she'd contacted a few days ago to come and inspect some broken tiles. As she listened to his lengthy message her gaze wandered to the other side of the hall where the drawing- and dining-room doors were closed, as usual, then on through the ornate archway opposite the front door where she could see into the sizeable and spectacular kitchen, and out to the garden beyond. A jingle on her mobile signalled an incoming text. It was from a friend saying she was glad Olivia was feeling better, but perhaps it was still too soon to be thinking of playing doubles just yet.

Swallowing her disappointment, Olivia wondered if that meant Sandie had found another partner who played better, and wanted to keep her. It made Olivia feel annoyed and frustrated, but she could hardly blame Sandie for moving on. She'd probably have done the same if the roles were reversed, but didn't Sandie realise how eager Olivia was to try and get back into the swing of things?

Saving the roofer's message, she spent a few moments texting Sandie back, watched over by the portrait of herself that Richmond had commissioned several years ago. She'd objected strongly when he'd insisted on hanging it here, in the hall; she was almost nude, it was far too intimate for public display, she'd argued, why couldn't he hang it somewhere a little more discreet, such as in his study, or in their bedroom?

'Because no one will see it there,' he'd pointed out, 'and I want everyone to see how beautiful you are.'

She looked like Bardot, according to him, and she remembered how thrilled and flattered, even awed, she'd felt when she'd first seen the painting. It did make her look a bit like the famous movie star. However, the children hadn't been thrilled about having such a moody image of their mother greeting them every time they came in the door, but over time, like Olivia, they'd probably stopped noticing it. She felt certain Richmond had too, or he'd surely have taken it down during these past few months when it had become an ordeal for her to see her once glorious mane of silvery-blonde hair mussed around her face, and tumbling randomly around her plump, bare shoulders.

Oddly, considering all that had happened to her body during these past months, it wasn't the suggestion of a nipple that she generally found the hardest to look at, or even the glossy luxuriance of her hair, it was the shapeliness of her buttocks and legs that seemed to affect her most deeply. She had no idea why losing so much weight should upset her this much, unless it was her mind's way of protecting her from the far more shattering loss of her hair and breasts.

Hearing a noise behind her she spun round, and terror exploded inside her. A man was standing in the arch to the kitchen. She tried to move, to tell him he could take whatever he wanted, just please don't hurt her. Then her senses shifted, and recognition began to filter in as though fog was clearing from a landscape she knew and loved well.

'Hello, Olivia,' he said.

As he smiled she felt herself falling back in time to a place she rarely allowed herself to think about now, into a tangle of memories that could trap her so easily and make her unwilling to let go.

'Sean?' she said hoarsely.

His once-familiar blue eyes shone with a humour that was so typical of him that almost without realising it, she started to smile. How could she not have recognised him right away? It seemed inconceivable when he'd hardly changed at all, provided she ignored the silvery strands that streaked his thick, fair hair, and the laughter lines around his eyes that had darkened and deepened. Almost sixteen years had passed since she'd last seen him. How insane and unsteadying to find herself awash with so much girlish joy.

'Surprised?' he enquired.

She put her hands to her burning cheeks. For a strange, exhilarating moment it was as though the burdens of the past year were being lifted, leaving her free to be the young woman he'd once loved and who had been crazy about him.

Trying to ground herself, she pushed through a torrent of questions and said, 'What are you doing here? How on earth did you get in?'

'Well, I had several methods planned,' he told her with gentle irony, 'but since we're in the middle of a very upright neighbourhood, you'll be happy to know that I settled on the conventional route.'

Knowing that conventional didn't always mean the same to Sean as it did to everyone else, she waited.

'The front door,' he explained. 'I knocked, the delightful Aisling answered and insisted I come in to wait.'

Olivia shook her head as she stared at him incredulously. In eight years of knowing Mrs Kelly she'd never once called her Aisling – and wasn't it just typical of Sean Kenyon to be on intimate terms with a complete stranger only minutes after first meeting her? So where was Mrs Kelly now?

'Oh, she had to go,' he replied, when she asked. 'She got a call from someone and told me to make myself at home in the garden.'

Olivia blinked. He really had charmed Mrs Kelly if she'd just left him here as if he were a long-lost member of the family. He was hardly that to Richmond, while to her he was …

Just thank goodness she'd come home first and not Richmond. Maybe he'd known Richmond was in London today – but how could he?

'So how are you?' he asked, tilting his head to one side as his eyes held hers in a curious, slightly teasing gaze.

Her smile wavered as she thought of how much she'd like to walk into his arms, to welcome him back and tell him … tell him what? They were different people now, knew nothing of each other's lives, so why on earth was she thinking she could gain some comfort from him?

She wondered what he was thinking as he looked at her. Was he remarking on how much she'd changed? She bolstered herself quickly with the reminder that though her hair was no longer thick, shining and blonde, the darker feathery cap that had grown back these past few weeks quite suited her, or so Sasha kept insisting. It even contrived – according to her father – to make her sky-blue eyes seem more dazzling than ever. Being her father he would say that, but even if it were true, she was still painfully thin, and the blemishes on her skin hadn't completely cleared up yet. However, a voluminous white linen shirt over loose capri pants, and a good Clinique foundation, were helping to disguise the worst of the surface travesty, and a shaken, but so far undefeated spirit was doing its best to take care of the inner mess.

'I know I look a wreck,' she began, in the blasé manner she generally adopted when discussing her appearance these days, 'but if you'd let me know you were coming ... ' Realising it probably wasn't a good idea to admit she'd have made an effort, she stopped, but his laughing eyes told her he'd read her anyway. So she said, with perhaps too much affection, 'I see you're still way too sure of yourself, Mr Kenyon, and how dare you turn up here, as though we'd all welcome you with open arms ... '

'Ah, now there's an idea I like the sound of,' he interrupted, and in a few quick strides he was across the hall, sweeping her into an embrace that was startling, almost overwhelming at first, then felt as though it was all she'd ever needed to hold her together. Not that she was falling apart, she'd never let that happen, but if she were ...

'So what are you doing in Kesterly?' she demanded, finally pulling away, and wondering what it was about him that always made a person feel safe, when he had to be one of the most unsafe people she knew.

'I came to see you, of course,' he replied, sounding amazed that she needed to ask. 'It's been a long time – too long, and since I've never been able to get you out of my mind ... '

'Sean Kenyon!' she protested. 'That is so not true.'

He looked hurt and amused and something else, she thought, and to her surprise she realised that it might be concern.

Had someone told him about her cancer? Did he know that when she'd thought she was going to die, seeing him again, spending time with him, if only a day, had gone to the very top of her bucket list? Of course he didn't know that, she'd barely admitted it to herself, never mind to anyone else, and she still wasn't absolutely sure she'd meant it.

'Come on through to the kitchen,' she said, needing to escape his scrutiny, 'lucky Richmond's not around today.'

He laughed. 'Are you saying he wouldn't be pleased to see me?' he teased.

Since he surely knew the answer to that, she simply threw him a look. 'Tea or coffee, or something stronger?' she offered, glancing up at the clock. Still only four fifteen, yet it seemed as though a whole lifetime was piling into the minutes.

'Whatever you're having,' he answered, going to perch on one of the bar stools at the centre island. 'This is a very smart place you have here,' he commented, taking in the elegant black laminate units, Gaggenau appliances, and glossy white Corian worktops.

'Since when were you into kitchens?' she enquired drily.

'Since you were standing in one,' he quipped.

She switched on the kettle, then turned back to face him. 'OK, so what's the real reason ... ' She broke off as her mobile started to ring. The decision not to answer came swiftly, for she wasn't about to let anyone spoil this unexpected and intriguing reunion. On the other hand, she needed to make sure it wasn't one of the children.

It wasn't, and after the ringing stopped their eyes met, his even more intense and knowing than she remembered; hers ... What were hers conveying, or betraying? Probably more than she was aware of; perhaps even more than she fully understood.

'So why are you really here?' she asked, folding her arms and feeling once again the absence of her breasts. She was getting used to not having them now, in the same way any amputee gets used to a part missing, but she still hated it, felt somehow diminished by it, and continued to question her decision to refuse a reconstruction.

No more hospitals, no more surgery, life needed to get back to normal.

'OK, I'm exploring a business opportunity,' he replied in a way that sounded both droll and slightly incredulous.

'Here in Kesterly?' She was certainly incredulous. 'I'd have thought we were far too small-town for you.'

'It doesn't take a big town to create a big project,' he responded. 'I flew over a few days ago for a board meeting at our London office, and while I was there we got a call about the expansion of Kesterly Marina. It was suggested that it might be something our organisation would be interested to take a look at.'

Knowing that major infrastructure projects were what his consultancy firm was mostly about, providing everything from design concept, finance management and manpower, this was making sense. The expansion of Kesterly Marina wouldn't be a large undertaking for them, however, and she guessed might not even have been considered had Sean, the senior partner, not been in London when the call had come in. So he was here either out of simple nostalgia, or because he knew that the project was being managed by Penn Financial – in other words Richmond Benting – and he wanted to see for himself why it was running into trouble. The most puzzling question was who had contacted Kenyon

Holdings, because she knew beyond any doubt that it wouldn't have been Richmond.

Deciding not to explore that potential minefield for the moment, she brought the subject back to a more personal place as she said, 'So how did you know where to find me?'

He cocked an eyebrow. 'Rena told me.'

Olivia had started to make tea, but stilled for a moment as she registered this, then continued calmly. 'So you've been in touch with my mother?' she commented, wondering why she was surprised when she probably ought not to have been.

'I've never really lost contact with her,' he admitted.

So her mother had been in touch with Sean Kenyon all these years and had never mentioned it? Like a couple of hidden pieces to a jigsaw an understanding came half into the light, but she still hadn't quite found the right place for them yet. Something was going on in the background of their lives, she'd sensed that for some time, though she'd never dreamt it might somehow draw Sean into the picture.

'So I'm fully aware,' he continued, 'that your children are growing up fast. There's Luke, who must be seventeen?'

'Eighteen,' she corrected.

'Eighteen,' he echoed in amazement. 'And there's you looking no older than thirty, when you must be ... ' He stopped and chuckled at the warning look she shot him. 'Not yet forty,' he conceded. 'And then there's Sasha, who's sixteen?'

She nodded.

'The same age you were when we met.'

Olivia couldn't stop herself smiling as she remembered that time. She thought of Sasha and realised it wasn't easy for her, as a mother, to imagine her daughter being as sure of herself and worldly and carefree as Olivia had considered herself back then. On the other hand, it wasn't difficult to see Sasha turning up at the marina excited about learning to sail and being swept off her feet by the instructor who'd come for the summer to organise charters for his father's boats, and to school young hopefuls in the hedonistic arts of water sports.

'So you and Richmond are still together,' Sean stated, a note of surprise in his tone, or maybe she'd imagined it.

Her eyes went to his, searching for sarcasm, but she found only friendliness and interest.

'He's a lucky man,' he commented with a twinkle.

'There are those who consider me to be the lucky one,' she countered truthfully.

'And would you be amongst them?'

Her eyes narrowed slightly. 'Of course,' she answered, and she felt herself flush, for he'd clearly

clocked her defensiveness, and was no doubt reading all sorts of things into it.

'So you have a PR company now,' he said, as
though sensing her desire to change the subject.
'Very successful, I believe.'

With a shake of her head, she said, 'My mother
can be prone to exaggeration.' Actually, it had been
quite successful when she'd had it, mostly because
it had been the only agency in town, but business
had already started to fall away even before she'd
got sick. It was austerity, of course, everyone was
feeling it, and the cutbacks were by no means over,
for her efforts to start rebuilding recently hadn't met
with positive results. 'I've been working with Andee
Lawrence lately,' she went on. 'You must remember
her and Martin from … '

'Of course I remember them. Didn't she join the
police?'

'She did, but she gave up being a detective a few
years ago, around the same time as she broke up
with Martin. She's with Graeme Ogilvy now, an
antique dealer and property developer based in the
Inner Courtyard. She does interior design for him,
and I'm helping her.'

He was regarding her intensely again, as though
listening to what was behind her words, a subtext
even she wasn't aware of. 'And Richmond is running Penn Financial?' he stated, as if this had been

the subject all along. 'How is your father, by the way?'

'He's fine, as I'm sure you know if you're in touch with my mother.'

'And Rena still has her dance school, which, she tells me, has been doing extremely well thanks to *Strictly*. Does she still dance herself?'

'Not so much any more, but she has about a dozen instructors and she's at the studio most days, apart from during the summer. It's closed now until September.'

'Do you dance?'

'Sasha and I go to tap and jazz/funk. We learned the flamenco last year. That was fun.'

'I'd like to have seen it.' Taking the tea she was handing him, he ignored the milk and sugar she pushed forward on a tray and began surveying his surroundings again. He seemed so relaxed, so unfazed by being in another man's house, with another man's wife, and so unaware of what coming back into her life now, at this time, might be doing to her.

Or was he?

Feeling another rush of happiness to see him, she put her mug down and went to open the fridge. 'Let's drink a toast to reunions,' she proposed, seizing a bottle of wine. Her doctor might have cautioned her against alcohol while she was taking tamoxifen, but he hadn't ruled it out altogether.

Apparently amused, Sean took the bottle from her and she felt momentarily dazed, as though all the years that had passed were blending themselves into some kind of an illusion, or a period of time that had no meaning at all. It might only have been a month since she'd last seen him, or even a week. She could still be a teenager, carefree, in love and ready to follow this man to the ends of the earth ...

She looked up and seeing him watching her, she turned to go and open the French doors a little wider. It was a warm summer's day, so why not let in some air? Indeed, why not flirt with him? It was making her feel good and who cared if Richmond wouldn't like it? Richmond did plenty of things she didn't like and she was sure he didn't much worry about it.

'Glasses?' Sean said.

Without looking round she went to take two from an overhead cupboard and set them down in front of him. After he'd filled them he insisted on toasting her, and old times – beautiful memories was how he put it – so she let him, and clinked his glass with her own.

'Now tell me about you,' she said, sliding on to a stool facing him. 'What have you been doing all this time? Actually, I saw you on the news a few years ago. You were flying planes for the Red Cross, ferrying refugees to UN medical centres in Ethiopia. How did that come about?'

He nodded slowly, almost as if he'd forgotten it, though she knew this was unlikely. 'I was there assessing a dam project,' he said, 'and when we saw what was happening, what was needed … It had to be done.'

They fell silent for a while, sobered by the tragedy that was no less real for being so far away. Eventually she moved them on by asking if he was married. He wasn't wearing a ring, but that told her nothing.

'Not currently,' he replied. 'Actually, that isn't strictly true, Alisha and I are still legally bound, but we're supposed to be in the process of a divorce. I say supposed to be, because neither of us ever does anything about it. We just live separately, her with her new partner, and me with my four kids when they come to stay.'

'Four?' she echoed, not sure why she was surprised when there was no reason on earth why he shouldn't be a father.

'One from my first marriage. His name's Tom and he's just turned fifteen. Two girls from my second marriage – Evie twelve and Grace, ten; and another boy, Noah, from my marriage to Alisha. He's seven next month.'

Olivia's eyes were round. 'You've been married three times!' she cried, laughing. 'Why aren't I surprised? Actually, I am. Or maybe I'm not. I can't be sure.'

'I promise I'm not trying to break any records . . . '

'Or hearts?'

'Definitely not hearts. I think all three of them were glad to be rid of me, but I'm happy to say that in each case we've managed to remain friends. It works better for the kids if we're civil to one another, we find.'

'You must have photos,' she insisted.

He grinned. 'Just a few,' he admitted in a tone that suggested he probably had thousands, and taking out his phone he did a quick search, landing on one that made his eyes twinkle as he handed it over.

Olivia couldn't help but gasp and laugh as she saw the crystal-clear shot of three women, all stunning in their own way, standing behind four laughing children who, the girls in particular with their blonde curls and blue eyes, bore such a remarkable resemblance to their father it was almost hypnotic.

'I positioned them that way,' he said, 'with the mothers' hands on their kids' shoulders, to remind me who belonged to whom.'

Knowing he wasn't serious, and easily able to imagine the female contingent groaning at his dad joke as the boys barrelled into him, Olivia passed the phone back as she said, 'It's quite something that you've managed to retain such a good relationship with them all. Have you been taking lessons from Rod Stewart?'

He laughed. 'The kids have no problem getting along, apart from all the usual sibling stuff, obviously. As for the mothers, I don't think they seek one another out much outside of family get-togethers – unless one of them wants to have a whinge about me, but in all honesty I can't imagine that happening very often.'

Loving the mock innocence of his reply, she said, 'And what about now? Are you making plans for wife number four, maybe?'

His eyes narrowed with amusement, but the light dimmed as he said, 'There was someone, but she died about eighteen months ago.'

Olivia immediately felt wretched. 'Oh, I'm sorry,' she said quickly. 'What happened?'

'We were in a helicopter crash. By some miracle I survived, but for a long time I wished I hadn't.'

She found herself looking at him more closely than ever, and could see from his expression that he truly meant what he'd said, he hadn't wanted to go on living. Shock rippled silently through her, followed by the devastation she'd have felt if she'd learned he'd taken his own life – if he'd lost his life at all. It wasn't something in all these years that she'd ever considered, not even during her illness, that he might die and she'd never see him again. It made her realise that somewhere in the back of her mind, beyond the reach of words or even conscious thought, she'd always believed their paths would cross again. 'What was her name?' she asked quietly.

'Isabella. She was Italian.' He opened his phone again and searched out another photo. 'I used to carry one of you,' he told her, as he scrolled. 'Not on my phone, obviously, we didn't have that facility then. It was a proper photo taken on board the *Calypso* with you at the helm, your hair blowing in the breeze, your bikini glittering in the sunlight. You looked so happy, so young and so damned sexy ...' He broke off, eyeing her carefully or maybe it was teasingly.

Remembering the photo and even the day it had been taken, it pleased her to know that it had meant something to him after they'd parted. 'And I expect you still have it,' she challenged playfully.

His grimace was answer enough.

Arching a humorous eyebrow, she reached for the phone and turned it to gaze down at a laughing, vivacious young woman with deep brown eyes, short inky-black curls, and a wide, voluptuous mouth. 'She's beautiful,' she murmured, easily able to imagine the two of them together, loving, living life to the full and ready to embrace all kinds of adventures. At least Isabella had found happiness with Sean before fate had dealt her such a cruel blow.

She looked up at him. 'I'm so sorry you lost her,' she said, meaning it.

He nodded and took the phone back, closing it without looking at the photo again. They sat quietly for a moment, until sensing his strain she reached for his hand, not sure whether she wanted to share some of his heartache, or to comfort him. Probably both.

His smile was flat and sad as he nodded inattentively, and she tightened her fingers around his. Moments passed, moments filled by a slow, gentle awakening of the connection they used to share, not in a demanding or even deeply felt way, but simply making her think of what it would have been like to have a brother. Someone who knew her so well they didn't always need words to communicate their understanding; someone who loved her, and whom she loved, come what may.

Eventually his eyes came to hers and she could see that he was no longer thinking of himself, or Isabella. He was focused wholly on her now, in the gently intense, almost consuming way that she remembered well. 'I'm not the only one who's sad, am I?' he said softly.

The words were so unexpected, and so insightful, that she felt a jolt of shock as her throat tightened with emotion. 'Why – why do you say that?' she asked, forcing herself to smile.

He didn't answer, just waited for her to confide in him if she wanted to, or not if she didn't.

She continued to look at him, her smile still in place as she wished he had the power to make it all go away, the pain, the anguish, the fear – most of all the fear. It overcame her in so many ways, fear of losing her husband, her children, her home and most of all her life. But she wasn't going to die. The cancer hadn't spread to any other part of her body, and she'd come through the treatment ...

His hand cupped around her face, and she found herself being transported back to another world, to a time before it all went wrong, when she was still a teenager and this man had meant so much to her. She'd never have been able to imagine life without him then, hadn't even tried, yet look at where they were now.

She put a hand over his, keeping it against her cheek. Then her eyes moved past him at the sound of the front door opening, and she quickly pulled away. It would be Sasha. She'd have to introduce her, but who would she say he was? A friend, of course. There was nothing wrong with that ...

To her dismay and unease she saw it was Richmond, and he wasn't alone. Cooper Jarrett, the too smooth, too cocky finance director for Penn Financial, was with him.

Registering her expression, Sean turned around, and seeing who was coming towards him he got to his feet. 'Richmond,' he said affably, as though he saw the man every day, when as far as Olivia was aware they'd only met once, at a conference in Dubai.

Richmond's cold eyes stayed on Olivia, as though cutting Sean out of his home, his entire existence, as he said, 'Get him out of here,' and turning away he directed Cooper to the door of his study and followed him through.

Chapter Three

'Are you going to be OK?' Sean asked, as Olivia walked outside with him.

'Of course,' she answered, gazing abstractedly down to the forecourt where Richmond's silver Mercedes was parked next to her multi-purpose hatchback. She didn't want Sean to know how furious she was, or how much she was dreading the showdown in store. God knew it would have been bad enough if Richmond had come in alone, that the detestable Cooper Jarrett had been with him …

Sean was scrolling through his mobile. A moment later hers rang. 'You have my number now,' he said, 'just in case.'

She didn't ask in case of what, or how he'd got her number; presumably her mother had given it to him.

'I should be coming and going for a while,' he told her. 'I'll be using an apartment over at the marina when I'm in town.'

She nodded and wanted to tell him she'd be in touch, that she was glad he was here, that she hoped to see him again, but decided that it might not be a good idea. Life was complicated enough already. She didn't need to make it any worse.

As Sean drove away, steering his rented black Audi through the well-heeled Garden District towards the seafront, his expression showed both concern and intrigue. He'd achieved more than he'd expected to today. Seeing Olivia was, of course, the best of it, but uppermost in his mind was Richmond Benting, who he hadn't imagined running into just yet. Did the man realise what had brought the Kenyon Group's senior partner to Kesterly? Had anyone told him it might happen? He was intelligent and quick-witted, presumably not slow in connecting the dots; however, Sean had come across many men in his time who'd considered themselves smart and ahead of the game, and they still made mistakes.

He'd find out soon enough which category Richmond Benting fell into.

Olivia was still standing on the front steps, staring towards the end of the square where Sean's car had vanished a few moments ago. She felt strangely empty, as though he'd taken some of her energy and her ability to think straight along with him. She was aware of how problematic his presence in Kesterly could become, but at the same time memories were beginning to absorb her, more easily recalled since he'd driven away, it seemed, than when he'd been with her. Now wasn't the time to let them dazzle and confuse her. She had to push them back into the safe place she'd always kept them, like an album in the attic that was there, unforgotten, but rarely enjoyed.

Going back inside she remained in the hall for a few moments, trying to decide what to do. Clearly there was no way she could talk to Richmond while Cooper Jarrett was around – why did that man always set her teeth on edge? – so maybe she should try to get on with some work. First, though, she should clear away the wine glasses. Richmond wouldn't need any reminders of what had greeted him.

As she started back to the kitchen her eye was caught by a photograph on the hall table that had been moved from its usual position. She went to straighten it, thinking maybe Sean had picked it up while he was waiting. It was a shot she'd taken during a family trip to Disney World several years ago – Richmond, Luke and Sasha playing in the hotel swimming pool. She remembered wondering during that trip what she would do if they ran into Sean and his wife and children, if he even had a wife and children. She'd become almost consumed by it at times, had seemed to see him everywhere, but of course she never had.

Pushing it from her mind, she returned to the kitchen and wondered what Richmond was thinking now. Was he able to concentrate on what he and Cooper were discussing, or was his mind too full of anger and the need to make her explain? He could be obsessing over a perceived betrayal, the way she probably would if the situation were reversed. She never used to be so insecure, but that had changed over time, particularly in the past year. Richmond invariably became impatient with her, said he wasn't going to waste any time on her delusions. Where Sean Kenyon was concerned it was unlikely he'd be so dismissive. And who could blame him, when she'd thrown Sean in his face more times than she cared to remember over the years.

Half an hour later she was upstairs in her studio, attempting to focus on the old chapel project she was helping Andee with, when she heard the front door slam. She tensed, and listened. It could be Sasha coming in. Or maybe Richmond had gone out with Cooper ...

Leaving her computer, she went to the window to look down into the street. There was no sign of anyone, but there were so many trees ... Then she saw

Cooper step off the kerb to cross the road. So she and Richmond were alone in the house.

She waited, expecting him to come and find her, but several minutes ticked by with nothing happening. In the end, unable to bear the suspense, she saved what she'd been working on, and ventured downstairs to face the music.

As she crossed the hall she could see him in his study, sitting at his computer, apparently engrossed in what he was doing. His mustard-coloured jacket that he always wore with raspberry-coloured cords was draped neatly over the back of his chair, his white shirt only slightly crumpled, his brown wavy hair perfectly in place. She no longer saw him as the almost tall, almost handsome man who wore success as easily as a tailor-made suit, and whose air of authority could make her heart beat faster. More often these days she saw him as someone she could never quite reach.

She watched his hands moving on the keyboard, waiting for him to acknowledge her presence, and tried not to let herself become angry when he didn't. Finally she said, 'Do you want to talk about it, or do we pretend it didn't happen?'

'Did you see Luke's email?' he asked without looking up.

With a pang of guilt for not checking, she said, 'No. Where is he?'

'Still in Bangkok. This gap year of his is going to end up costing a fortune.'

'Is that what you're doing now, sending him money?'

He nodded.

'How much?'

'Five hundred.'

Her eyes widened. Luke was going to be delighted with such a generous sum. She just hoped he wasn't in some kind of trouble that required his father's financial assistance. It wouldn't have been the first time.

'No trouble that I know of,' Richmond responded when she asked. 'Still in love, apparently.'

'With the same girl, or has he met someone else?'

'Same girl. You can read the email yourself, he's copied it to you and Sasha.'

A surge of longing for her hopelessly romantic son, with his gangly limbs, easy laughter and boundless affection, swept through her so forcefully that it almost brought tears to her eyes. She missed him so much. It was so very hard letting go, and accepting that she was no longer needed in the way she once had been.

'So,' Richmond said, finally looking at her. 'Maybe you'd like to tell me what that man was doing in this house?'

Bristling at being spoken to like a child, she met his forbidding grey eyes with a steely look of her own. His expression showed only anger, but he was nothing if not a master of disguising his feelings. 'He turned up unexpectedly,' she said, failing to keep the bite out of her voice. 'I had no idea he was even in the country ... '

'But as soon as you did, you just had to see him.' His tone was so scathing that her eyes flashed with fury.

'I'm sure you'd like to make something out of this,' she snapped. 'It would let you off the hook then, wouldn't it?'

'Oh for God's sake!' He shot to his feet, sending the chair crashing into the wall of books behind him. 'I might have known that would come up, but I'm not getting into your fantasies again. I thought you'd finally put them behind you, or at least got them into some kind of perspective ... '

'You might want to belittle my feelings, or pretend you've never been anything but faithful, but it doesn't change the truth, nor does it go away because other things come up that you think are more important.'

He put his hands to his head in despair. 'Exactly. More important. Your life comes top of that list, and thank God, you're through the worst of it, we're getting our lives back on track, so why are you trying to sabotage things by inviting that man into the house?'

Deciding not to ask if he actually knew why Sean was in town, or to mention that she did, she was about to try and calm things down when she registered what he was saying.

'... and as for your insane paranoia about me having affairs, I've told you before that you need to get that nonsense in check, and now would be a very good time to begin, because I really don't need to be dealing with it while I've got so much else on my plate.'

She wanted to hit him, to strike out with all the resentment and hurt he'd inflicted on her over the years, never really soothed by the love she knew was also there. He could be a cold and complicated man, and yet he was also warm and caring, generous and understanding in a way that rarely failed to remind her of why she loved him too.

She didn't love him right now, she detested him as they stood glaring at one another, pain and anger simmering so close to the surface that the effort to hold it in was almost too hard for them both. Yet what were they going to say that hadn't already been said? How could they find the way back to one another when their physical closeness had never been everything it should, and when she wasn't even beginning to forgive him for not always being there during her treatments, for holding himself aloof in his own shell of self-protection instead of sharing hers.

As he continued to look at her she could detect no thawing in his manner, nor any kind of inclination to soften, so, mindful of how damaging stress could be to her health, she turned away.

'You still haven't told me what Sean Kenyon was doing here,' he reminded her.

'Do you mean in this house, or in Kesterly?' she countered.

His eyes darkened. 'Let's start with the house.'

Gathering her patience like a cloak of calm, she said, 'I've already told you ... '

'So I'm expected to believe that he just turned up? How very convenient, when it was only this last weekend, I believe, that you told me what a huge mistake you'd made marrying me instead of him.'

As her heart twisted with guilt, her eyes darkened with fury. 'I never said any such thing,' she protested. 'What I said was maybe I should never have got married to you and run off with him instead, because *you* might be happier with another kind of wife.'

'There are times you make the prospect quite tempting,' he told her harshly.

'I'm sure you've already got someone lined up, so why not just go? Perhaps you're already there. I mean, how do I know what you're doing all those nights you're away in London? And where were you last night until gone ten o'clock? I couldn't get hold ... '

'You know damned well where I was.'

'You told me you were dining with a banker, but why should I believe that?'

His eyes were chilling. 'Nothing I do is right, is it? I've told you a thousand times that I'm not having an affair, but maybe you want me to so you can justify your own with Kenyon.'

She didn't bother to deny it, he knew very well it wasn't true.

His eyes remained hard as he stared at her, until finally seeming to understand that this was getting them nowhere, he dashed a hand through his hair and shook his head. 'I'm sorry,' he said gruffly. 'It's just that sometimes ... ' He took a breath. 'Sometimes I don't know what to say to you ... '

The depth of the inner struggle she could sense in him, the suspicion that his business problems were even greater than she'd feared, pushed aside her anger as she said, 'I'm sorry too. We shouldn't fight.'

'No, we shouldn't.' Coming to take her face between his hands, he said, 'You're through the worst of it, that's all that really matters, OK? Everything else we can learn to cope with.'

As relief washed over her she sank into his arms, feeling both drained and disoriented by the last few minutes.

'Tell me how you feel now you've seen him again?' he asked after a while.

Knowing what he wanted to hear, she looked into his eyes and said, 'I feel glad that I'm married to you.'

Appearing uncertain he regarded her steadily, as though trying to find a way past the doubt. 'But?' he prompted.

'No buts.'

His smile was flat and rueful as he said, 'God knows what Cooper must have thought, seeing you like that with Kenyon of all people.'

'Does Cooper know him?'

'Not personally. He wouldn't have recognised him, but I had to tell him who it was.' He glanced at his watch. 'I have to go back to the office, but maybe we could steal a few minutes and go and lie down for a while? Nothing else, I promise, I'd just like to hold you.'

Because she knew it would make the gulf between them even wider if she refused, she said, 'Let's go.' They almost certainly wouldn't make love, because they rarely did, and she knew very well that his mind was elsewhere, anyway. Nevertheless, if he was prepared to make an effort to restore some sort of closeness between them then she should be too.

They had got no further than the foot of the stairs before the front door banged open and Sasha all but exploded into the hall.

'Hey, Dad, I thought you weren't back until tomorrow!' she cried, dumping the bags she was carrying and going straight to the mirror to check her newly waved hair that was cascading around her shoulders in nymphlike fashion. 'Doesn't this look cool?' she demanded, flicking out her abundant blonde mane as she turned from side to side. 'Gina did it, at The Salon, and I think it's a really great look for me to go to college with in the autumn, don't you, Mum?'

Olivia had no chance to respond before Sasha burbled on. 'I need to talk to you, Dad. I just dropped into Grandma Imogen's and she says she'd love to come for dinner tomorrow night. You remember, you said you'd help me cook?'

'I remember,' Richmond replied, keeping an arm around Olivia. 'But I don't recall setting a date.'

'Oh no, don't say you can't make it,' Sasha protested, fixing him with a plaintive version of Olivia's stunning blue eyes. 'I've been looking forward to it and I've invited Parker. He's seriously impressed by women who can cook.'

Olivia glanced at Richmond. 'I'm not sure I can believe what I'm hearing,' she muttered. 'Did you know about this?'

'Kind of,' he replied.

Olivia returned her gaze to Sasha. 'Since when did you decide to become Parker's chattel?' she enquired, moving on towards the kitchen.

'Oh, Mum! Don't see it like that. I expect you wanted to impress Dad once, and I enjoy cooking, so what's wrong with doing it for my boyfriend?'

Knowing the answer she'd like to give wouldn't go down well, Olivia decided to stay silent.

'OK, I know you can't stand him,' Sasha cried, 'but it's not up to you, is it? I'm sixteen now, so I can make my own decisions, and Dad likes him, don't you, Dad?'

'I hardly know him,' Richmond responded, checking something on his phone.

'Precisely,' Olivia said. 'You've never brought him here ... '

'You haven't exactly wanted any visitors,' Sasha reminded her tactlessly. 'And I'm bringing him tomorrow, so what's all the fuss?'

Richmond said, 'Sasha, if you want things your way, you need to learn some manners.'

'Well, she always has a down on people without even getting to know them,' Sasha complained.

'Don't talk about me as though I weren't here,' Olivia warned.

'Parker is a really nice guy,' Sasha ranted on, 'and you said yourself, when you first met him, that he was really fit, so if ... '

'Being good-looking can hide a multitude of sins,' Olivia responded drily. 'I mean, look at your father.'

Richmond started to laugh, then he caught Sasha in a bear hug as she declared him so not fit, it was embarrassing. 'Stop, stop,' she begged, 'you're messing up my hair. Mum, have you seen my college brochure? There's something I need to check.'

'It's in the TV room,' Olivia told her, used now to Sasha's growing excitement over the private college in London where she was going to spend the next two years. 'When you're done, perhaps you'd like to come up to my studio and help me choose some wallpaper samples.'

'You're using wallpaper? In an old chapel? Mum, your career is over.'

'You need to keep up with the times,' Olivia informed her. 'Are you at home for dinner tonight?' she asked Richmond.

'Probably not. I'll get a pizza or something delivered to the office.' Taking out his mobile as it rang, he headed back to his study.

'Dad, don't forget, we've got to put a menu together,' Sasha called after him.

'As long as you do the shopping.'

'Yeah, like I've got time. Will you do it, Mum? If I give you a list.'

'No way. I'm too busy. Get Grandma Rena to take you.'

'She's got a spa day tomorrow, and some important event tomorrow night. I think she's just trying to get out of coming, because she can't stand Grandma Imogen.'

Olivia flashed her a sweet smile, which Sasha would know very well meant *she's not the only one,* then sweeping on past her she returned to her studio.

As she reached the mezzanine she heard Richmond ending his call, so leaning back over the banister she said, in a moment of rashness, 'How do you fancy going to Paris this weekend, if we can get the flights? Just the two of us?' As soon as the words were spoken she knew she didn't want to go, for some reason the time just didn't feel right, but she needn't have worried.

'I can't think of anything I'd like better,' he mumbled, eyes back on his phone, 'but I've got such a heavy workload right now ...'

When don't you? she almost asked, but since it would have been unlike him to forget it was her birthday on Saturday, there was a good chance he had something else planned that he was keeping a secret.

OLIVIA. I didn't pursue anything then about the reason Sean was in Kesterly. To be honest, I didn't know enough about what was happening with the marina expansion, only that building had come to a stop and whatever had caused it was keeping Richmond awake at night.

It irritated me a lot, the way he accused me of paranoia every time I mentioned his affairs. I'm certain they were real, even though I'd only ever found evidence of one, several years before, and I guess you'd have called it more of a fling than a full-on affair. Maybe if he'd shown more interest in having sex with me I wouldn't have been so suspicious. The times we did make love it was good and I felt sure he thought so too, but he never really had a high sex drive, and after we moved to Kesterly he was always so busy, so tired and preoccupied; and of course he was at the London office for much of the time.

He didn't seem to realise that I needed some reassurance after the mastectomy, that he had it in his power to help me deal with the trauma of it. We never even discussed it, which is of course as much my fault as his. I found it much easier to talk to my mother, and reached all the decisions I made with her support and guidance. Nevertheless, I should have brought it up with him, at least given him a chance to prove that he wanted to be there for me, even if he couldn't actually face it. Maybe I didn't because I was afraid of his response; his conscience, his empathy were unpredictable at best. He could react one way over something one day, and another way altogether the next.

Chapter Four

Olivia was on the restaurant terrace of Kesterly's Royal Hotel, soaking up the warm summer sunshine and watching the glittering bay with all its surfers, sailors and swimmers. In some ways it was like watching an old-fashioned postcard come to life, making her feel nostalgic and quietly happy in a way she hadn't for some time.

Her London friends couldn't understand why she loved this place, for it was really just an ordinary coastal town with donkeys plodding slavishly up and down the sandy beach, tourist trains ferrying people in from caravan parks and guest houses, and a dearth of designer shops and Michelin-starred eateries. Which wasn't to say that all of Kesterly lacked sophistication, for there were plenty of independent boutiques tucked away in the inner courtyard and cobbled streets of the old town, and a handful of restaurants that, OK, might not be starred, but they had some good TripAdvisor reviews. There was also a theatre (mostly local productions), a restored art deco cinema, several golf courses on the outskirts of town, and two tennis clubs to which everyone who was anyone in Kesterly and the surrounding areas belonged.

Reminded of how few games she'd managed to get in this past year – zero – Olivia took a sip of iced water and tried not to mind that it was proving harder to get back into the swing of things than she'd imagined. When she'd first been diagnosed her friends had seemed unable to do enough to support her, but over the last couple of months she'd come to realise that many of them were getting on with their lives while she convalesced. She and Richmond weren't even being invited to as many dinners and cocktails as before, although he was quite glad about that, he said, given how busy he was.

She let her gaze drift across the bay to the marina and the sleek apartment blocks fronted by cafés, boutiques and of course a cornucopia of sailing vessels. The new construction site was hidden from view, but she knew that the foundations had been laid, and from here she could see the towering necks of cranes set against the clear blue sky. She wondered if Sean was over there now, and what exactly he might be doing. She'd googled his company earlier that morning, so she had a clearer idea now of just how much it had grown over the years. He, apparently, was executive chairman, which she guessed made him the overall boss, but there was also a CEO, Timothy Creek, based in London, and a COO working from Dubai. The eight other board members operated between London, Dubai and Sydney and comprised five men and three women. Beyond that there were group boards covering development, finance management and construction, with strategic hubs in the Middle East and North Africa, North America and Asia. It was impossible not to be impressed by the size of the projects the company undertook, from vast shopping malls in the US, to a new world of student accommodation in China, to airport terminals in India, and a defence project in Australia that had had no details attached to it, presumably because they were classified.

It seemed the services offered by the Kenyon Group were as far-reaching as any global airline, providing everything from 'sector expertise' 'industry insights' and 'estates rationalisation'. In truth, it was all way beyond her, and what was troubling her more right now than the reason Sean was in Kesterly, was the phone call she'd received from Andee on the way here. It had even managed to eclipse the positive results from the hospital check-up she'd just had – and the fact that Richmond had apparently forgotten about the appointment because he'd neither wished her luck before he'd left this morning, nor texted to find out how she'd got on.

Glancing at the time, she wondered what was keeping her mother. They'd gone to the clinic together earlier, so Rena was already aware that the check-up had produced the right results, but she'd needed to call into the studio on the way here. This meant that, as yet, Olivia hadn't had a good opportunity to tackle her about never mentioning that she'd stayed in touch with Sean.

'About time,' she said, when Rena finally sat her graceful, willowy self down with a small sigh of satisfaction. Aged sixty-three, Catrena Penn had the gentle beauty of a woman almost half her age, and in many ways as youthful a spirit. With wide blue eyes, a playful mouth and thick chestnut hair usually held back by an Alice band, she was as capable of turning heads these days as her beautiful granddaughter, Sasha, though it had to be said most of her admirers were silver-haired and slightly stiff in the joints.

'How come you've changed?' Olivia asked.

'The dress I had on earlier was too warm for this weather,' Rena replied, filling a glass with iced water. 'Oh, I'm so thrilled about this morning's news. I never want you to go through chemotherapy again in your life, and I'm absolutely certain you don't either.'

'Your insight floors me,' Olivia informed her drily.

Rena twinkled, took a sip of water, then shuddered. 'I've just remembered Imogen's coming to your place for dinner tonight, isn't she?'

Before Olivia could respond Rena was gesturing to the waiter who was searching the room for the destination of two glasses of champagne. 'I thought we should celebrate,' she explained, as Olivia regarded the lunchtime extravagance in surprise. 'You don't have to go to the clinic again for three whole months. That's such wonderful news. Dad sends his love, by the way. He's just dropped me off and would have come in, but he wanted to get to the office.' After the waiter had left, she raised her glass and said, 'To you, my angel.'

Aware that this was the second time in as many days that she'd drunk a toast, Olivia took a sip and said, 'So, Sean Kenyon's in Kesterly.'

Rena's face lit up. 'I take it that means you've seen him,' she smiled, clearly thrilled by the idea.

'I have, and what I'd like to know is why you've never told me you stayed in touch with him all these years?'

Rena waved a dismissive hand. 'I'd hardly call the odd Christmas and postcard staying in touch, or not in the way you seem to mean it ... Ah, menus. What are you going to have?'

After they'd made their selections, Rena picked up her champagne glass again and said, 'By the way, I told Sasha I was going to be at the spa all day, just in case she asked me to shop for her dinner party. I could see it coming, and honestly, darling, as much as I adore my only granddaughter, nothing in the world could persuade me to set foot in a supermarket for Imogen Benting – unless I was allowed to lace my goods with something unpleasant of course.'

Olivia had to smile. Her mother's dislike of Imogen was only matched by her own; in fact she sometimes wondered if anyone really liked Imogen. She guessed this morning's phone call had given her the answer to that, but she hadn't yet finished with the subject of Sean Kenyon.

'But I didn't *send* him to see you,' Rena protested when Olivia accused her. 'He asked where you were living now, so I told him.' She met Olivia's eyes and shook her head fondly. 'Honestly, darling, there hasn't been much to cheer you up lately, has there? What with all the awful treatment you've had to go through, and Richmond not really understanding how much you've needed him at home. Not that we don't appreciate how much pressure he's been under with the marina and everything, but I'm afraid I have questioned his priorities at times, and I'm sure you have too.'

Olivia didn't deny it.

'And then there was Luke taking off around the world,' her mother ran on, 'that was a big thing ... It was so sweet of him to call this morning, wasn't it? Fancy remembering you had a check-up today. He's such a good boy. I'm very proud of him, you know.'

'Mother,' Olivia said darkly.

Rena gave an innocent shrug.

Olivia waited.

Accepting they still weren't done with the subject of Sean, Rena said, 'Tell me you weren't pleased to see him.'

'That's not the point.'

'Oh, I think it is. It's wonderful reconnecting with old friends, especially when they've meant so much in your life.'

'It was a long time ago ... '

'I appreciate that, but it doesn't make it any less pleasurable to see him. Is he married these days?'

Olivia eyed her carefully. 'Yes, he is, but they're separated. I expect you already knew that.'

Rena's smile seemed to sparkle. She didn't have to say what was in her mind, for Olivia had no problem reading it.

Sighing with fond exasperation, Olivia said, 'Yes, it was good to see him, but I don't think Richmond was terribly thrilled.'

Rena's eyebrows shot up. 'Oh, they've come face to face already, have they?'

'They have, and maybe you'd like to tell me what you know about the reason Sean's here.'

Rena threw out her hands. 'All I can tell you is what your father told me – that the marina expansion needs more investment and more experienced players to get it back on track, so they contacted the Kenyon Group to see if they could help.'

'Who's they? Richmond would never have contacted them.'

'Why not? He probably didn't expect to be dealing with Sean himself, given that Sean's based in Sydney, and, so Dad tells me, there are really only two UK-based consultancies specialising in this kind of construction that might be interested. I expect both were approached and for all I know the other one – I think they're called Mace – is also assessing the project.' She smiled mischievously. 'Does that satisfy you?'

'Satisfy?' Olivia repeated, surprised by the question. In truth she hardly knew what she felt about it, so deciding to change the subject, she said, 'Wait till you hear who walked into Graeme Ogilvy's antique shop this morning.'

Rena was all intrigue. 'Have you been there today?' she asked, perplexed. 'I thought you were coming straight here.'

'I got a call from Andee while I was in the car,' Olivia explained. 'She happened to be in the shop earlier checking on an order when she looked up, and there was Ana Petrov staring right at her.'

Rena's jaw dropped. 'Ana Petrov,' she echoed, clearly as appalled as Olivia had felt when she'd received the call. 'I've always remained hopeful that we'd seen the last of her, and now here she is stalking us again?'

Olivia's eyebrows rose. 'You can hardly call a visit to Ogilvy's stalking. For all we know she has no idea Andee and Graeme are friends of ours.'

Rena's expression was still showing unease. 'But she does know that we live in Kesterly. Did Andee find out what she's doing here?'

'They don't actually know one another, but Andee did learn that she's been here for several days, and I imagine Richmond's mother could tell us the rest.'

Rena was looking more dismayed by the minute. 'I expect she could,' she murmured abstractedly. 'I'm sure it'll be where she's staying.'

Certain her mother was right, Olivia tried to erase the worry from her face as she said, 'We have to remind ourselves that time has moved on. We all have. Ana was very young when all those awful things happened. She's probably a very different person now. In fact I'm sure she is, because we all are ... '

'Did she ever get married?'

'I've no idea. If she did, it's something Imogen has failed to tell us, but then that's exactly the kind of detail Imogen would keep to herself.'

Rena picked up her glass. She was looking so concerned that Olivia was regretting even mentioning her old nemesis.

In the end it was Rena who said, 'You know, I don't think we should make too much of this. We don't want you getting stressed, not after all you've been through. She'll no doubt be gone again before we know it, and it's not like we have to see her.'

Agreeing, Olivia sat back as a waitress delivered their salads, then decided to move on to the matter of Sasha's boyfriend. 'What do you make of Parker?' she asked. 'I take it you've met him.'

'A couple of times. He seems a nice enough lad to me. Why?'

'I don't know. I wish I could put my finger on what bothers me about him.'

'It wouldn't be a little touch of snobbery, would it?' Rena suggested lightly.

Olivia blinked. 'You mean because he comes from the Temple Fields estate? Absolutely not. If anything, that's probably the best thing about him, if you consider how well he's done to get into Edinburgh Uni after growing up in such a rough neighbourhood with no parents and virtually no money.'

'So who brought him up?' Rena asked.

'His grandparents, I believe. That's why he's here in Kesterly. He's staying with them for the summer, apparently, and he's picked up with Sasha again.'

'So they were in touch while he was in Scotland?'

Olivia nodded. 'Apparently, yes, but you have to wonder why he's hanging about with a sixteen-year-old when there must be any number of girls his own age he can choose from.'

'You could have once said that about you and Sean,' Rena reminded her, 'but as we're discussing Sasha, I'd say it's because she's beautiful and fun and who knows, maybe he is playing around a bit when he's in Edinburgh, but they're young, it's what you do at that age. I'm sure it's just a summer fling before she starts college.'

Olivia treated her mother to a despairing look as she fished into her bag to retrieve her phone. Seeing it was Sasha she clicked on.

'Mum, I can't get hold of Dad,' Sasha cried belligerently. 'He is going to help me tonight, isn't he?'

'I'm sure he is.'

'So where is he?'

'In meetings, I expect. That's how it goes in his world, you know that. How are you getting on with the shopping?'

'I think I've got everything. What time will you be home?'

'Around five. Have you emailed Luke yet?'

'No, but I will. Did you see the picture of his girl-friend? She's gorgeous, isn't she? It's no wonder he's staying in Bangkok. I was thinking, we should all fly out there to meet her.'

Olivia's eyebrows went up. 'I dare you to put that to Luke, see what he has to say. Now, I'm in the middle of lunch with Grandma so I'll talk to you later, OK?'

'I thought Grandma was having a spa day.'

'Ah yes, she is. That's where we are, at the spa.'

'OK, send her my love, and be nice to Parker tonight, *please.*'

Rena was looking pensive again. 'You know, I've never been able to work out what Imogen expects to gain from alienating you the way she does,' she stated. 'All these years ... She's such an unpleasant woman, and she never does anything to change our opinion on that. She surely knows that it's hurtful for Luke and Sasha to see how awful she is to you sometimes.'

'I don't think she sees it through their eyes,' Olivia replied. 'And you know that she manages to block out the fact that I'm their mother. As far as she's concerned they're wholly Richmond's. Remember, she says quite openly that they don't resemble me at all, either in looks, behaviour, mannerisms or character.'

'Except Sasha's the image of you.' Rena sighed. 'Let's not talk about her any more. I'd rather hear more about Sean and whether or not you're planning to see him again.'

Experiencing a small fluttering inside, born more of nerves than anticipation, Olivia said, 'Why would I?'

'Why wouldn't you?'

'For one, Richmond wouldn't like it.'

Rena shrugged. 'Well, at least we can say that Sean didn't go barmy when you two broke up, nor did he ever threaten to hurt you or Richmond.'

Olivia picked up her wine. 'Let's hope Ana's experiences in Asia and America have sailed her a long way past that particular time in her life. In fact, better still, let's hope she's already on her way back to London and taking Imogen with her.'

ANA. It was interesting being in Kesterly at that time, a very different world to the more cultural and exotic playgrounds I was used to. Quite a dull place really. I felt sorry for dear Imogen having to live there. I'd visited a few times before, always to stay with her, and as far as I was aware Olivia never knew I was nearby. Unless Richmond told her, of course, but I don't think he did.

On my previous visits I'd spent some time watching Olivia coming and going from the Folly, attacking her day as a PR consultant with great energy, promoting various businesses, visiting celebrities or attending charity events.

She seemed to have a lot of friends, was quite popular I'd say, and as far as I could make out her relationship with Luke and Sasha was good.

I was careful never to let her see me; I didn't want to scare her, only to satisfy myself that I could be in her world if I wanted to be, without her knowing. Of course, I was anyway, but having her in my sights could be faintly thrilling.

Yes, Richmond knew I was there. His mother would sometimes complain that he didn't visit her nearly as often when she was alone, but I have no idea if that's true.

Of course you want to know the reason I was in Kesterly then. In a nutshell, it was because Richmond needed my help. This was something of a turnaround, because until then it was me who'd needed his.

Yes, I knew what was going on at Penn Financial, or more specifically with the marina project.

Did I know that Sean Kenyon's consultancy had been invited to advise on the expansion? Not immediately, but when I did know I could see right away what an effect it was having on Richmond, and it wasn't good. I thought the Mace Group, who have an equally stellar reputation in that field, some would say even better, was being called in. I heard later that they had been approached, but at that point they were still carrying out due diligence from their desks and conference rooms in London. It seemed the Kenyon Group moved faster and it wasn't hard to guess who'd contacted them. It could only have been David

Penn, Olivia's father, because he was the only partner at Penn Financial who'd had any previous dealings with them. There are other reasons it would have been him, but there's one to start with.

Yes, Richmond valued his marriage. You can be forgiven for thinking otherwise; I did myself for a long time. I'm not sure even he knew how much it meant to him, but I do know it was never as much as the children did. He wasn't ever going to leave them and he knew she wouldn't give them up, so that was why he stayed. Then we reached the point where the eldest flew the nest and the other was about to try her wings. You could say that was what brought things to a head, but there were so many other factors playing into it all by then that focusing only on the domestic would be rather pathetic.

So, I returned to Kesterly two years ago to help move things along. I knew that everything had to be approached delicately, subtly, in a way that created as much clarity in some areas as it did confusion in others. It's the way I operate best, how I've earned my reputation in the art world, bringing people together with similar interests, goals, ambitions, making sure everyone gets what they want by whatever means it takes.

It's important, don't you think, for everyone to get what they want?

It's just a shame that things don't always work out that way.

Chapter Five

It was well past seven thirty by the time Sasha raced up the stairs to drag Olivia out of her studio. 'I told you what time we were eating,' she cried worriedly. 'Grandma's been here for ages, and everything's going to be spoiled if you don't come down now.'

'Darling, I'm sorry,' Olivia responded distractedly. 'I have to finish these plans for the plumber tonight, or he can't start work tomorrow. I didn't think it would take so long.'

'You have to leave it now,' Sasha insisted, her face flushed with annoyance. 'Daddy's given everyone a drink, but it looks rude you not being there. Grandma's already making comments about it, you know what she's like.'

'She would make comments whether I was there or not,' Olivia reminded her. 'Can I have a few minutes to put on some lipstick and tidy up my hair?'

Sasha appeared about to protest again, but after giving her the once-over she reluctantly relented.

'OK, but make sure you use the Sunset Shimmer lip-gloss, you know the really pink one, because it's a great colour on you, it brings out the blue of your eyes. And no more than a couple of minutes. What do you want to drink? Everyone else is having gin and tonic.'

'Neat tonic for me,' Olivia told her, starting to follow her down to the mezzanine level. For one heady moment, as the relief of that morning's doctor's appointment washed over her, she wanted to grab Sasha in her arms and dance her around with the sheer joy of it. She'd suffered so horribly during chemo that it was as though her whole life had gone into darkness for that time, but now, at last, she was seeing light at the end of the tunnel. However, it wouldn't be fair to make this evening about her, when Sasha and Richmond were probably going to feel awful once they found out they'd forgotten she'd been due for a check-up today.

Olivia was just peeling off towards her bedroom when Sasha said, in a whisper, 'Mum!'

Olivia turned back.

'You didn't say anything about my dress. Is it OK? I bought it specially for tonight.'

Olivia surveyed her appreciatively. Although it was too short and the neckline too low, she accepted it was the fashion, and being so young and shapely Sasha could get away with it. 'You look gorgeous,' she told her. 'You've probably already wowed Parker off his feet.'

Sasha glowed. 'Even he said I look cool,' she confessed, 'which isn't like him at all. You know what men are like, you're never sure if they notice these things.'

Olivia's eyebrows went up, but she refrained from pointing out that they seldom failed to notice when so much slender bare leg and youthful cleavage was on show. Out of nowhere she wondered what Sean would think of her daughter, if Sasha would remind him of those exhilarating times when they were young, but she quickly pushed the thought away again.

Once in her bedroom, with its stylish black Peter Maly bed and matching closets, she quickly tore off the linen trousers and shirt she'd been in all day, discarded her underwear and padded through to the twin-showered limestone bathroom. As she rapidly hosed herself down she grimaced at the paleness of her skin, which was badly in need of some sun, though she was relieved to see that the eczema on her hip had all but gone. As for the scars from her operation – well, there was no doubt the surgeon had done a great job all those months ago because they were definitely fading, and maybe, over time, she might reconsider her decision not to undergo a reconstruction. For the moment, however, she was sticking fast to her determination to avoid any trips to the hospital that involved anything more than a check-up.

Realising she still hadn't seen Richmond this evening, apart from when she'd all but flown in and out of the kitchen before disappearing upstairs to her studio, she made a sudden conscious decision to feel upbeat about the evening ahead. It was a shame about Imogen, but as long as she didn't manage to cast a dampener on things, the way she usually did, there was every reason to have a good time.

In fact, as she wrapped herself in a towel and padded back into the bedroom, she was even wondering if she dared dig out some of her sexier underwear in an attempt to get both her and Richmond in the mood. No sooner had the thought entered her head than her heart sank to think of how pathetic, even absurd, she might look in it.

Dismayed by the rollercoaster of emotions that continued to swoop her from the heights of confidence to the depths of insecurity in the space of a heartbeat, she tried not to resent Richmond for his failure to help her through any of this. It would have made the world of difference to her if he at least showed some sensitivity towards her anxieties, or even asked how she was feeling, but he rarely did.

'Mum!' Sasha exclaimed, storming into the bedroom. 'Oh God, you're not even dressed yet. Why are you doing this? I wanted everything to go so smoothly and now you're ruining it.'

'I'm sorry,' Olivia said, hurriedly drying herself. 'Just grab me something to wear and I'll be right there.'

As Sasha flounced off to the wardrobe, Olivia caught the sound of voices downstairs, and feeling a pang of guilt for spoiling her daughter's evening, she said, 'Sasha?'

Sasha looked round, her expression one of frustration and resentment.

Olivia walked over to her, feeling painfully aware of the gulf that had opened up between them this past year, partly because of Sasha growing up, but also because Sasha's way of dealing with the fear of her mother's illness had been to try and withdraw, almost defiantly, from their closeness, as though letting her know she could cope just fine without her.

'What?' Sasha demanded.

Olivia touched her face. 'You really do look lovely, darling,' she told her. 'He's a very lucky young man.'

Sasha's cheeks immediately glowed. 'You will be nice to him, Mum, won't you?' she begged. 'You know how daunting Grandma Imogen can be if she starts going off on one, so he needs us all on his side.'

'I promise.' Olivia smiled.

Giving her a quick kiss, Sasha grabbed a dress from the wardrobe dropped it on the bed and skipped out of the room.

Quite what the always fastidiously turned-out Imogen was going to make of her daughter-in-law's hastily thrown-together appearance Olivia had no idea, nor did she much care. The only person she really wanted to please tonight was Richmond, in the hope of bringing back to the surface some of the tenderness and caring that she knew would always exist between them, come what may.

When she finally walked into the drawing room she managed to keep her smile cheerful and welcoming, even though Imogen was the first person she saw, perched on the fender in front of the fireplace, looking every inch the supercilious nightmare she was. She was so prim and fussy and ludicrously overdone with all that heavy make-up and bulky jewellery. On the other hand, when she was laughing, as she was now, it wasn't hard to see why she'd once been considered a beauty.

Looking up as the door opened, Imogen said, in mellifluously superior tones, 'Good evening, Olivia.' Without waiting for a response she returned her attention to Richmond. Sitting on one of the sofas, his back was turned to the door as he talked to the person beside him.

When she saw who it was Olivia's heart virtually stopped beating. Some kind of madness must have gripped her, because surely to God that wasn't Ana Petrov sitting beside Richmond. It just couldn't be – and yet it was. The woman's behaviour in the past had been so grotesque it would cause anyone a lifetime's embarrassment, so how could she have found the nerve to come here? She had to know how unwelcome she'd be – yet it was hardly appearing that way, when Richmond was so clearly wrapped up in what she was saying that he'd failed to hear his wife come into the room.

'Here's your drink, Mum,' Sasha said, putting a glass in her hand.

Olivia mumbled something as she took it, then aware of Imogen slyly registering her shock, she made a valiant effort to pull herself together. 'How's dinner coming along?' she asked Sasha. 'Do you need any help?'

'No, everything's fine. Are you OK? You look a bit strange.'

Olivia forced a smile. 'I'm fine,' she assured her.

'So are you going to say hello to Parker?'

Olivia looked at the young man sitting on the other sofa, one scuffed Nike trainer resting on the opposite knee, a skinny elbow propped on the sofa back, and a can of beer clutched in his pale young fist. He was wearing the customary oversized T-shirt and jeans of his age group, and his handsome face was carelessly unshaven. However, for once she didn't baulk at his vaguely offensive air of boredom, in fact she felt almost pleased to see him.

'Hey, Mrs B,' he said, raising his can to greet her. 'This is a really cool room. I've never been in here before. Did you do it yourself?'

'Mm, yes,' Olivia murmured, and turned round as Richmond said, 'Ah, Olivia, there you are. We have a surprise guest.'

'So I see,' Olivia responded evenly.

'Olivia,' Ana said warmly, getting to her feet. 'How lovely to see you. You're looking wonderful, especially considering everything you've been through.'

Appalled that she would even know about the cancer, much less mention it, Olivia tried not to imagine the kind of conversations she and Imogen must have had about it.

'You have a lovely home,' Ana breezed on. Her throaty voice, mesmerising sloe-eyed stare and exotic dark beauty were having a most unsettling effect on Olivia, reinforced by the unmistakable air of confidence that seemed to emanate from every inch of her slender frame. At five foot nine she was the same height as Olivia, but had always been a much more angular shape, not at all voluptuous; indeed, Olivia would have preferred to describe her as thin. However, this evening her exquisite long limbs and naturally olive skin were being shown off to devastating perfection by tight black hipster jeans and a pale blue top that hugged the hard points of her nipples as though they were shrink-wrapped.

Feeling she had no choice but to take the hand Ana was holding out, Olivia shook it, saying, in a voice she barely recognised as her own, 'I had no idea you were coming this evening, Ana.'

Ana laughed softly. 'Nor had I,' she confessed, 'but Imogen insisted you wouldn't mind, and she checked with Sasha first, to make sure it would be OK.'

Olivia felt a moment's anger with Sasha for not mentioning it, even though she obviously had no idea who Ana was. Besides, the fault was all Imogen's, who'd have known damned well how unwelcome Ana would be, which was, of course, why she'd done it. 'So what brings you to Kesterly?' Olivia asked, trying to sound polite, though not particularly caring if she failed.

Ana glanced at Richmond and smiled, and Olivia's heart clenched with misgiving. Such an intimate exchange was indicating something she really, *really* didn't want to understand, because no way in the world could he be responsible for Ana being here, which was what the look had seemed to suggest. No, no, she was being paranoid, because he was showing zero interest in Ana's answer as he checked his phone while Sasha and Parker took off for the kitchen.

'Summerville's are thinking of opening a saleroom here,' Ana replied, referring to a renowned international auction house.

Olivia didn't disguise her astonishment. 'Here, in Kesterly?' she said, finding it hard to believe.

Ana smiled. 'They have subdivisions all over the world,' she explained, 'and because of my connections and background in the art world they've asked me to start things rolling down here. Actually, I'm considering running it, if things work out.' Her smile seemed to say *wouldn't that make you happy?* 'If I do, I won't take up the position until the beginning of October, so I'll have plenty of time to look for somewhere to live.'

There was a moment's silence as Olivia stared at her, hoping beyond hope that she wasn't hearing this right.

'Isn't it marvellous?' Imogen chimed in silkily. 'She'll be staying with me until she finds a place of her own.'

Of course she will, where else would she go?

Ana said, 'No, I really can't impose on you for so long, Imogen. A month at the most. If I haven't found anywhere to rent by then, I'll move into a hotel.'

'You'll do no such thing,' Imogen protested fondly. 'You know you're most welcome to stay with me for as long as you like.'

Apparently just catching up with the conversation, Richmond said to Ana, 'I'm afraid you might find Kesterly a bit dull after the kind of places you've been used to.'

Olivia's head was starting to spin as she wondered if she was the only one in the room who found this odd – or even remembered what had happened all those years ago, because looking at Richmond, he apparently didn't. Either that, or he suddenly thought it was fine to entertain a woman who'd slashed Olivia's car tyres, made her terrified for her baby, slapped her round the face in a coffee shop, and even threatened to kill her.

'We're all absolutely delighted that she's considering Summerville's proposals,' Imogen was saying. 'Of course it doesn't mean she'll be giving up her wonderful gallery in Bond Street, she'd never do that, would you, my dear, she's had so much success with it. You know people come to her from all over the world either to buy, or to seek advice on oriental paintings and ceramics. No, she'll be dividing her time between London and Kesterly, and while you're here you really must think of yourself as one of the family,' she instructed Ana, 'mustn't she, Richmond?'

Stunned, Olivia looked at Richmond.

'Of course, she practically is,' Imogen chuntered on, 'I've known her parents for so long, and she and Richmond were very attached to each other when they were growing up, as I'm sure you know.'

'But that was a very long time ago,' Ana came in swiftly. 'And I'm afraid I made a bit of a fool of myself when Richmond and I broke up, which I do hope you can both forgive me for now.'

Again Olivia looked at Richmond, and could only imagine he was having some kind of mental black-out as he said, 'Don't give it a moment's thought. We've all but forgotten it, haven't we, darling?'

'No,' Olivia replied woodenly. Everyone else might want to labour under some kind of weird delusion here, but she was damned if she would.

'Of course she hasn't,' Ana said. 'I wouldn't either, if I were in your shoes, Olivia. I behaved very badly indeed, so I won't blame you at all if you are unable to forgive me.'

Though slightly thrown by such frankness, Olivia knew exactly how she wanted to respond, but since she was getting no support from Richmond, she didn't want to risk the humiliation of ordering Ana out of the house and finding him lining up on his mother's side. So instead she said, 'I'm sure you'll have a wonderful time with Imogen. She's always been so fond of you.'

Ana's smile was steeped in affection as she turned to Imogen and held out her hand. 'The feeling is mutual,' she said.

Taking the hand, Imogen held it between her own, saying, 'You will be joining Bridget and me for lunch tomorrow, won't you? You'll like her enor-mously. We're planning a little shopping expedition after to find some ideas for freshening up my house. The painters are due to start next month, and we're thinking about throwing out all the old furniture, so I would greatly value your advice in setting things up again, if you have time, Ana dear.'

'Olivia's into interior design these days,' Richmond piped up loyally. 'Maybe you should take her along.'

Olivia could hardly believe it. He surely had to know how much she'd loathe every minute; however, she was saved from objecting as Imogen said, 'Oh no, Olivia's tastes are far too *modern* for me. She wouldn't enjoy shopping for my style of furnishings one bit, would you, my dear?'

'Not one bit,' Olivia assured her, and almost instantly wished she'd had the presence of mind to foist herself on the old bag, if only to make her squirm her way out of it.

At that moment Sasha pushed her way through the double doors that opened into the dining room, and throwing them wide, announced, 'OK, dinner is served. Dad, would it be all right for Parker to do the wine?'

'I've already brought it up from the cellar,' Richmond told her, standing aside for Ana to go ahead of him.

'I know that,' Sasha said, as though he was stupid. 'I just mean can he open and pour it.'

'I think it's a great idea for Parker to take charge,' Olivia told her. 'It'll leave Dad free to catch up with his old girlfriend.'

Sasha's eyes immediately rounded. 'Like in *girlfriend*?' she mouthed.

Olivia nodded confirmation and glanced at Richmond, who had apparently either ignored her remark, or simply hadn't heard it, as he was now holding out a chair for his old girlfriend to sit down.

'Dad used to go out with her?' Sasha whispered in her mother's ear.

Olivia nodded again.

'Wow!' Sasha murmured.

Though Olivia could have cheerfully slapped her, she somehow managed not to, and walked on into the dining room where the black lacquer table, which would seat fourteen when opened to full stretch, was currently set for six. Olivia was in her usual place at one end, with Richmond at the head, his mother and Ana either side of him, leaving Sasha and Parker to sit either side of Olivia. Were it not for that 'wow' Olivia might have suggested that Sasha and Parker take each end of the table – in fact, now she came to think of it, it might seriously embarrass Sasha if she did, which would be no more than she deserved for such atrocious disloyalty.

The first course passed off reasonably well, though to Olivia's mind Ana's praise of Richmond's rather ordinary starter was cringe-making, while his pleasure in the compliments bordered on the ridiculous. Fortunately, though, the conversation centred mainly around the much safer territory of Luke and what he might be up to in Bangkok. Imogen was obviously delighted that he kept in such regular contact, particularly as she'd bought a computer and learned how to email for no other reason. She could, however, have tried to be a little less embarrassing in her shameless boasts about her grandchildren's various talents, most of which, as usual, she was managing to attribute to Richmond's guiding influence or perfect genes.

To Olivia's surprise, Sasha didn't seem to mind being discussed as if she were some kind of gifted puppy, but then she was probably lapping it up because of Parker, whose table manners were making Olivia dislike him even more. She wondered how Sasha could bear him being so loud about chewing his food and slurping his wine, already on his third glass while the rest of them were still on their first. Were Richmond not so engrossed in conversation with his old flame Olivia felt sure he'd have noticed this too, but since his attention seemed wholly focused on Ana, or his mother, she had to accept that he was going to do nothing to bring the situation under some kind of control.

So why should she?

'Is there something wrong, Mum?' Sasha said, when it came time to clear the plates. 'You've hardly eaten anything.'

Imogen immediately responded. 'Oh dear, Olivia, are you not feeling well? Is this perhaps a little too much for you?'

Showing no sign of having caught the barb, Olivia stored it away with the many others she'd received over the years and said, 'I'm perfectly fine, thank you. Just saving myself for the main course. Would you like a hand, Sasha?'

'No, Parker can bring the rest,' Sasha responded pointedly.

Rising up from the slouch he'd fallen into, Parker obediently collected the remaining plates and followed Sasha out to the kitchen. Olivia watched him go, wondering what it was that she disliked so much about him apart from his table manners, the way he dressed, his arrogance and the thought of him slathering himself all over her precious girl.

Realising those at the other end of the table were now reminiscing about the many Benting and Petrov family holidays that had taken place over the years, Olivia tried to decide whether she should walk out, try to join in, or hurl a drink at someone. Then quite suddenly Imogen clapped her hands excitedly and said, 'You know, I have a marvellous suggestion. Ana and I are driving to London this weekend to see her parents who are going to be in town, so why don't you come with us, Richmond? It will be just like old times. We will have such fun, all of us.'

Olivia was stunned. She knew she'd heard right, but surely not even Imogen would go so far as to invite Richmond to London with his ex-girlfriend and her family, and expect him to leave his wife at home.

'Sounds like a great idea to me,' Richmond replied, pouring more wine.

Olivia stared at him, dumbfounded. 'But I thought you were working this weekend,' she reminded him.

He shrugged. 'Sometimes plans have to be changed,' he responded mildly, and raising his glass to no one in particular he drank deeply.

Olivia watched him, hurt cutting hard through the shock. She could scarcely believe he'd just said that. Having turned down her suggestion that they go to Paris for her birthday weekend, was he seriously now contemplating going to London with his mother and Ana?

Sasha and Parker were returning with the main course. Hardly registering what was happening, Olivia watched Parker setting down the plates, while Sasha put the serving dish at the centre of the table. Somehow she managed to add her praise to the presentation, but as everyone else helped themselves and started to eat, she could only look down at her food and wonder if she was losing her mind. She was trying to tell herself that the past few minutes hadn't happened, or that she'd somehow misunderstood their content, but she knew she hadn't.

The conversation continued around her, moving lightly from one topic to another, as friendly and natural as if they were all the very best of friends and no issues had ever occurred between them. She kept glancing at Richmond, who was apparently oblivious to how much he'd just hurt her, and yet somehow she felt sure he wasn't. Then she realised: this could be his payback for finding her with Sean.

She wanted to scream at him, but nothing in the world would induce her to create a scene in front of Imogen. Later, though, Richmond was going to have a lot of explaining to do, because this sort of revenge wasn't only petty and unmanly, it was completely unnecessary.

In the end, after forcing down as much food as she could take, and half listening to Parker's inane drunken babble, she excused herself and went upstairs to her studio. For a while she merely sat staring at the blank screen of her computer, still reeling from what had happened, and going back over it in her mind. She tried to recall exactly what Richmond had said, how he'd sounded, if he'd been paying full attention to what was actually going on around him. Given how distracted he always was by whatever was playing out in his head he might very well have missed all the nuances, if not the actual words, and deciding it was better to go along with his mother than to fall out with her and spoil Sasha's evening he'd simply said what had been expected of him.

There still remained the fact that he must have known Ana Petrov had been invited this evening, and instead of stepping up to say it was a bad idea, he'd let it happen.

Wishing she could talk to Andee, who lived just across the square with Graeme, she took out her phone and sent a text instead.

To her surprise, since she hadn't expected to hear back tonight, she received a reply within minutes. *Neither Graeme nor I have heard that Summerville's are opening up in the area. Can investigate further if you like.*

Olivia considered that for a moment, then sent another text saying, *Yes please. Will call tomorrow to explain more.*

As she put her phone down she heard the front door open downstairs and voices outside. Presumably Imogen and Ana were leaving, so it was going to be interesting to find out what Richmond had to say for himself.

Somehow switching her mind to the plans she'd yet to finish for the plumber, she made a few changes and sent them on their way. Next she opened up the work schedule, ran through what was due to happen over the following week, then sent messages to the builder, electrician and kitchen designer. Everything was currently on target, but she knew only too well that anything could happen at any time to put them behind.

It was almost midnight by the time she finally turned off the computer and went downstairs to look for Richmond. There was no sign of him in the kitchen or dining room, and the doors to the drawing room had been pulled together. Sliding them open, she stepped through and came to an immediate stop as Sasha and Parker sprang apart.

'Where's Dad?' she asked, trying to ignore the fact that Parker was holding a cushion over his lap and Sasha was on her knees in front of him.

'I think he went up to bed,' Sasha said, her cheeks so red they looked painful.

'You need to finish clearing up,' Olivia told her.

'The dishwasher's already full, so I can't do any more.'

'Don't argue, just do as you're told,' Olivia snapped, and closing the doors she crossed the hall to Richmond's study. He wasn't there either, so perhaps he *had* gone to bed.

Though it seemed crazy to think he might have left with his mother and Ana, that was exactly what she was thinking as she approached the TV room. Hearing the sound of voices she pushed the door open, expecting to find him watching a video, but the screen was dark and he was on the sofa with Ana. They weren't touching, in fact there was quite a distance between them, but the fact that Ana was there at all was making Olivia's head spin.

'Oh, there you are,' Richmond said, glancing over his shoulder. 'I thought you'd gone to bed.'

'Not yet,' she heard herself say, in a tone she barely recognised.

'We were just catching up on old times. Why don't you come and join us?'

Was he out of his mind? Go over old times with *Ana Petrov*? She'd rather put a gun to her head. And what the hell would he say if she suggested he do the same with Sean? How ready would he be to join a tender trip down memory lane where he had nothing of any value to offer and didn't even belong? 'I've got an early start tomorrow,' she said. 'I thought you did too.'

Richmond glanced at his watch. 'Christ, I had no idea it was so late,' he said. 'We're due on site at eight.'

Unable to stop herself, Olivia said, 'Are you meeting Sean?'

Richmond's eyes darkened. 'No, we're not meeting Sean,' he replied coldly.

Ana got to her feet and approached Olivia. 'I'm so sorry if I've overstayed my welcome,' she said, reaching for her hand. 'It's been lovely to see you again after all these years, and I appreciate you not throwing me out the minute you laid eyes on me.'

Olivia looked at her dispassionately.

Ana smiled, as Richmond said, 'Come on, I'll call you a taxi.'

'Perhaps you'd like to take Parker with you,' Olivia suggested. 'He's someone else who's outstayed his welcome.'

Though Richmond looked at her sharply, he made no comment, merely followed Ana into the hall while scrolling through his contacts for the number of the firm they generally used. 'So where is Parker?' he asked.

'They were in the drawing room,' Olivia told him. 'I suggest you knock before you go in.'

He didn't have to, Sasha and Parker were already on their way out, and when a car turned up a few minutes later Richmond went to pay the driver in advance.

The instant they were alone Sasha rounded on Olivia, clearly livid that she'd been treated like a child in front of her boyfriend. '*Just do as you're told*,' she repeated through her teeth. 'Don't you ever speak to me like that again in front of him ... '

'Get up to bed now,' Olivia cut in.

'I'm not ... '

'*Go*, Sasha, and be thankful I'm not telling your father what I walked into.'

Sasha's cheeks burned. 'It's none of your business what I do,' she retorted.

'I'm not arguing with you,' Olivia told her. 'Not now. We'll discuss it tomorrow,' and turning on her heel she walked into the kitchen. Finding it in an even worse state than she expected, she simply walked out again and took herself off upstairs.

When Richmond came up, some ten minutes later, he found her in Luke's room, lying on the bed. For a while she'd thought she was feeling sorry for herself, but she wasn't, she simply felt vulnerable, she realised. Life had shown her once with her cancer diagnosis not to take anything for granted, and she knew it could do it again at any time.

Just please don't do anything to hurt the children.

'What are you doing in here?' Richmond asked from the door.

'It makes me feel close to him,' she answered, aware of a longing for her son so deep that she didn't want to share it, not even with Richmond. He'd probably only tell her to pull herself together, or stop being so clingy. On the other hand he might understand just how strange and unsettling she'd found this evening, and even tease her for believing that he'd actually go to London at the weekend without her.

It didn't matter. Whatever games he might be playing, or misunderstandings he'd caused, she didn't want to discuss them right now. It was best to say nothing.

'Are you going to sleep there?' he asked, managing to sound both impatient and worried.

'I think so.'

He hesitated a moment longer, seeming unsure what to do, then coming to kiss her goodnight, he whispered a perfunctory 'love you', and turning out the light he closed the door behind him.

Chapter Six

Olivia left the house just after six the next morning to go and open up the old chapel before the workmen arrived. Considering how upset she'd been last night she'd slept surprisingly well, and while she wasn't feeling exactly relaxed this morning, she wasn't particularly stressed or agitated either. She had no idea how Richmond was, since he'd already left the house by the time she'd got up, so he was presumably at the office by now, preparing for whatever his day had in store.

As she drove over to the north headland, a giant lion's paw of a grassy peninsula, she was reflecting on how events over at the marina – or lack of them – were proving that he'd bitten off more than he could chew with the expansion. He hadn't admitted it to her, but he wouldn't anyway, out of pride and probably because he'd want to protect her from the stress of it. But the fact that major construction consultancies had been drafted in, or at least approached, presumably to help with some sort of rescue package, confirmed just how serious things had become. She had no doubt that Richmond's biggest concern would be for the clients of Penn Financial, many of them friends and neighbours, who'd invested in the project, though she guessed that share of the investment was nothing compared to the loan provided by the bank.

As she pulled up outside the old chapel, where a clutter of builders' paraphernalia was fenced in by orange plastic nets and the two-centuries-old stained-glass windows were coming colourfully to life in the early morning sunlight, she gave a small sigh of frustration. She wanted to help Richmond, she really did, but apart from moral support she had nothing else to offer. And even if she did, she knew he wouldn't welcome her interference any more than he was welcoming Sean's. Or her father's, who'd called on the Kenyon Group for assessment of a project that she knew he had had doubts about in the first place.

Knowing that the only sensible course for her to take now was to let them sort this out between them, she pushed open the car door and drew focus on her own day. She couldn't control every-thing, and she most certainly couldn't influence a situation that she had scant understanding of, so she would simply let it go the way she'd been taught by her counsellor, and hope that the worst

Richmond suffered as a result of his bad management, or faulty judgement, or whatever had caused the problems, was a bruising of his manly ego.

When Olivia returned home some three hours later she found the kitchen was still a disaster zone from last night, so she set about tackling it, since there was no sign of Sasha, and she knew there probably wouldn't be this side of midday.

As she worked, the unpleasant and worrying prospect of Ana Petrov starting up a new business here, in Kesterly, began coming over her in waves. She knew very well that having the woman in the vicinity wasn't something she could live with, last night's dinner was proof enough of that, but how could she stop it? Ana Petrov had the right to live and work wherever she chose; but the fact that she'd chosen Kesterly ... Well, what other reason could there be for her arrival here than to cause mischief? None whatsoever that Olivia could see. Indeed, it had already started with Imogen's ludicrous invitation to London this weekend. Olivia just knew that Ana had put her up to it, but what bothered her more than their petty little mind game was the way Richmond had agreed to go.

He wouldn't, of course, Olivia was certain of that, if only because it would mean leaving Sean Kenyon's investigation of the marine project's problems unsupervised by their architect, namely Richmond. Her father could work with Sean, of course, and was probably already doing so, but that particular pairing was even less likely to make Richmond want to leave town. So, whatever trouble Ana had hoped to cause this weekend, she was out of luck.

Looking up as Sasha padded into the kitchen, Olivia was on her way to a rebuke for not clearing up last night when her heart sank at the black scowl on her daughter's face. She said nothing, only returned to scouring a pan, reminding herself that confrontations and emotional explosions were rarely helpful to anyone, least of all someone such as herself, who had no heart for them.

After tossing an empty drink bottle and her mobile phone on the counter top, Sasha went to dash a helping of cereal into a bowl. 'I still haven't forgiven you for last night,' she muttered angrily. 'You made a real fool of me, and now, thanks to you ... '

'If I were you I wouldn't bring it up again,' Olivia cautioned. 'I know what you two were up to in the drawing room, and frankly, I find it ... '

Sasha spun round furiously, 'I'm old enough to do what I want,' she shouted.

'That's what you wanted, was it? It was your idea, not his?'

Tight-faced, Sasha flounced over to a stool and banged her bowl down. 'You know what your trouble is,' she snapped, 'you're jealous.'

Olivia blinked with astonishment.

'You are!' Sasha insisted. 'You're jealous because Dad was being nice to Ana last night, and now you're taking it out on me. Well, frankly I don't blame Dad if he finds her attractive. You're always in such a bad mood, and picking on him for the least little thing. You were better when you were actually ill, at least you were nice to us all then.'

Olivia stared at her, too stunned to respond.

'It's no wonder Luke took off halfway across the world as fast as he could,' Sasha ranted on recklessly. 'He couldn't wait to get out of here ... '

'At least Luke bothered to find out how my check-up went yesterday,' Olivia retaliated.

Guilt flickered in Sasha's eyes, but she wasn't backing down yet. 'So you want me to ask now, do you?' she retorted. 'Well I'm not going to, because that's just playing your game.'

'Game?'

'Yes, game. You keep making us all ask what's going on instead of just telling us. Well, I'm sick of everything always being about you and your treatment and your results ... '

'I didn't realise that was how you were seeing it,' Olivia said quietly.

'No, because you never think about anyone but yourself. You don't care how much you hurt other people. Like last night, you just got up and walked out right in the middle of something Parker was saying, then you came barging in on us ... '

'I didn't know you were in there, and frankly, you should be relieved it was me and not Dad, or that boy would never be allowed here again and you know it.'

'What makes you think he wants to come?' Tears were starting down Sasha's cheeks. 'You were so horrible and rude to him that he's saying he might not want to see me any more.'

Olivia stared at her in despair, her conscience so torn that she had no idea what to say to make things better. Should she go and comfort her? She probably wouldn't welcome it, but on the other hand at least it would show she cared.

'Get away from me,' Sasha sobbed, slapping at her. 'I don't want you to touch me or come near me ever again.'

Olivia took a breath to respond, but Sasha suddenly began to rant so furiously that it was hard to make sense of what she was saying.

'Sasha, stop!' Olivia cried. 'You're going to make yourself sick.'

'And what would you care if I did? I'm nothing to you. Luke's always been your favourite ... '

'Don't be ridiculous.'

'Everyone knows it. He's only got to ask and he gets everything he wants.'

Olivia was incredulous. 'Sasha will you ... '

'Five hundred quid! He just sends an email saying he's running low, and next thing Dad's wiring over five times what he was expecting – and I'll bet it was you who told him to do it.'

'Then you'd lose, because I didn't – and I'm not arguing with you any more about this. You need to pull yourself together ... ' As Sasha's mobile started to ring she made to snatch it up, but Olivia got there first.

Sasha's eyes blazed. 'Give me that phone,' she demanded.

'Not until ... '

'Give me that phone or you'll be sorry!'

Shocked, Olivia said, 'Don't you dare threaten me.'

'It'll be Parker, now let me have it.'

The ringing stopped.

'I hate you!' Sasha screamed at her.

'You're grounded,' Olivia told her, tucking the phone into her pocket.

'That is so not going to happen,' Sasha seethed, and to Olivia's relief instead of coming to try and wrest the phone back, she stormed past her to the stairs.

Taking out her own phone as it rang, Olivia saw it was her mother and clicked on.

'Hello, darling,' Rena said warmly. 'How are you feeling today?'

With her head still spinning from the past few minutes, Olivia hardly knew how to answer. 'OK, I think,' she said.

'Mm, you don't sound it, but you can tell me all about it tonight. We're still on for the theatre, aren't we? You haven't forgotten?'

'No, of course not,' Olivia lied. 'I'm looking forward to it.' For the life of her she couldn't remember what they were going to see, but she did know that she hadn't been involved in promoting the show. She'd always looked after the theatre's publicity, but it seemed Bob Aisley, the manager, and his wife Susie were either doing it themselves now, or they'd found someone else.

That hurt probably more than it should, but she would have to get used to the way people had moved on. For all they knew she might never have been able to take up her old life again.

'Is it OK if we find one another in the foyer?' Rena asked. 'Dad and I are meeting Sean for an early drink beforehand, so we'll already be nearby.'

Olivia's heart flipped as she wondered why she wasn't invited for the drink. Did she want to be? Of course she did, but with all things considered maybe it would be better if she didn't go. 'That's fine,' she said stiffly.

'So we'll see you at seven?'

'Lovely,' Olivia replied. 'Mum, tell me, was I really horrible to you when I was a teenager?'

Rena sighed. 'Oh dear, have you had a falling-out with Sasha? I wouldn't worry too much, it's normal between mother and daughter when girls reach her age.'

Olivia took no comfort from that. 'I think she's harbouring some kind of grudge or anger about my illness,' she said. 'Maybe we didn't pay her enough attention. It was right through her GCSEs, but we always helped with her revision ... '

'Of course you did, but she was scared out of her wits, as we all were. It's not such an unusual reaction to be angry with someone who's frightened you. Think of the mother who slaps her child for running into the road without looking. Relief and anger can be two sides of the same coin. Where is she now?'

'In her room, I imagine. She's furious with me because her boyfriend's apparently broken up with her. She says it's my fault because I don't like him ... '

'You don't,' Rena confirmed, 'but if you ask me this isn't any great romance, it's her attempt to acquire a little sophistication and experience before she goes to college.'

'I get that, but I didn't much enjoy catching her giving him oral sex last night. What was more, he didn't seem to mind that I'd walked in.'

'Oh dear,' Rena murmured. 'I must admit, that's not too pretty a picture to be confronted with as a mother, but you can't tell me you didn't do anything like it with Sean when you were that age.'

Olivia was thrown, even shocked. However, it was true, she and Sean had been intimate when she was sixteen; it had happened within three weeks of them being together, but she'd never once felt that he was using her. In any case, she wanted her mother to take her side over this, not Sasha's. In the end, she said, 'Actually, it's not just Sasha ... Something else happened last night that I need to talk to you about. I won't tell you on the phone, I'll save it for later, but I need some advice.'

'All my worldly experience is at your service, my darling,' Rena assured her.

Olivia was still smiling as she clicked off the line, then scrolling to another number she went through to her father's mobile.

'Ah, it's the other woman in my life,' he said cheerily. 'If you're calling to remind me it's your birthday tomorrow your mother's beaten you to it, but she needn't have bothered, because I have a knot tied in my hanky.'

Olivia laughed, and felt some of the tension unfurling. Sometimes all it took was the sound of her dad's voice, or one of his special hugs, to make the world feel all right again. Thank God she had him and her mother, because there were times when they felt like the only calm waters in very stormy seas. 'I don't suppose you're at the office, are you?' she asked him.

'I am indeed. Why?'

'I was just wondering ... Is Richmond there?'

'I saw him earlier. Why, can't you find him? I can go and look if you like.'

'No, no, it's fine. I'll track him down. You're OK, are you?'

'Never better. Looking forward to seeing you later.'

'Me too.' It was on the tip of her tongue to ask about the marina project, but in the end all she said was, 'Love you,' and rang off. It really wasn't going to help anyone for her to be drawn into the problems, especially if she was right about her father and husband being on opposing sides of the solution. She wondered who she'd choose if she had to. Right now she felt sorry for Richmond, for she remembered how excited and confident he'd been about the expansion at the outset. It was a project he'd cooked up with Cooper Jarrett to make Kesterly the go-to coastal resort post-Brexit, when it was believed the end to cheap flights and border-free travel would create a huge boost for staycations. He'd truly believed in the idea, and it would appear the local authority, who owned the marina, had too, for they'd granted planning permission in record time.

At first, in fact for over a year, as land was cleared and reclaimed and plans were modified and even expanded, the venture had seemed to go from strength to strength. But now, with no more than the foundations in place, work had ground to a halt, and it seemed the only way of saving the day was to hand everything over to an organisation that possessed all the necessary skills and reach to see it through.

This level of public humiliation was going to half kill her husband, particularly if he was forced to accept help from Sean Kenyon. She didn't even want to think about what the future held, she only knew that she would be there for Richmond in any way she could, and she hoped, prayed, that when it came right down to it her father would be too.

It was just over an hour later, as Olivia was responding to an email from a lighting company, that Richmond rang. She was upstairs in her studio, where she'd been trying to work against the thunderous music coming from Sasha's room next door – though thankfully the volume had gone down in the last few minutes.

'Hi, darling,' he said, when she answered. 'Are you OK?'

Feeling an immediate lightening of her spirits at the tone of his voice, she said, 'I think so. How about you?'

'I'm fine,' he replied. 'Hectic, but I just received a text from Sasha telling me you two had a row and you've grounded her.'

'Did she tell you how she spoke to me?'

'She admits she said some pretty horrible things, but she's feeling really bad about them now.'

'Then she can apologise. I'm in the next room.'

He sighed gently. 'Don't be too hard on her. She's been through a tough time lately, what with everything, and I hate to think of you two being bad friends.'

Already feeling guilty for prioritising her work for the past hour when she should have tried to make up with Sasha, Olivia said, 'That's not what I want either, and you're right to remind me of how difficult this has been for her. I can see now that I probably haven't understood enough of what it's been like for the rest of you. She said I've been horrible to you too, always picking on you ... Is that true? Have I become a monster?'

'Only some of the time,' he teased, 'but I can take it. So, how were things at the old chapel this morning?'

Surprised, since he rarely asked about her work, she said, 'OK. Everything and everyone arrived on time, which is always a bonus. How about things there?' *Have you seen Sean? How's that going? Are things really so bad?*

'It's all fine,' he told her. 'I just popped out of a meeting to make a few calls, and when I found Sasha's text I thought I'd better get hold of you. So here I am. By the way, I missed you last night.'

Feeling nothing but relieved to hear those words, she said, 'I missed you too.'

'So does that mean you'll be back in your usual place tonight?'

'Of course.'

'That's what I want to hear. I'll try to be home for seven if I can.'

'OK, but I'm going to the theatre with Mum and Dad, remember, and we're having dinner after so I probably won't be back until late.'

'No problem. I'll order pizzas or Chinese for me and Sash if she's grounded. Are we going to stick to this? I'll back you if your mind's made up.'

Feeling awful as she thought of Sasha's outburst, and the horribly conflicting emotions she was try-ing to cope with, Olivia sighed as she said, 'I'll talk to her.'

'Good. Let me know how it goes. I'll wait up for you later. We can have a nightcap together.'

'It's a date.' She smiled, and deciding that that would be a better time to bring up what had happened with his mother and ex-girlfriend last night, she rang off.

After quickly finishing the email she picked up Sasha's mobile and went to make peace.

'Can I come in?' she asked, peering cautiously into the room when Sasha didn't respond to the knock.

Her daughter was sitting on the big iron-framed bed they'd found while on holiday in France last year. Her legs were crossed, and her long crinkly blonde hair was falling over her face, masking it completely. She appeared to be listening to something through her earpods while staring down at her iPad, but when she looked up Olivia saw right away how hard she'd been crying.

'Oh, darling,' she said, going to her as she started to cry again.

'Oh, Mum, I'm really, really sorry,' Sasha choked into Olivia's shoulder. 'I shouldn't have said all those terrible things. I didn't mean them, honestly. I was just so angry, and it's not your fault you got cancer. I shouldn't blame you ... '

'Sssh, ssh,' Olivia soothed. 'I'm sorry too, and nothing's your fault, darling. None of this has been easy, but it's going to be all right. The doctor was very pleased with me yesterday ... '

Sasha's arms immediately tightened their hold. 'Oh, Mum, I'm so glad, and I'm so sorry I said wouldn't ask. I was just afraid ... I mean, it all seemed to be OK, but then I kept thinking what if it wasn't?'

'I should have told you right away,' Olivia said. 'I should tell Dad too.'

'You mean you haven't yet?'

'Maybe he's someone else who's fed up with asking,' Olivia said wryly. 'I think it's more likely he forgot I was going, though.'

Sasha clasped her hands round her mother's face and gazed hard into her eyes, seeming to see her anew, or differently, or maybe she was just really seeing her. 'If you'd died, Mum,' she said, her eyes filling with tears again, 'I would have wanted to die too.'

Olivia smiled tenderly. 'It's not going to happen, sweetheart, or not yet awhile, so let's put it out of our minds, shall we?'

Though Sasha nodded, the way her eyes went down prompted Olivia to say, 'There's something else, isn't there? I'm guessing it's Parker.'

Sasha nodded. 'Don't let's fight about it, Mum, please. That was really bad earlier ... I got so mad and I don't want to be like it again.'

'We're not going to fight,' Olivia assured her. 'You're just going to tell me what's really going on with him.'

Sasha swallowed and sobbed on a breath. 'Apparently some friends have invited him to go backpacking around South America,' she said, and her face started to crumple again. 'He says he's going to go, and I thought ... I thought he really liked me ... Oh, Mum, what am I going to do?'

Olivia held her close and wished she knew how to answer in a way that would be helpful.

'I've been emailing Sophie,' Sasha said, 'and she doesn't think it's really true about South America. She says he's only saying it to make me .... To get me to ... You know.'

Not liking the sound of that, Olivia tilted Sasha's chin up to look at her. 'Is that what you think as well?' she asked.

Sasha shrugged.

'Darling, you can't let him blackmail you into something so important. It's a horrible thing to do ... '

'I know it might seem that way, but I don't want to be the only virgin when I get to college ... '

'Who says you're going to be?'

' ... and it's not blackmail if he loves me, and he says he does.'

'If he really loved you he wouldn't put you under that sort of pressure.'

'But he's nineteen, Mum, and he's done it lots of times before, and men have those needs, don't they? And it's not as if I don't want to, because I do.'

Olivia sighed as she struggled again for the right response.

'You've never had a problem with Luke sleeping with his girlfriends,' Sasha pointed out.

'But I'm pretty sure Luke never blackmailed anyone into it.'

'How do you know? He might have. Loads of my friends say it's happened to them, and then they've been really glad that they did it.'

Though she doubted that, Olivia decided that it probably wasn't going to help to argue about it, so all she said was, 'I don't think this is the right way for you, Sasha.'

Sasha's eyes welled again. 'If he finishes with me I might as well kill myself,' she wailed.

'Don't talk silly.'

Sasha's eyes darkened. 'I mean it,' she declared.

Knowing full well that she didn't, Olivia said softly, 'I wish I knew what you saw in him. Yes, he's good-looking, but ... '

'Oh, Mum, that's just a stupid thing to say. I mean why do you love Dad? You can't explain those things, they just happen, and if you knew how it felt ... '

Knowing very well how a first love felt, Olivia stroked her daughter's face and wished with all her heart that Sasha could have found someone more like Sean. There had never been any ugly game-playing with him; she'd always known what their relationship was about, and all she'd had to do was enjoy it.

Wresting her mind back from those halcyon times, she thumbed away Sasha's tears as she said, 'I'm afraid we'll have to continue this later, but I want you to think long and hard about the way Parker's persuading you to do things, because I think, in your heart, you know it isn't the right way to go.'

Chapter Seven

'Hey, Mum! Happy birthday,' Luke shouted down the line. 'Are you awake yet?'

Struggling to come to, Olivia glanced at the clock on the nightstand and could hardly believe her eyes. 'Luke, darling,' she answered, sitting up to get another angle on the clock to make sure it really was twenty past ten in the morning, 'where are you?'

'Still in Bangkok. So what are you doing today? Anything special planned?'

'I'm not sure yet,' she replied. 'I wish you were here.'

'I do too, but only for the day. I'm having the best time, Mum, and now you're past all that chemo stuff I can really throw myself into this. I reckon I'm going to spend about four weeks in India, then maybe I'll go on to New Zealand.'

'You're not exactly taking the most direct route,' Olivia commented, carrying the phone across to the bathroom. 'Have you received the money from Dad yet?'

'Yes, I picked it up this morning. Is he there?'

'It doesn't look like it,' she replied, finding the bathroom empty and Richmond's towelling robe hanging on its usual hook.

'Oh well, send him my love, won't you, and tell him to make sure he gives you the best birthday ever, or he'll have me to reckon with.'

'If I don't find him soon, he'll have *me* to reckon with,' she responded drily. 'Take care of yourself, darling, and thanks for calling.'

As she rang off she was remembering how she'd found Richmond already in bed and fast asleep when she'd come home last night. She hadn't been that late, so he must either have forgotten their nightcap date, or had been so tired he simply couldn't stay awake any longer.

She was about to try calling him when the bedroom door burst open and Sasha announced herself with a 'Dah-dah!' as she transported a very prettily laid breakfast tray over to the bed. 'Happy birthday, Mum,' she sang out. 'I thought you were never going to wake up. Dad and I went out jogging first thing, then he said to let you sleep, but I just heard your mobile ringing ... Is this OK? I've got you a present too, but it wouldn't fit on the tray so I have to go back down to get it. The postman brought some cards, I'll bring them up with me too, shall I?'

'If you like,' Olivia answered, sitting down on the bed next to the tray. 'Where's Dad now?'

'He went to the office, I think.'

Since Richmond regularly worked at weekends, Olivia let it go and narrowed her eyes as she said, carefully, 'You seem in a very good mood this morning.' It no doubt had something to do with Parker, and she wasn't sure she wanted the details.

Sasha shrugged. 'I'm cool,' she replied airily. 'Oh my God, you don't think Dad's forgotten it's your birthday, do you? That would be so bad. He didn't mention it when we were running round the park. He's going to be in such trouble ... By the way, we bumped into the *old* girlfriend while we were out. You were so funny the way you said that the other night. I didn't know you could be a bitch, not like that, anyway. She was running too, so she joined us for a while.'

Aware of a slow freeze closing over her heart, Olivia tried to sound casual to the point of uninterested as she said, 'That was nice. So what did you talk about?'

'Nothing much, really. The weather, my college, Grandma Imogen's refurb plans. She seems quite cool.'

Imagining how stunning Ana had probably looked in her jogging gear, while wondering if she and Richmond had arranged to 'bump into' each other and had ended up having some private time spoiled by Sasha's decision to join her father, Olivia said, 'Did she mention anything about going to London today?'

'No. She wasn't with us for very long before she cut off down towards the canal. Then Dad said he had to get to work, so I turned back and came home. Do you think I ought to let him know he's in trouble about your birthday?'

Olivia said, 'Why not? Give him a call at the office. He must be there by now.'

'Oh easily,' Sasha agreed as she connected to Richmond's direct line. As she waited for an answer she rolled back on the pillows, letting her T-shirt ride up over her hips and stretching out her long, slender legs. After three rings his voicemail picked up. 'Hi, Dad, it's me,' she said. 'I hope you haven't forgotten Mum's birthday, because if you have, you are going to be so dead.' As she rang off she said, 'Shall I try his mobile?'

Olivia nodded.

Once again Sasha received a recorded message. 'Dad, call home fast,' she said. 'It's a big day for Mum and I think you might have screwed up.' Then clicking off the line, she rolled on to her front and propping her chin in her hands she said, 'Do you know what, Mum? I really, really, really, really love you.'

Though Olivia smiled, a growing sense of unease was distracting her. Why wasn't he answering his phone? Where was he? He surely to God hadn't gone to London with Ana and his mother?

'Hello, remember me?' Sasha sang. 'I just told you I love you.'

Giving her full attention, Olivia smiled more warmly as she said, 'I love you too, and I'm guessing you've seen Parker which is why you're in such a good mood.'

Sasha sighed dramatically and rolled over on to her back. 'I might have,' she countered. 'There again, I might not.'

'Please tell me you haven't given in to his blackmail.'

'It's not blackmail, it's just him being crazy about me and not finding the right way to say things.'

Olivia forced her tone to remain neutral as she said, 'So based on that you're going to have sex with him?'

Sasha coloured. 'I don't know, I haven't made up my mind yet.'

Knowing in her heart that Sasha didn't really want to do it, Olivia thought back over the advice her mother had given her last night and decided to follow it. 'If you're going to give in to him,' she said, 'then there's nothing I can do to stop you, but I'd like you to go on the pill first, and to make sure when it does happen that he wears a condom.'

Less fazed by this than Olivia had expected her to be, Sasha said, 'I've already thought of that, so you've got nothing to worry about.'

Apart from the fact that you don't really want to do it, Olivia wanted to say. Taking a sip of coffee instead, she said, 'By the way, did you borrow my pink lipstick? I don't mind if you did, I'd just like to have it back.'

'Not guilty.' Sasha opened an incoming text.

Puzzled by the loss, since she normally kept the lipstick in the bathroom, Olivia tried to remember if she'd put it in her bag. It wasn't there now, because she'd already checked, so maybe it had fallen out. 'I'll look in the car,' she said, as Sasha finished with the text. With a sigh, she added, 'I wish I knew where Dad was.'

'Oh, he'll call any minute,' Sasha assured her. 'Or he'll turn up with some surprise or other, which he's probably gone out to get. He's always been good at those things, you know that, so just chill out and enjoy your breakfast.'

After Sasha had gone down to fetch the present and cards Olivia tried Richmond's numbers herself, but he still wasn't answering. Then, hating herself for it, she went back to the bathroom to make sure his shaving gear and toothbrush were still there. She didn't really think he'd gone to London, but she still couldn't help feeling relieved to find everything where it should have been. Apart from the lipstick, that definitely wasn't there, and the gap in her memory was unsettling, for it wasn't the first time she'd mislaid something lately.

It was in the middle of the afternoon, while Sasha was out shopping with friends, that Andee Lawrence brightened the day by dropping in with a card and some chocolates. She was a tall, striking woman with exquisite aquamarine eyes and dark curly hair, and a reassuring air of capability and calm behind the glamorous facade that probably came from her time as a detective. Since Olivia had known her for most of her life, she trusted her in a way she didn't always trust her other friends, maybe because she'd never known Andee to gossip or let someone down. And over this past year, each time Olivia had needed a shoulder that didn't belong to one of her family, and more recently a job to start getting her out again, Andee had been there for her.

Now, having decided to treat themselves to an early glass of wine, Olivia's drowned in soda water, they wandered into the garden to sit under the vine-covered pergola. 'So have you heard any more from Sean?' Andee asked, stretching out her long legs to catch some sun.

Feeling an odd sort of twist inside, Olivia said, 'No. He had drinks with my parents last night, so he's still in Kesterly, but he hasn't been in touch with me.'

'Did your father mention anything about the marina assessment when you were having dinner?'

'Only to say that various meetings have been set up with the builders and the local authority, but they haven't happened yet.' After a beat she added, 'I guess Sean hasn't been in touch with you, or you'd have said.'

'Not with me, he hasn't, but Graeme's heard from him. He was looking for an objective view on the expansion from a local independent developer.'

Olivia nodded vaguely. 'So what was Graeme able to tell him?' she asked, aware of how tense she was without exactly knowing why.

'Well, he admitted that he'd always had doubts about the project's viability, but that was really all he could say.'

Saddened by Graeme's lack of faith in the project, though it certainly wasn't news, Olivia said, 'I'm sure it was my father who contacted the Kenyon Group, and if I'm right it means he has no confidence in Richmond's ability to sort things out.' It was more upsetting than she wanted to admit, even to herself, to think of how betrayed by his own family Richmond must be feeling over this.

'What about Mace?' Andee prompted. 'Any idea who might have contacted them?'

Olivia shook her head. 'Unless that was also my father, or someone acting with his blessing.' She reached for her drink and swirled it slowly around the glass.

'I have some news about Summerville's,' Andee said, changing the subject.

Olivia looked up. *Summerville's. Ana Petrov.* Her mouth turned dry.

'Apparently,' Andee continued, 'they were looking into turning the old Assembly Rooms over on Colston Road into an auction house, but after an initial feasibility study the plans were abandoned.'

Olivia swallowed as her mind clawed towards unpleasant conclusions. 'So what do we deduce from that?' she asked, trusting to Andee's more objective viewpoint.

'As far as Ana Petrov is concerned?' Andee responded. 'It's hard to know. Did she specifically say Summerville's?'

Olivia nodded, and felt a chill running through her as she sipped her wine and wondered where Richmond was today. He still hadn't been in touch, and it wasn't like him not to respond to messages, even if he couldn't get back right away.

By the time she'd finished telling Andee what had happened at Thursday night's dinner, when Imogen had suggested Richmond should join her and Ana in London for the weekend, she was feeling more uneasy than ever.

'Are you sure he actually agreed to go to London?' Andee asked, clearly doubting it.

Olivia was perfectly sure. 'And now I can't get hold of him.'

Andee looked perplexed.

'I talked it over with my parents last night,' Olivia told her, 'and they think that if Ana Petrov really is planning to move here then I should try to make a friend of her.'

Andee blinked in astonishment. 'After the way she behaved when Richmond dumped her for you? I mean, your parents could be right, it might be the best way to go, but I don't think it'll be easy.'

'Actually, I might find it easier to make a friend of her than I ever have of my mother-in-law. I wouldn't be at all surprised if Imogen contacted Ana the minute she knew I had cancer. She probably saw it as a vacancy opening up.'

Though it wasn't funny, they both laughed.

'Well, luckily there's not, but you ... Is that someone at the door?'

Going to answer it, Olivia checked her mobile on the way, but there was still no word from Richmond. She was half tempted to turn the phone off so he couldn't get through even if he tried.

'Mrs Benting?' It was a florist's delivery lad, holding out a simple bouquet of old-fashioned roses.

'Thank you.' She smiled, taking it from him, and turning back inside she searched for a card.

Finding it, she read, *Where is the Life we have lost in living?*

Frowning, she read it again. Something about it was stirring her memory … and then it came clear. It was a quote: T.S. Eliot's *Choruses from 'The Rock'*. She remembered with a sweet pang of nostalgia where she and Sean had been the first time they'd read Eliot's poems together, on the deck of his father's yacht, *Calypso*, in Tortola. They'd read them again many times after, had even memorised some, but she wasn't sure she could recite any now.

Taking the flowers through to the garden, she put them on the table and said, 'Guess who?'

Andee's eyes narrowed. 'I'm going to say not Richmond?'

Olivia shook her head.

Breaking into a smile, Andee said, 'Then it has to be Sean. I'm impressed he remembered after all these years.'

'I'm sure he didn't,' Olivia retorted. 'He saw my parents last night and no doubt they told him. So this is less impressive than mischievous, because I'll now have to explain who they're from.'

'You might also have to call to thank him,' Andee pointed out.

Olivia frowned darkly. 'That,' she decided, 'would be manipulative.'

Andee shrugged. 'True, but don't you want to speak to him?'

Olivia gave it some thought. 'No, I don't think I do,' she replied, 'not with the way things are. They're complicated enough without doing anything to add to it. I'll send a text.'

Andee picked up her wine and regarded Olivia in a way that seemed faintly amused, but also serious. 'I was about to say, before the doorbell rang, that the stars seem to be positioning themselves rather curiously over your world at the moment.' She smiled.

Olivia sighed as she laughed. 'Tell me about it. First Sean turning up, then Ana ... ' After a moment she added, 'I could feel quite unnerved by it if I allowed myself to. It's like too much is happening at once, and I've forgotten the right way to react to things. Maybe the chemo frazzled my brain, because I don't feel like myself at all.'

Andee looked up at the sound of the front door opening and closing. Realising it was Richmond, Olivia's heart flooded with relief. 'Please say the flowers are from you,' she whispered quickly.

'Of course,' Andee agreed. 'Actually, I should be going. I promised to take over at the shop at four.' As she got to her feet Richmond came out of the kitchen door in a crumpled pale blue shirt and red corduroy jeans, looking tired, harassed, but nonetheless pleased to see her.

'Please don't go on my account,' he said, embracing her.

'Nothing to do with you,' she assured him. 'I have an appointment to keep.' To Olivia she said, 'I'll meet you at the old chapel on Monday?'

After seeing her out Olivia returned to the kitchen to find Richmond helping himself to a glass of wine. He seemed unaware she was there until she said, 'Where have you been all day?'

Sighing, he dropped his head to massage the back of his neck as he said, 'At the marina and the office. I should still be over there, but when I picked up Sasha's messages ... '

'Why didn't you call? If you got her messages?'

'Because I wasn't alone ... '

'So who was with you?'

He seemed confused and irritated. 'Cooper, Gerraint, Philippa,' he said, naming Penn's finance director, and the marina's senior board members.

'And they stopped you picking up a phone?'

'Olivia ... '

She wasn't liking herself for this, but she seemed unable to stop. 'I've been worried,' she informed him. 'Why didn't you wake me before you left this morning?'

'What is this?' he exclaimed. 'I didn't wake you because you didn't have to get up ... ' He stopped abruptly and lowering the tempo he went on, 'I'm sorry. As you know, there's a lot going on right now ... '

'Why don't you tell me about it?'

' ... and as this is the first time in twenty years that I've forgotten your birthday ... '

'It's not about my birthday,' she interrupted angrily. 'It's the way you dropped out of contact, the fact that you're hardly speaking to me these days, that your project's in trouble, that *Ana Petrov* has suddenly turned up ... ' She wouldn't mention Sean, that really wouldn't be a good idea. 'If you knew what's been going through my mind ... '

'I'm sure I can guess,' he said tightly, 'but let's not get into that again, eh? I've said I'm sorry. If I'd known it was going to lead to this I'd have woken you, but ... '

'But you'd arranged to meet Ana while you were out for a run. I guess it rather spoiled things when Sasha said she was coming too.'

He regarded her through narrowed, scornful eyes.

'Tell me I'm wrong,' she challenged.

'I'm not telling you anything,' he countered. 'It seems you already have the answers, so why bother?'

'I thought she was supposed to be going to London with your mother today.'

'As far as I know they've gone.'

'But you didn't go with them?'

His brow drew into a puzzled frown. 'Evidently not. Why would you think I had?'

'Because you told your mother on Thursday night that you'd go. You turned me down flat when I suggested Paris, but suddenly, when she suggests London, it becomes a great idea – and if Ana Petrov is going to be there ... '

He took an irritated breath. 'I really don't need this right now.'

'And you think I do? You think I liked watching my husband fawning over his ex-girlfriend the way you did on Thursday night?'

'Jesus Christ, Olivia,' he shouted. 'She was a guest in our house, what did you want me to do, throw her out?'

'Yes! That's exactly what I wanted. Have you forgotten what she put us through all those years ago?'

'*Precisely*, all those years ago. Isn't it time you got over it? She's obviously managed to ... '

'It wasn't me who threatened to kill her, it was the other way round, in case you've forgotten, and have you asked yourself why your mother brought her here?'

His hands gripped the edge of the sink as he took a steadying breath. 'I've tried to say I'm sorry about your birthday. I want to make it up to you, so please stop making it so hard.'

Wanting nothing more than to let it go, even to wipe it out, she went outside to collect the glasses, needing to give herself a moment to calm down. 'Have you eaten?' she asked, when she came back again.

'We had food sent in.' He was reading the card for the flowers. 'Who's this from?' he asked, a hard edge to the smoothness of his tone.

Realising he'd already guessed, she said, 'Sean.'

He looked at her in a way that made her wish she'd lied. 'You have the nerve to stand there ranting on about Ana and the nonsense that goes around in your head, while all the time you're the one who's being deceitful. You claim not to have invited him here to this house, but I know you did ... '

'You can't know that when it isn't true,' she cut in angrily, 'but I'm not sorry he came. There's nothing underhand about the relationship I have with him, if you can even call it that. He's not here to try and break us up, nor is he lying about *why* he's here. I don't think you can say the same for Ana Petrov.'

His eyebrows rose in disdainful surprise. 'Don't tell me you've been checking up on her? If you have, I hope you realise how sad that makes you.'

'Don't patronise me. And she isn't here to open a saleroom for Summerville's, so why did she say she was?'

'How would I know? Maybe it was the plan, but plans change.'

'You know that's not a good enough answer.'

'It's the only one you're going to get from me.'

'I don't want her in this house again,' she shouted after him.

'I'll agree to that as long as you don't bring *him*,' he retorted over his shoulder.

As he disappeared she put a hand to her head as though to stop it from spinning. She needed to take deep breaths, to try and centre herself and let go of all the anger and resentment that was building to a terrible pitch. It was hard, so hard when she was besieged by questions that needed answers, and doubts that were undermining her at every turn.

It was a moment before she realised he'd come to stand behind her, and as he wrapped her in his arms she leaned into him and closed her eyes. 'I'm sorry,' he murmured. 'Not a good time with all that's going on, but today should be about you. I only wish I'd said this earlier: happy birthday.'

Wanting no more than for the tension to disappear from between them and from inside her head, she turned her face to his as he tightened his embrace.

There was a note of amusement in his voice a few moments later as he said, 'You didn't really think I'd gone to London with them, did you?'

Irked that he seemed to find it funny, she said, 'What else was I supposed to think when we couldn't get hold of you?'

He gave a protracted sigh, and letting her go he turned to pick up his wine. 'What would you like to do this evening?' he asked. 'Shall we go out, or stay in and I'll prepare dinner? Where's Sasha?'

'Out with her friends.' After a moment she added, 'She wants to sleep with Parker.'

His eyes started to darken, showing his disapproval, but his words when they came surprised her. 'Well, I guess we should have seen that coming.' Refilling his glass, he went to sit on one of the bar stools.

She watched him staring into his glass for a while, and wondered if he was even thinking about Sasha any more. In the end, apparently coming back to the present, he said, 'I guess if it's OK with you then it had better be with me. But probably best not to mention anything to my mother, because she definitely won't approve.'

Olivia's amazement could hardly have been greater. 'Why on earth would I tell her, when we barely even speak?'

He seemed distracted again as he said, 'I don't … I … Sorry, not really thinking … ' He took a sip of wine, and after a moment he went on, 'You know, my mother was quite concerned about you when you were having your treatments?'

Olivia's surprise went to new heights. 'I think you'll find,' she countered, 'that she came up with all the right things to say, because she felt she ought to, but genuine concern? You know how she feels about me, why else would she have brought Ana Petrov here? Did you know Ana was in Kesterly before Thursday night?'

He drank some more wine. 'Yes,' he admitted.

And he hadn't mentioned it. She felt thrown by that, and foundered for a moment as if a lifeline had fallen out of her reach. Then, understanding why he'd have kept it to himself, she said, 'Was Thursday night the first time you saw her?'

'Olivia, you're getting yourself worked up ... '

'Was Thursday night the first time you saw her?'

'Yes, it was. Does that satisfy you?'

She wasn't sure if it did or not, since she had no idea if she believed him.

Picking up the landline as it rang, he said, 'Benting residence.'

'Hey, Dad,' Sasha cried down the line. 'So you're home at last. Is Mum giving you a hard time for taking off early this morning?'

'You could say that,' he responded. 'Where are you?'

'In Fruit of the Vine. I was just ringing to let you know that I'm going to stay over at Sophie's tonight.'

He turned to Olivia as he said, 'Are you sure it's Sophie's?'

'Of course I am, I don't tell lies, unlike some people I could mention.'

He frowned. 'What's that supposed to mean?'

'Don't worry, your secret's safe with me. Anyway, you and Mum are bound to be going out somewhere tonight so I'd just be on my own. Oh, before I go, tell me, did you really forget her birthday?'

'I'm afraid so,' he confessed.

'Oh wow! You've got some serious making-up to do. How did you remember in the end?'

'When I got your messages at lunchtime.'

Sasha chuckled. 'OK, well good job someone reminded you. Did she give you the good news yet, by the way?'

Richmond's eyebrows rose. 'No, I don't think so.'

'Well, you're going to love it. Anyway, got to go. See you tomorrow.'

After he'd rung off Richmond was about to ask what the good news might be, when Olivia said, 'If you got Sasha's messages at lunchtime, where have you been since then?'

Closing his eyes, he shook his head in despair.

'I'm sorry, Richmond, but none of this is adding up very well,' she told him. 'Not to answer the phone, and then not to call once you got the messages ... '

'This is where I was,' he said, pulling a small package from his pocket.

The moment she saw the velvet box her cheeks flushed with colour. Then her eyes went back to his, and she felt such a surge of awkwardness mingling with too many other emotions that she hardly knew what to say. Covering her confusion with a mock scold, she said, 'This is so typical of you. Just when I'm so mad I could have ... Oh hell, I don't know what I wanted to do ... '

'Open it,' he said. 'I think you'll like it.'

Fumbling the lid from the box, she gave a quiet exclamation of pleasure when she saw the antique gold bracelet with a single charm in the shape of a heart. 'It's beautiful,' she told him.

'Here, let me,' he said, taking it from her.

As he fastened it around her wrist she said, 'I love it, but I don't feel as though I deserve it after the way I've behaved today.'

'Just as long as I'm forgiven for forgetting, that's all that matters. Now, Sasha tells me you have some good news.'

Olivia smiled as she felt a renewed surge of relief. 'I had another check-up on Thursday, and it went well,' she announced.

Immediately his eyes closed. 'Jesus, I forgot that too,' he groaned. 'What kind of husband am I?'

Laughing, she teased, 'It's a question I often ask myself, but the answer is always the same – the only one I want.'

A while later they were sitting together on one of the garden sofas, soaking up the evening sunshine and already into a second bottle of wine, when she asked, gently, 'Why don't you tell me what's going on at the office, or with the marina? I can see … '

'Sssh. It's your birthday … '

' …how much it's getting to you, and you can't keep shielding me from the difficulties you're facing. I'm fine now, and you're obviously not. So please, let's talk about it.'

Taking a deep breath, he looked down at his drink, as he said, 'There's nothing much to tell you, really. We've hit a few problems that are taking more time to resolve than I expected, and frankly, I wish people weren't trying to interfere in things that are no concern of theirs.' He didn't mention Sean's name, but she knew that was who he meant. 'Now I want to forget it for a few hours if you don't mind, and talk about something else. Have you spoken to our son today?'

Knowing that if she tried pushing things any further they'd end up falling out again, or more likely he'd walk out on her, she decided to give in to the change of subject. 'Yes, he called this morning. He got the money.'

'Good.'

'You were very generous in the amount you sent.'

Sighing, he let his head fall back and stared up at the blue, impervious sky, seeing only he knew what, but she was certain it contained more demons than angels.

Unable to stop herself, she said, 'You're treating me as if I'm an outsider, or someone with no under-standing or feelings ... '

'This isn't about understanding or feelings, for Christ's sake, or about where anyone is positioned. In fact, it's not about you at all, so can we please agree that all you have to do is carry on getting well and leave everything else to me?' He looked down as her mobile rang, and seeing it was her mother he handed it to her.

'I'm going to run a bath,' he said shortly, and pulling himself to his feet he carried his drink back into the house.

'Are you having a good birthday?' Rena asked fondly.

'I've had better,' Olivia admitted. 'Richmond's quite stressed.'

'Mm, when isn't he these days? It's a stressful time, but we're hopeful Sean and his colleagues will come up with some answers to set the build in motion again.'

'I still don't know exactly why it came to a stop,' Olivia said. 'I mean, the money obviously ran out, it doesn't take a genius to realise that ... '

'It did, thanks to the bank pulling the plug, but Dad assures me it's not unusual for projects of this size to run into trouble, especially when you don't have any real experience of managing them. Richmond will be finding it hard to swallow his pride and accept that he needs more experts on board, but if he wants to find another bank and save the project, not to mention all our private investments and the jobs that have been lost, I'm afraid he'll have to.'

Her mother was making everything sound so simple, worrying, of course, but actually quite easily resolved – Richmond's pride notwithstanding – that Olivia could feel some of the knots starting to loosen.

'I was ringing to ask if you and Richmond have booked your flights to France yet,' Rena said. 'The villa's already reserved, as you know, the same one we always rent, but I wasn't sure whether we're all flying down together ... '

'I'm sure it's all in hand,' Olivia replied, relieved to know that her father was apparently relaxed enough to be continuing with their plans to go away in a couple of weeks. 'I'll check with Richmond and get back to you.'

After ringing off she went upstairs and came to a stop at the bathroom door. Richmond was already stripped down to his boxers, and standing in front of the mirror cleaning his teeth. She stayed where she was, watching him and feeling almost envious that he was still in as good shape now as he'd been when they'd first met. She would have been too, if things hadn't gone the way they had.

'So how come you didn't tell me your good news on Thursday?' he asked, catching her reflection in the mirror as he reached for a towel.

An ironic look came into her eyes. 'I was saving it for when we were together, in the evening,' she replied, 'but then your mother showed up with Ana ... '

He groaned his understanding. 'Terrible timing,' he muttered. Then, looking at her again, 'I'm sorry it put such a dampener on things for you.'

'It wasn't your fault.'

'No, but if I'd known you had something like that to tell me I'd have thrown them both out.'

She took a moment to enjoy the image of him marching Imogen and Ana out of the door while she stood by watching, then wondered briefly what they might be doing in London now. However, she soon pushed the thought away, for she really didn't care.

'Is there any chance of a back scrub?' he asked, as he sank down into milky water.

She massaged him for a good long time, watching his eyes close until she realised he was sleeping, and pressing a gentle kiss to his forehead she stole quietly away to begin making dinner.

The sun had barely gone down by the time they'd finished eating and wandered back upstairs again, mellowed by the wine and music they'd been dancing to. Their arms were around one another until he closed the bedroom door behind them, and she went to light the candles she'd placed on each of the nightstands.

As she turned back she was trying to ignore the tension starting to build inside her. She wanted to make love so much, but she could never really be sure that he did.

As she watched him undress she waited for him to notice that she was taking off her clothes too. Soon she was wearing only a camisole and panties, and though she was nervous about going any further, she was aware of how much they needed this closeness and reassurance.

She opened a drawer and took out the cream she'd been given to help her with intimacy, then slipped between the sheets.

He sat down on his own side of the bed and dropped his head in his hands.

'Are you all right?' she whispered.

'Yeah,' he replied, looking up. 'Are you?'

'I think so. Will you come and lie next to me?'

Swinging his legs up on to the bed, he moved over towards her, and drew her into his arms. For a long time they lay quietly in the darkness, barely moving, merely listening to the distant sounds of footsteps or cars passing, and the occasional plane overhead. Someone was having a party not too far away, and next door's sprinklers were soaking the lawns. She could feel his breath on her cheek, and tightened her hold on his hand. When there was no response she realised he was already asleep.

OLIVIA. There was a lot about my marriage to Richmond that was good, and in spite of how difficult he could be, mercurial even, I loved him…

Yes, I knew he lied, and that he was very good at covering it, but I lied too. Sometimes you have to in order to spare someone's feelings, or to avoid a confrontation that doesn't have a chance of a happy outcome. I used to think of it as damage control, if I thought about it at all, but I didn't really, not then.

ANDEE. I can't say that Ana Petrov's appearance in Kesterly unnerved me right away, it intrigued me more, especially when I discovered that she'd lied about Summerville's. It was such a careless lie, one that she must have known would be easily exposed, so she apparently didn't care about being found out.

The fact that she'd turned up at the same time as Sean Kenyon was no more a coincidence than the fact that they both, for different reasons, had an interest in the marina expansion. Like many others, my mother and Graeme's sisters included, Ana had invested in the project through Penn Financial, so presumably she was trying to find out what was happening to her money. However, she could have done that from London. Instead, she'd chosen to come to Kesterly, and, at the first opportunity, she had managed to insinuate herself into Olivia's home.

Although she was causing me almost as much concern at that time as the potential, even imminent collapse of the marina expansion, *this* wasn't something I discussed with Olivia. On the face of it Olivia and Richmond's marriage was strong; there was no reason to suspect an affair between him and Ana – although I know he'd had them with others in the past – in fact as far as I was aware, there wasn't even a platonic relationship of any standing between them.

Nevertheless, almost from the moment Ana walked into Graeme's shop, my detective's sixth sense warned me to keep a careful eye on her.

Chapter Eight

Richmond was at his desk early on Monday morning, taking the opportunity to catch up on some of his normal workload before the others arrived. Though the place was quiet, with no distractions, he was finding it hard to focus, and before long he was standing at the window gazing down over the town's clutter of rooftops and alleyways and on out to sea. The marina expansion site wasn't visible from here, but he could sense it, almost smell it, as though it were a predator with a malevolently beating heart already sucking the life from the town. A predator he had brought here.

He didn't go to the site now if he could avoid it; the silence, the stillness of machinery and the ghostly abandoned foundations were too hard to take. It was no easier standing here thinking about the many jobs that had been lost, the dreams that had been crushed into the harsh reality of no more income, combined with debt. A dozen of the project's private investors weren't only clients, they were friends, neighbours, people he and Olivia often socialised with, and even, in some cases, had holidayed with. He'd taken care of their portfolio management, trust services, estate and retirement planning, asset protection, pensions, wills, mortgages – there was almost nothing that Penn Financial hadn't handled for them since he'd taken over from his father-in-law. The company had grown considerably under his stewardship; even the London office had doubled in size.

As far as Richmond was aware no one in Kesterly knew yet that the Serious Fraud Office had been in touch with senior staff in London, but it was only a matter of time before word got out. Knowing where the inevitable investigation of the company's dealings could end was making him feel sick to his soul. Sean Kenyon turning up when he had was making it a hundred times worse. What he didn't know yet was how much Kenyon knew, or had managed to find out since coming here. Whatever it was, Richmond kept reminding himself that he needed to keep a level head, do as little as possible to antagonise the man, and hang on to Cooper Jarrett's reassurance that they were going to come out of this intact.

Jarrett was a fool if he believed that.

'Good morning,' Jarrett said from the doorway.

Richmond turned round to find the man looking as spruce and relaxed as he always did, with his slicked-back silver hair, handsome, perma-tanned features and black pinstriped suit. His insouciance was an irritant Richmond was finding increasingly difficult to live with, but the last thing he needed was to alienate the man now.

'What news?' Richmond asked, as Jarrett came to set two takeaway espressos on the desk.

'Mace have turned us down,' Jarrett replied, as though it was a foregone conclusion.

It was, nevertheless Richmond's insides knotted so tightly he felt unable to breathe. 'Did they give a reason?' he asked, not wanting to hear the answer, but knowing he had to.

'Actually, it was surprisingly non-specific. They simply said that their board had voted against it.'

Richmond inhaled deeply as he turned away. His head was throbbing, his fists clenching and unclenching at his sides as though readying to thump someone and losing nerve at the last minute. 'So we're left with Kenyon,' he stated, biting out the words as if they were nails stuck in his teeth.

'For the moment, yes, but we haven't exhausted all other possibilities yet. There are potential investors we still haven't spoken to ... '

Richmond cut him off as he heard someone coming out of the lift. 'How was your weekend?' he asked, picking up the coffee and downing it in one.

'When I finally got round to having one,' Cooper sighed, 'I guess it was OK. How about yours?'

Richmond merely shrugged.

As his mobile rang, Cooper took it from his breast pocket and waving a hand in farewell he ambled towards his own office, leaving Richmond to return to the build-up of stress in his head. What a fool he'd been to get involved in this damned project in the first place. He should have listened to his father-in-law, and the senior partners in the firm. They'd never had confidence in it, nor had he if the truth were told, but none of them had been facing the kind of problems he'd been facing then, problems that he'd been persuaded could be resolved by the marina expansion, instead of which they'd simply got worse.

Looking down at his phone as a text arrived from Sasha, he felt the band round his head tightening. There was no let-up in his world right now, every-thing was stressing him, right down to the fact that his daughter had told him that his secrets were safe with her. What the heck she'd meant by that he still didn't know, and he wasn't even sure he wanted to. She had something on her mind though, that much was certain, but she hadn't been forthcom-ing yesterday morning when she'd returned home much earlier than expected from her sleepover. She'd brought the Sunday papers, takeaway coffees and croissants with her, and had sat at the end of his and Olivia's bed hardly seeming to hear what either of them asked her, or showing any inclination to chat, or go away. In the end, Olivia had said, 'If you don't tell us what's wrong, we can't help you.'

'Nothing's wrong,' Sasha had protested. 'It's just, I don't know … People can be really weird sometimes.'

'In what way?' Olivia prompted.

Sasha shrugged, and she'd looked so young and vulnerable in that moment that in spite of the tenderness in his heart, Richmond had wanted to shout at her to go away. He'd do anything to protect her, give his life if need be, but her petty teenage issues were grating on him badly these days, especially when he had so many more important things on his mind.

'Like one minute they're your friend and the next they don't want to speak to you,' Sasha complained.

Olivia glanced at Richmond as she said, 'Are we talking about Sophie, or Parker?'

'Neither of them. It's just some of the others … ' She threw out a hand, as though batting the problem away. 'It doesn't matter. I'm going to have a shower.'

Richmond had made no comment as he and Olivia returned to the papers; he'd simply nodded when Olivia had sighed, 'She's in her own little world.'

Later in the day they'd gone for a birthday lunch at the Mermaid. A couple of friends had pulled out at the last minute, but Andee and Graeme had come, and of course Olivia's parents. Richmond was so angry with his father-in-law who he'd guessed was behind Sean Kenyon's presence in Kesterly that he'd had a hard time hiding it, but he'd somehow managed to, mainly by keeping out of his way. There was nothing to be gained from a showdown he couldn't win, at least not at this point.

How long would it be before someone at the London office informed David Penn that the SFO was asking questions they were finding hard to answer?

As the morning wore on Richmond struggled to keep his anxieties under control, forcing himself to focus on the day-to-day business of Penn Financial. To a degree he succeeded, until the sound of his mobile ringing hit him like a fist in the gut and he was right back in the middle of his worst nightmares.

Seeing it was Sasha, he almost choked on his frustration and relief.

'Hi, darling, sorry I forgot to call back,' he said cheerily. 'Is everything OK?'

'Yes, I'm cool,' she responded. 'Is there any chance of having my pocket money a couple of weeks early?'

Money, money. It was all anyone ever wanted. 'I don't see why not,' he replied affably, 'provided you remember how long it'll have to last.'

'Yeah, right.'

Registering her tone, he felt a stirring of annoy-ance. 'What is it?' he asked, trying to be fatherly. 'Still having problems with your friends?'

'No, yeah, it's OK. So, how are things with you?'

'Everything's fine with me,' he assured her. 'Couldn't be better.'

'Good. Right. I'm glad.'

Sensing that she wasn't ready to ring off yet, he heard himself saying, 'You told me the other day that my secrets were safe with you. What did you mean by that?'

There was a moment's pause before she said, 'I was just winding you up. Why? Have you got secrets?'

His laugh sounded jarring even to him; he hoped not to her. 'If I told you, they wouldn't be secrets any more.'

'Cool,' she said, and after asking him to pay the money into her account she rang off.

At eleven he was about to leave his office to go into a meeting when Olivia called. 'It's not a good time,' he told her shortly. 'Can I ring you back?'

'Just tell me if you're free for lunch. Paula's had to bail on me, and Mum's not free ... Sorry, that's mak-ing you sound like a last resort.'

'Maybe tomorrow,' he suggested, looking up as Rosalind came in to let him know that his eleven o'clock was waiting in the conference room.

'I'll let you go,' Olivia said. 'See you later.'

After ringing off he thought about Paula Mitchell bailing. She was the wife of Harry Mitchell, one of the marina's private investors. He was in to the tune of fifteen thousand – a drop in the ocean compared to the overall sum – but it would obviously mean a lot to Mitchell, and like the other investors he was understandably concerned.

Dismissing it, Richmond picked up his laptop and a slim blue file, and started across the main office.

'I've just taken in coffee,' Rosalind told him, coming out of the conference room as he reached it. 'Shall I hold calls or will you take them?'

'Put them through if they're urgent,' he answered.

As he went inside he smelled the familiar perfume right away and after glancing at the woman who was leaning casually against the table, holding a cup of coffee in one hand, the other tucked inside the back pocket of her white low-rise jeans, he closed the door.

Ana smiled and took a sip of her coffee.

He put down his laptop and file and poured himself some water. He drank deeply, then said, 'Well?'

'You shouldn't look so worried,' she chided. 'It'll just upset people and make them more nervous.'

He stared at her stonily.

Turning from him, she picked up the expensive snakeskin briefcase she'd brought in with her and laid it on the desk. She didn't open it, simply tapped it, ruminatively, before holding out a hand for him to put something into it.

Without a word he took a key from his pocket and gave it to her.

Smiling, she reached into her shoulder bag, drew out a long white envelope and passed it to him. 'I hope you like the name,' she said, and picking up her bag and briefcase she touched a playful finger to his cheek and let herself out of the room.

His head was throbbing as he looked down at the envelope she'd left with him. After examining the contents he felt his chest burning with so many recriminations that he was physically shaking as he tucked the envelope into his inside pocket and returned to his office.

This was a spur-of-the-moment thing, Olivia was telling herself, as she sat down in the hairdresser's chair. She'd been passing, and had decided to put her head in the door to say hi to Gina. When Gina, The Salon's owner, had beckoned her in she'd felt so uplifted by the welcome that she'd hugged the slight, beautiful woman far too hard.

'It's good to see you out and about,' Gina said softly. 'Your mum told me what a rough time you had with the chemo.'

'It wasn't the best' – Olivia grimaced – 'but here I am now and I thought ... ' She looked around the stylish salon with its intriguing oriental *objets*, lush green foliage and scented candles. 'If you could fit me in ... '

'You're in luck,' Gina told her. 'I'm on my own today, and I just had a cancellation. So what would you like? Highlights? A little shaping?'

'Sounds perfect.'

After flicking through some magazines to decide on a look, she settled down to enjoy the pampering and anticipation, wishing she'd come weeks ago.

'So how's Vivienne?' she asked, referring to Gina's daughter, as Gina eventually cleared away the solution.

Pride shone in Gina's eyes. 'She's doing really well, thank you,' she replied. 'Apparently there's a chance she'll head up the legal team where she is by the time she's thirty.'

'Thirty?' Olivia echoed disbelievingly; Gina hardly looked much older than that herself. 'How old is she now?'

'She was twenty-six in April.'

'Wow, how time flies. Is she still loving London?'

'Every minute of it, but she travels a lot with her job, she loves that too. Of course, I never see enough of her now, but if it's what she wants ... '

Hearing how much Gina clearly missed her daughter, Olivia said, 'And what about that gorgeous son of yours? How's he getting on at uni?'

'Yes, he's doing really well too.' She gave a girl-ish sort of laugh. 'Funny how one day they can't do anything without you and the next you're lucky if they remember to call.'

Realising that was exactly where she was heading, Olivia rolled her eyes in sympathy and tried not to feel saddened by the prospect of an empty nest.

For the next two hours as Gina performed her magic, they talked about their children, various events in Kesterly and about Gil, Gina's estranged husband, whom she clearly still loved and saw all the time. Why they'd split up was a mystery to everyone, but Olivia didn't ask, she simply felt glad for Gina that Gil remained a big part of her life. Gina didn't mention Richmond, so Olivia didn't either; she just hoped that Gina and Gil hadn't invested in the marina project.

Finally she was gazing at her reflection in the mirror, feeling so thrilled with her new blonde hair and its pixyish style that she broke into a dazzling smile. 'I love it,' she declared warmly. 'Not too different, but different enough to make me look healthier, even younger,' and she wondered with some elation what Richmond would think of it, just before she wondered the same about Sean.

The sun was staging a welcome return through a pur-plish batch of storm clouds as Sean parked his Audi in the marina car park and walked hand in hand with Elise Jansen over to the Waterfront Café. The tables were set out on a shady terrace overlooking the maze of boats and glittering estuary beyond, and several locals and tourists were either finishing their lunches or consulting maps. They'd just driven from Bristol airport, where Elise's flight had arrived from Amsterdam over an hour late, so in spite of being eager for some private time together, they'd decided to postpone it for now in favour of food.

As usual Elise was turning heads, for she was a beautiful woman with shoulder-length platinum hair, an athletic figure and a readiness to her smile that was as beguiling as the sparkle in her olive-green eyes. That she was good-natured and kind showed in her face, just as the eroticism of her body showed in the graceful way she moved.

After they were seated at a table for two and drinks were ordered, Sean propped his chin on one hand and smiled at her.

'What?' she prompted.

'It's good to see you,' he told her. 'It's been too long.'

Her eyebrows went up, but it was clear she was pleased to see him too. 'Just over a week since I flew to Amsterdam and you left London to come here,' she reminded him. 'I'm intrigued to know how things are going.'

Sitting back, he said, 'Still too early to say for certain, but what I've learned so far is certainly interesting.' He broke off as a chilled bottle of rosé arrived with two glasses. After pouring, the waiter propped up a small chalkboard detailing specials, and left them with menus and a glass bowl of olives.

When they were alone again she said, 'Interesting as in worrying?'

He nodded slowly. 'It's certainly that,' he confirmed. 'The construction board at Kenyon in London is doing due diligence as we speak, but we heard last night that Mace have kicked it back.'

Her eyes widened. 'Do you know the reason?'

'Not yet, but we'll find out soon enough. Meantime, I still haven't got to the bottom of why the funds have dried up.'

'But you have your theories?'

'I do indeed, and I hope I'm not right. What I need next is to find out exactly what steps Penn Financial are taking to get the build going again.'

'Hasn't Olivia's father been able to help with that?'

He smiled. 'You could have called him David Penn,' he commented wryly, 'but as he's not directly involved in the project he's being kept in the dark.'

'But he has access to the offices and computers, surely?'

'The offices yes, but the computer files are password-protected. His main fear is that the private investors, a lot of them good friends of his, are in danger of taking a serious hit if things don't get sorted out.' He paused for a moment, assessing whether or not to continue. In the end he said, 'Between us, I'm pretty sure it's his son-in-law who stands to take the biggest hit, and not just financially.'

Her eyebrows rose. 'Are you saying he might go to prison?'

'That's certainly one possibility.' His smile was humourless, his eyes half-narrowed as he considered the other possibilities, should his theories prove correct. Then tapping his glass to hers, he sat back in his chair. 'Enough about that,' he declared, 'we should choose what we're going to eat and then you can tell me where we're going in Italy. Actually, what I really want to know is how long I'll get you all to myself?'

She grimaced awkwardly. 'I've a confession to make. I told Max he could drop in if he was going to be in Tuscany while we're there and he called yesterday to say he probably will be.'

Sean shrugged. 'It's OK, I like Max. And if you can put up with my ex-girlfriend's family for the time you're here, I think it would be churlish of me not to put up with your ex-husband.'

'Not that it's particularly important,' she said, 'but technically Max and I are still married.'

'Of course, I was forgetting and thinking of you as all mine.' As she laughed and blew him a kiss, he said, 'I'll tell you later how many of my kids are threatening to descend on us ...'

'You're not serious.'

'It's winter Down Under,' he reminded her. 'They're in school. Now, bringing us back to this hemisphere, we've been invited for an early supper with Olivia's parents tomorrow evening. Would you like to go?'

She took a moment to consider it, then nodded decisively. 'Yes, OK, why not? Will Olivia be there?'

'No, just them.'

'You've seen her, though, since you got here?'

'I have, and we need to choose what we're going to eat.'

After making her selection, Elise returned to her wine. 'So I guess now is as good a time as any to ask you ...'

'Ask me what?' he prompted when she didn't go on.

'To ask you ... Now you've seen Olivia again, do you think you still have feelings for her?'

He gave a laugh of astonishment. 'After all these years?'

'Why not? Maybe it just wasn't the right time for you two back then.'

'It was,' he corrected, 'for the time it lasted. Now we're different people and we belong to entirely different worlds.'

'Neither of which precludes having feelings,' she pointed out.

He picked up his wine and drank, wanting to buy himself some time before answering as truthfully as he could. It was true he'd felt something when he'd seen Olivia again, but putting whatever it was into words ...

In the end, waving the question away, she plucked a Niçoise olive from the bowl and regarded him carefully as she ate it. 'There's a possibility all this could end in her leaving her husband,' she declared. 'Is that something you'd want?'

Leaning across the table he planted a kiss on her lips. 'What I want,' he said, 'is for you to put all that out of your mind and change the subject.'

Since their food arrived then, they poured more wine and allowed their conversation to ramble around the more neutral and familiar territories of their long-distance relationship, from the people they knew, and the places they'd been, to their plans to spend some time in Italy before he returned to Sydney.

'Last night,' he said, when they finally strolled to the apartment he was renting, 'Rena asked me how serious it was between us.'

'Rena? Olivia's mother? And what answer did you give?'

'I told her you were too good for me.'

She laughed.

Swinging her round to face him, he said, 'What I should have told her was to ask you.'

Her eyes stayed on his, but though they were shining with amusement, they held a hint of seriousness too.

'What answer would you have given?' he prompted.

She tilted her head to one side as she thought, then she said, 'I'd probably have asked her why she wanted to know.'

He groaned and let his head drop to hers. 'Which tells me nothing at all,' he objected.

'Of course not, because you don't really want to know,' and slipping out of his arms, she waited for him to open the front door of the apartment block so they could go upstairs for their much-anticipated siesta.

Chapter Nine

Olivia and Richmond were in the dining niche of the kitchen finishing the last of a fruity Sauvignon Blanc as Sasha cleared the table. They'd eaten bouillabaisse, one of Richmond's favourites, with fresh fish from the beach stall, and a delicious rouille made by Olivia using the Niçoise method that included cayenne pepper and saffron.

When Sasha had come in she'd immediately gushed her approval of Olivia's new hair, making Olivia feel light-hearted and lovely. However, when Richmond had returned he'd had to be prompted by Sasha to notice, and although he'd told Olivia it was good to see her as a blonde again, and that the style suited her, his lack of enthusiasm had been deflating.

Now, as she watched him reading something on his phone, she waited until Sasha announced she was going to her room, and said, 'I was wondering if we're still going to France with my parents.' It seemed so unlikely, all things considered, that she could hardly believe she was asking, but something had to be said about it, and this seemed as good a time as any.

'There's no reason for you and Sasha not to go,' he replied, putting his phone away. 'Once I get things sorted out here I'll drive down and join you, but it's unlikely I'll make the flight.'

She pretended to yawn as she shook her head. She didn't want to make a big deal of it, but she couldn't just leave it there either. 'I'd rather wait for you,' she told him, meaning it.

He sounded irritated as he said, 'But you always complain that I drive too fast. I thought you might welcome a chance to escape it.'

Or was he trying to grab at a chance to escape her?

'Ah, but you'll slow down if I'm with you' – she smiled – 'and I don't want to be worrying myself silly from the minute you set off about whether or not my children are still going to have a father at the end of the journey.'

His colour deepened as he snapped, 'That's a stupid way of putting it.'

Getting up from the table she muttered, 'If you say so.'

Draining his glass, he set it down hard and took a breath. 'I just want you to know that if you do decide to go on ahead, it's fine with me.'

The following day Olivia pulled up outside her parents' house, a self-designed homage to the New England style of architecture that Rena loved, with gable-pitched roof, dormer windows and an open front porch that ran the full width of the property. They'd had it built over thirty years ago, and in that time very little had changed; the garden was still surrounded by a neat picket fence, and the brick facade was regularly painted a deep, warm grey, with white window frames and a white front door.

Rena and David adored the place, and so did Olivia.

As she pushed open the gate she was searching in her bag for her ringing phone, certain it was Andee calling, and trying to get to it before it flipped to voicemail.

'Hi,' she said, just making it. 'I should be there around three. Is that OK?'

To her surprise there was no immediate response, then she came to a stunned halt as the caller said, 'Hello, Olivia. It's Ana. I hope you don't mind me ringing, but I ... As I mentioned while I was at your house the other day, I'd really like us to be friends. Of course, I understand if you don't feel the same way, but I'm hoping we can put the past behind us and start afresh.'

Olivia was so thrown she couldn't think of a thing to say.

'Perhaps we could have lunch sometime?' Ana continued. 'As you know, I'm a bit of a stranger to this area, but I've heard the Waterfront Café is very good. It'll be my treat. Shall we say one o'clock on Thursday?' and before Olivia could even think of an objection the line went dead.

She stared down at her phone, wondering if there was anyone in the world she'd less like to have lunch with, never mind make friends with. Yet, as her parents had already pointed out, maybe having Ana Petrov in plain sight would be better than having her lurking about in the shadows, and never knowing when or where she might strike.

It was just that she'd expected to be the one holding out the olive branch, not the other way round.

Letting herself into her parents' kitchen she found them either side of the table, both on their computers, glasses perched on the ends of their noses and website password books beside them. 'You're never going to believe this,' she declared, going to put the kettle on.

'Try us,' her father challenged, closing down his laptop. He was a gentle man with ruddy cheeks and birdlike blue eyes, known for being slow and careful in reaching a judgement. He was also someone who was well liked in the community, not only for how patiently and skilfully he'd handled investments, pensions and wills, but for how touchingly proud he always seemed to have the beautiful Rena as his wife.

'I've just had a call from Ana Petrov inviting me to lunch on Thursday,' Olivia informed them.

Rena peered over the top of her reading glasses.

Olivia said, 'I'm thinking I might go.'

Rena and David exchanged looks.

'Have you told Richmond?' her father asked.

'I've only just had the call, and why would I tell him? It's me she's invited.' Catching sight of herself in a large oval mirror, she gave a groan of dismay. 'Still loving my hair, but please tell me my face isn't as red as a baboon's bottom.' The cancer treatment had thrown her into early menopause, and she wasn't enjoying any aspect of it.

Rena smiled. 'You are looking a little flushed.'

'I'm on fire,' Olivia complained, taking the newspaper her father was passing her to use as a fan.

'Did Mum tell you we had a bite with Sean and his young lady yesterday evening?' he asked.

Olivia stopped fanning. Her parents were socialising with Sean – *and his 'young lady'*. She felt unaccountably thrown by that. She wondered if it was someone who'd come with him from Australia, or maybe she lived in London. Surely not someone he'd met since arriving here? 'No, she didn't,' she said, looking at her mother.

'She's a lovely girl,' David continued. 'Dutch, but she speaks perfect English, with a bit of an American accent, because apparently she lived there as a child.'

'So what's her name?' Olivia asked, hearing her own voice at a distance as she wondered if she really wanted to know.

'Elise Jansen. She's a doctor with the World Health Organization. Very high-powered job, by all accounts. Takes her all over the world.'

'How interesting,' Olivia commented, thinking how like Sean it was to have found someone so fascinating. *Of course he's found someone. How could you ever have thought otherwise?* And what difference did it make? It wasn't as if she wanted him herself. 'So have they been seeing one another long?' she asked, turning to drown a fruit tea bag.

'I'm afraid I didn't ask,' David replied.

Rena said, 'They seemed quite close. We liked her, a lot.'

Realising her mother was rubbing it in, Olivia managed to summon a smile as she said, 'Good. That's good.' She was aware that her parents' ambivalence towards Richmond had grown over the years, and not just because of recent events, but it was a subject only ever lightly touched on and certainly never discussed in depth. Not wanting that to change, she said, 'So how come you're not at the office today, Dad?'

'Oh, there was no reason for me to go in, and when your mother's finished there we're going to start packing ready for our trip.'

Rena was looking at her laptop again. 'Enrolment numbers are down this year compared to last,' she said worriedly. 'By now most classes would be fully booked for the autumn season.'

Coming to look over her shoulder, Olivia said, 'Have you done all the usual advertising?'

'Yes, although we get so many people coming back each year that I hardly need to these days. Tickets aren't selling for the Christmas ball either, or for the New Year Gala.' Catching a scowl from her husband she said, 'Maybe it'll pick up over the next few weeks while we're away.'

Realising from her tone that she wasn't convinced, Olivia said encouragingly, 'I'm sure it will. Everyone loves their classes; like you said, they come back every year, so you mustn't let it spoil your holiday. Actually, Richmond's trying to persuade me to leave ahead of him and go with you.'

Rena appeared impressed with the idea. 'So why don't you?' she prompted.

'Because I've got this project on the go with Andee, and anyway, I'd rather wait until he's able to come with me.'

Spotting her parents exchanging glances again, she felt irritated by it, and said, 'I want to be on hand if things don't go the way he hopes with the marina project. If I left, it would feel like I was running out on him.'

Though her father's face darkened, all he said was, 'I'm sure it'll be cleared up soon.'

'By Sean's company taking it on?' she challenged.

'If that's what turns out to be necessary.'

'What about the other group? Mace?'

His eyes remained fixed on hers. 'They've turned it down.'

It felt like a blow, as though a rug had been pulled from under her, or more accurately from under Richmond. 'Why?' she managed to ask. 'I suppose it's too small for them.'

'Possibly.'

'But that's not what you think.'

He took a breath. 'What I think is that the project needs to be handed over to someone who knows what they're doing.'

Feeling the slight on Richmond's behalf, she snapped, 'You could have chosen someone he'd be able to work with.'

'I did when I contacted Mace. It was only after someone on the board there warned me it wasn't looking good that I got in touch with the Kenyon Group.'

Olivia stood stiffly, aware of them watching her, and wishing she couldn't feel their sadness. 'And what does Sean have to say so far?' she demanded.

'He's still talking to people,' her father replied, 'but he's worried.'

'About what exactly?'

'He hasn't given me a full account yet. I'm sure he will when he's ready.'

Olivia let several moments pass, looking from her father to her mother and back again. In spite of feeling defensive and angry, she could see the strain they were under, how afraid they were that this was going to end up causing a rift between themselves and their daughter. She couldn't, wouldn't, let that happen, not now, not ever, but she had to ask the next question and she could tell from the tightness around his mouth that her father was expecting it.

'What if Sean turns it down too?' she said.

David's eyes remained on hers, gentle and worried, but showing her that he had no regrets for his actions. 'We just have to hope that doesn't happen,' he replied quietly, and picking up his laptop he left the room.

Andee Lawrence was listening closely to what Sean was telling her.

Seeing him again after so many years had brightened her day in a way she hadn't expected when he'd come through the door. Not that it had been a bad day until then, but the way he'd embraced her, as if she were a long-lost sister, had brought back memories of how pleased she always used to be to see him.

They were in the leafy, patio garden that opened off the kitchen of the elegant town house she shared with Graeme. He was also listening, and looking as concerned as she felt.

'According to my due diligence team in London,' Sean was saying, 'the bank pulled the plug on the build almost a year ago ... '

Graeme's eyebrows shot up with surprise.

'Which immediately begs the question,' Sean continued, 'how did it keep going for the next six months until it shut down?'

Andee's eyes moved to Elise, the chic, quiet woman, both beautiful and elegant, whom Sean had introduced as a friend. Since he was speaking to them in front of her it wasn't hard to deduce that their relationship went deeper, but if Sean trusted her so did Andee.

'I still don't have a definitive answer to that,' Sean admitted, 'but I can tell you this: the Russian investment bank in question is not one we've ever used, nor would we. They are what you might call a resource of last resort, given their connections to some dubious finance institutions in Moscow, Cyprus and Tel Aviv.'

Understanding right away where this was going, Andee said, 'You think they were using the project to launder money?'

Sean didn't deny it. 'My discussions with the builder have proved interesting,' he went on. 'There was a lot of cash changing hands in the early days, and I mean a lot. Enough to make him take his concerns to the marina's board, but no one ever got back to him. Soon after that, which was about three months into the build, funds began coming in through normal channels. So, as he could now see where the funds were coming from – a bank we've all heard of in London – he set aside his suspicions and continued work. It was about four months later that the transfers started to dry up, and when they didn't resume it wasn't long before our builder was forced to pull his guys off the job.'

Graeme said, 'So after the Russian bank pulled out Richmond found a backer here and then lost them?'

'On the face of it that's how it looks, but no record of a second deal has come to light.'

Graeme frowned hard, bringing his thick dark brows together as he said, 'So where was the money coming from?'

'That's what we're trying to find out,' Sean replied.

'I take it you've talked to David Penn?' Andee asked.

Sean nodded. 'He can't help us because the marina accounts are password-protected, and as he's not involved in the project ... '

'What I'd like to know,' Graeme said, 'is why Richmond got involved with this foreign bank in the first place. Given the time frame he surely couldn't have exhausted all the usual property investors before work began.'

'Unless we can access the files,' Sean replied, 'we won't know who he approached, but I can tell you this, in my view the project was never viable anyway. It's far too ambitious given the location, local demographic, tourist numbers, current turnover of the marina ... I could go on. The point is, the only way I can see that he was able to sell the idea to the marina's board, and to the local authority, was because he already had funding in place.'

Graeme's eyes widened in astonishment.

Taking a breath, Andee said, 'You mean it was a money-laundering scheme from the start?'

Sean gave a brief nod. 'It's possible.'

'So why did the Russian bank pull out?' Graeme wanted to know.

'There could be any number of reasons for that, and given the way they work I doubt we'll ever find out. The big question we're left with is, where did the next tranche of finance come from? Or, put another way, who was paying the funds into the London bank that were used to pay the builder?'

Andee waited.

'That,' Sean told her, 'is where you come in.'

She blinked in surprise.

'Apparently the reason our competitors, Mace, pulled out is because they got wind that the Serious Fraud Office are already sniffing around this. That makes it untouchable for us too. However, for David and Olivia's sake, or call it old times' sake, I'm prepared to look a bit deeper. So, given your police contacts, do you think you can find out exactly what the SFO are looking for?'

Andee's mind was racing ahead as she nodded slowly. 'I can try,' she replied, thinking of whom she could approach amongst her old colleagues, and how she should frame her request. It wasn't going to be easy, for much time had passed since her days with the Met, but she had some good contacts in Kesterly who might be able to open some doors.

Later, as Sean and Elise were leaving, Andee said, 'By the way, Sean, do you happen to know anyone by the name of Ana Petrov?'

With the flicker of an eyebrow, he said, 'No. Should I?'

'She's Richmond's ex from before Olivia,' Andee explained. 'She was a bit of a stalker and had to be whisked out of the way. Long story, it was years ago, but she's recently turned up here in Kesterly. She claims to be setting up an auction house for Summerville's, but we know that's not true.'

His eyes narrowed in puzzlement. 'So what's the real reason she's here?' he asked, clearly realising she wouldn't have brought this up if she didn't consider it relevant.

'I don't know,' she admitted, 'but given her history with Richmond – their families have been close for decades – and her ethnicity – I'm pretty sure her father's Russian ... Well, now you've told us about the first bank Richmond was involved with, I thought this was worth mentioning.'

Nodding his understanding, Sean said, 'Email me her name and what you know about her, and I'll forward it to the research team.'

As Sean drove them back towards the marina, Elise said, 'How much have you actually told Olivia's father so far? Is he aware that things could turn out to be much more serious than he feared?'

'Not yet.'

'So when are you going to break it to him?'

'Not until I have to.'

She turned to look at him. 'Aren't you afraid it might be too late by then?'

'What I'm afraid of,' he replied, 'is that it's already too late.'

Chapter Ten

As soon as Olivia arrived at the Waterfront Café she spotted Ana seated beneath one of the bamboo parasols, looking as sphinx-like and exotic as an Egyptian goddess, and as relaxed as if this was where she came every day. She was so effortlessly beautiful that it was virtually impossible for Olivia, in spite of her new hair and improving complexion, not to feel like a fading passport photo beside her.

'You came,' Ana declared huskily, appearing delighted and surprised as she got up to greet her. 'I'm so glad. I was hoping you would.'

Momentarily stunned by the vivid pink lipstick, Olivia could only stare at the woman and wonder which of them was going mad – Ana for wearing a colour that was so blatantly wrong for her, or Olivia for thinking it was the one she'd lost.

Gesturing to a chair, Ana said, 'Please sit down. We're in the shade, so not too hot. What would you like to drink?'

Tearing her eyes from the lipstick, Olivia looked up at the waiter. 'Iced water, thank you,' she told him, and checked her phone to find out who was calling. Seeing it was Sasha she said, 'Please excuse me. I ought to take this.'

'Oh, don't mind me,' Ana responded generously. 'It might be important.'

'Darling,' Olivia said after clicking on, 'I'm at lunch now, so can I call you back?'

'OK, no problem,' Sasha responded chirpily. 'I just wanted to let you know that I'm about to go surfing.' It was a rule that she always had to tell one parent before she went off to do water sports, although she usually sent a text, so there was probably more. 'And?' Olivia prompted.

'And can I borrow your purple top with sequins tonight? It's Ruby's birthday party, remember?'

'All right, but don't put it in the machine when you're done. It's hand wash only.'

'No problem. Who are you having lunch with?'

'Ana. You remember, who's staying with Grandma Imogen.'

'You mean, the *old* girlfriend, Ana? Wow! How's that working out?'

Keeping her tone neutral, Olivia said, 'I've just got here, so I really ought to go.'

Making a pretence of turning the phone off, she put it face down on the table as she said, 'Sorry about that. It's one of the drawbacks of her getting older, I never seem to have any clothes to myself.'

Ana smiled fondly. 'She's a very beautiful girl. A very talented cook, too.'

'I'll tell her you said so.'

'You know it makes me feel very strange to think of you and Richmond with children who are already so well into their teens. It's quite frightening to realise how much time has passed.'

Wondering if she was thinking that Richmond's children should have been hers, Olivia found herself transfixed by the lipstick again, as though it had become somehow brighter, more garish in the last few minutes.

Ana continued to smile.

Olivia looked up as a waiter delivered her water. 'Thank you,' she said, the words seeming to break her out of a trance. Then to Ana, as she picked up the glass, 'What shall we drink to?'

Ana's half-moon eyes narrowed as she gave it some thought. 'How about to friendship?' she suggested, almost, but not quite making it a challenge, before watching Olivia carefully.

Reminding herself that it was the reason she'd come, Olivia joined in the toast and took a small sip before opening the menu.

'Have you eaten here before?' Ana asked, still watching her.

'Once or twice,' Olivia replied. 'It's quite new.'

'So is there anything you can recommend?'

After pointing out a couple of salads, Olivia made her own choice and handed the menu back to the waiter. As Ana did the same, duplicating Olivia's order, Olivia silently repeated the advice, *keep your friends close and your enemies closer.*

'So how are things going with the new auction house?' she asked when they were alone again. She was prepared to go along with the charade for as long as Ana was, and it was going to be interesting to find out how long that would be.

Ana waved a dismissive hand. 'You know how things are, they start out one way then become something else altogether. I believe you're working in interior design? You've done a wonderful job with your own house, it's so stylish, but also very ... individual. I was wondering if you might be able to help me create something special when I find my own place.'

Knowing that working with her was the last thing she wanted to do, although it was actually a very good way of keeping an eye on her, Olivia said, 'I'll mention it to Andee. It's her company, so she makes those decisions.'

Smiling her understanding, Ana peered at her over the rim of her glass as she drank more wine.

Annoyed by a fleeting sense of discomfort, Olivia let the gaze go, as though refusing the silent contest.

She hadn't expected Ana to behave with such confidence, as though she were the one who'd been born here and Olivia was the outsider. Or as though she was the one who'd been stalked and slapped and threatened. Olivia needed to right the situation, to assert herself somehow, but couldn't think how to without making herself appear petty and foolish.

With a gentle sigh of pleasure, Ana turned to take in the bustle and colour of the marina. 'You know, I'm finding Kesterly far more agreeable than I'd expected,' she declared. 'In fact, I'm beginning to feel at home here already.'

Olivia only smiled, unable to think of a suitable response to that, at least not one that was going to help things along in a friendly way.

'Of course I shall still be up and down to London quite regularly,' Ana continued. 'I'll need the adrenalin fix, I'm sure. Doesn't Richmond have an office there?'

Suspecting she already knew the answer to that, Olivia said nothing and wondered what this lunch was really about. Ana had some sort of an agenda going on, the obfuscation over the auction house was proof enough of that, but right now Olivia didn't feel even close to understanding the rules of whatever game she might be playing.

'I suppose it's harder for you to get away, being a mother,' Ana commented sympathetically.

'Sometimes, not always,' Olivia responded, and deciding it was time to change the subject, she said, 'Have you made any progress at all with an apartment? Are you planning to rent, or buy?' Was she even intending to stay, or was this some warped sort of tease that only she was enjoying?

Ana's smile became mischievous, like a child who was winning without even trying. 'In the short term I think it's a better idea to rent,' she replied. 'If things work out ... Well, we'll see what happens, and then I'll be able to make a decision.'

Deciding to brush past the subtext rather than give Ana the satisfaction of trying to decipher it, Olivia said, 'Would you mind me asking if you have someone special in your life?' Not subtle, but stomping over the nuance and innuendo was perhaps the only way to wrest some control of this farcical pretence of friendship.

Ana's eyes shone with a sublime sort of pleasure as she said, 'Considering the past, I don't blame you for wanting to know that, so I'm sure you'll feel relieved when I tell you that there is.'

Not feeling quite as relieved as she'd expected to, Olivia said, 'Will he be moving down here with you?'

'Once again, that will depend on how things go. For the moment we're making things work very well as we are.'

'Can I ask his name?'

Ana tilted her head, appearing intrigued by the question, or perhaps she was deciding whether or not to answer. 'Adem,' she replied, seeming to enjoy the sound of it. 'Like Adam, but not quite. Adem Bekker.'

So not British – or not British-sounding anyway. 'Is he in the same line as you?'

Ana nodded, and nodded again. 'You could say that,' she replied, as though confirming it to herself.

Olivia glanced down at her phone as it rang. 'I'm sorry,' she said, 'I thought I'd turned it off.' Seeing it was her mother, whom she'd primed to call in case she needed an out, she let it go to voicemail and waited as their salads were delivered. If she'd answered the call she felt sure Ana would have guessed it was a set-up, and she didn't want to give her the satisfaction of that.

As they ate Ana seemed to loosen the control she'd exerted, talking easily, vainly, of her Bond Street gallery and the many art deals she'd pulled off over the years. She was someone who understood what her clients – her collectors – wanted, she claimed, and always found a way to get it. She dropped names that mostly sounded foreign, though whether they were buyers or artists Olivia had no idea. However, she was clearly supposed to be impressed, and if the figures Ana was dropping liberally into her boasts were true, her accomplishments certainly had been remarkable.

'Connecting someone with something they want most in the world,' Ana rambled on, sounding exceptionally pleased with herself by now, 'is the most elevating of experiences. It isn't always easy, sometimes it can lead to difficulties that would have been impossible to predict at the outset, but over-coming those difficulties, mastering a situation and reaching the point where you can finally see it all coming together ... ' She gave a small sigh of con-tentment as she allowed her eyes to reconnect with Olivia's.

'Do you always win?' Olivia asked, feeling both repulsed and fascinated by this other-worldly creature.

Ana's knowing smile returned. 'Always,' she confirmed.

Olivia looked away, keen to extricate herself from the moment, and her heart contracted as she saw Sean coming into the restaurant. A beat later she realised it wasn't him. In fact, it didn't even really look like him, but she waved anyway, because it *was* someone she knew.

Ana continued to talk up her accomplishments and travels, her few disappointments and many desires, apparently unstoppable, until finally she dabbed the corners of her exquisite mouth with a napkin and said, 'This has been such fun. I had no idea we'd get along so well.'

Wondering what she was really thinking, Olivia watched her pay the bill, and made all the right noises about them getting together again. Would it really happen? Was it actually what either of them wanted? She knew she didn't, and felt sure Ana didn't either, in spite of her words.

As Ana started to leave a waiter stepped in quickly. 'Miss? Is this your briefcase?'

Ana gave a small gasp as she realised she'd almost left it behind. 'Oh, thank goodness you spotted it,' she told him, as he handed it to her. 'This is not something I would want to lose. Thank you.' She took it from him and smiled sweetly at Olivia.

'It's lovely,' Olivia commented, thinking the snake-skin was probably one she'd sloughed off earlier.

Apparently pleased by the compliment, Ana held the case to her chest as if she'd just recovered a lost child, and left.

'I really don't know what it was about,' Olivia told her mother when she called into the dance studio to update her. 'She says she has someone special in her life, and that may be true, but frankly I still don't trust her. I felt like I was playing chess with someone who knows how to bend the rules, and as we know, I can't play at all. It's a shame you're going away tomorrow, because I think you should come if I see her again.'

'Do you think you will?'

'I'm not sure.'

'If you do, take Andee. It'll be interesting to get her take on the woman,' Rena advised, and reaching for her phone as it rang, she said, 'It's Sasha.' A moment later she was saying, 'Hold on, hold on, sweetie. Take a breath and tell me again what's happened.'

Alarmed, Olivia put her own ear to the phone, and her heart sank as she heard Sasha sob ' ... they went without me, Grandma. Not only that, one of them actually said they didn't want me to come.'

'Who are we talking about?' Rena asked worriedly.

'My friends. Sophie, Constance, Ruby ... I don't know what I've done. Parker says I should ignore them, but it's all right for him, it's not his friends who are being so mean.'

'Where are you now?' Rena asked.

'At home.'

'I'm on my way,' Olivia told her, 'and don't worry, darling, I'm sure we can get it all straightened out.'

ANA. After the lunch with Olivia I returned to Imogen's and went upstairs to remove the awful lipstick from my mouth. You're wondering why I did it, and how I got it, aren't you? I did it because I knew it would disturb her, and I got it the night I was at the house for dinner.

I was still mulling over what had been said during our lunch as I lay down on the bed, enjoying a wayward breeze wafting in from the open window. I felt tired, but refreshed; satisfied that Olivia had come and that it had gone so well. I'd expected it to be more difficult, but in the end I felt we parted ... friends? Perhaps not quite that, but hopefully the meeting had served its purpose.

It was about an hour later that I received a text from Richmond confirming that he'd gone home while the place was empty. He had several things to collect and it couldn't be done in one go, but a start had been made, that was what really mattered.

Richmond was in a black mood as he returned to his office after a quick trip home, followed by a chance encounter with a representative of the marine-expansion private investors group. He'd managed to fob the man off with an assurance that a new backer was on the point of signing, and he'd be in touch as soon as the ink was dry.

He could only feel thankful that it wasn't one of the contractors he'd run into, someone whose carpentry or plumbing business had collapsed, or was on the verge of it, thanks to him. The physical threats some were making by email and text were terrifying enough; he didn't have much doubt that at least one of them would be prepared to carry them out. It might not bring back their jobs, or their businesses, but beating him senseless would very likely afford them some degree of satisfaction.

Finding a message on his desk asking him to call Crispin Blake, the London-based lawyer acting for the company, he felt his head starting to throb. What now, for God's sake?

Before picking up the phone he turned to check his emails. Nothing from Cooper, who was at the London office today. However, there was a message from one of the fraud investigators requesting a meeting the following week.

Presumably Crispin Blake wanted to discuss strategy ahead of the meeting, and he hoped to God Cooper was already prepared.

'Fully,' Cooper assured him, when Richmond finally got hold of him. 'I swear, as far as Penn Financial is concerned, this will be nothing more than a bad memory by the end of next week.'

Richmond wanted to believe that, he really did, but while Cooper Jarrett's delusions might work for some, they held little sway with Richmond.

Olivia was sitting in a purple vinyl banquette at the back of a noisy pizzeria, somewhere near Paradise

Cove, an area just outside Kesterly, jammed with tourists, caravan parks, amusement arcades and fish and chip shops. It was Sasha's choice, or more probably, Parker's, so for the sake of an easier life she was doing her best to grin and bear it.

Richmond was going to hate it.

Spotting him at the door she waved to show him where she was, and watched him weave through the tables full of teenagers and raucous families to join her.

'Why are we here?' he asked, sliding into the seat next to her. He was clearly irritated to the point of anger at being made to suffer such an undesirable venue. Didn't she realise he had more important things to do than come to a place like this on the whim of a sixteen-year-old daughter, he seemed to be saying. 'And where's Sasha?' he barked.

'In the loo. Parker's on his way, apparently. I've ordered a glass of Pinot Grigio for you – it's the best they could do. You look tired.'

'I'm fine. So what's this all about? Couldn't we have gone somewhere else to cheer her up? What's wrong with her, anyway?'

'She had an upset with her friends today. They're turning against her for some reason, you know what teenagers are like, so I said she could choose where we went.'

Checking a text message, he read it quickly then returned the phone to his pocket. 'And this is the kind of place ... '

'Sssh. She's coming.'

As Sasha reached the table it was clear that she'd been crying, and as Olivia reached for her she buried her face in her hands. 'Parker's gone back to Scotland,' she sobbed, mascara pooling around her eyes. 'We only came here because of him ... Oh, Mum! Why is everyone being so horrible to me?'

Wrapping her in her arms, Olivia looked at Richmond and felt a flash of irritation when she saw that he was checking his phone again. Couldn't he at least give his daughter a moment of his attention?

'I don't want to stay here now,' Sasha wailed. 'Can we go home?'

Thankful for small mercies, Olivia left Richmond to pay for the wine that had just arrived, and took Sasha across the road to her car. It was like carnival night with all the blaring music, flashing lights and crazy costumes, but fortunately no one seemed interested in them. It was only as she was about to drive away that they heard a bang on the roof, and she'd have put her foot down hard had Sasha not shouted, 'It's Dad.'

'I came by taxi,' he explained, as he took over the driver's seat and Olivia climbed into the back.

'I wasn't going to leave my car parked anywhere around here. I might never have seen it again.'

By the time they'd inched their way out of the cove there was some sort of argument going on in the front between Sasha and Richmond that Olivia thought was about pocket money, but she couldn't be sure. Nor was she inclined to find out. She simply rested her head on the seat back and wondered why it was Richmond's fault that Parker had taken off with barely a word, since that was what Sasha seemed to be saying now.

As she closed her eyes she thought back over her lunch with Ana, trying again to get a sense of what it had really been about. On the face of it she'd seemed like any normal person who needed to make friends in a town she didn't know, but Olivia knew very well that it had been far from that simple. The most obvious motive for the relocation to Kesterly and friendly overtures was that she was trying to get close to Richmond. She already had his mother onside – had *always* had her onside – if she got his wife too … Except why would she want to insinuate herself into the family, if her aim was to get Richmond out of it?

She really had no idea and as the row in the front seat was becoming more heated, it was difficult to concentrate on anything else.

By the time they got home Sasha and Richmond were no longer speaking, and as soon as they were inside Sasha stormed off to her room while Richmond went into the kitchen to pour himself a drink.

'I blame you for the way she is,' he snapped as Olivia came in after him. 'You let her think everything's about her, so she has no sense of other people having issues that might matter. Luke's just as bad. Are you listening to me?' he demanded as she walked past him to make herself some tea.

'Maybe it's you who needs to understand that other people might have issues,' she said tartly. 'Teenage spats might seem nothing to you, but to her they can feel devastating, especially when her boyfriend ends up bailing on her.'

'So what do you want me to do, call him up and ask what his problem is?'

'Don't be ridiculous. You just need to be a bit more sympathetic.'

Knocking back the large whisky he'd poured, he dashed another into his glass and downed that one too. 'I'll go and talk to her,' he said.

When he remained focused on his phone, Olivia said, 'Who are you messaging?'

'It doesn't matter,' he growled, putting the phone away. He was clearly still angry, and she got the impression he was hardly connecting with his own words as he said, 'So when were you planning to tell me that you had lunch with Ana Petrov?'

Her eyes opened wide with surprise. 'How do you know?' she said sharply.

'How do you think I know?'

Her first thought was that he'd spoken to Ana, but then rolling her eyes she said, 'Your mother, of course.'

Though his expression was harsh, she could see that his mind was still partially elsewhere.

'What's Ana Petrov really doing here?' she demanded evenly.

His frown deepened as he said, 'How the hell am I supposed to know?'

'Hasn't she, or your mother, told you?'

'Isn't it something to do with a saleroom?'

'That's what she said, but she's being very vague about it now, and apparently Summerville's aren't looking to open up in the area. So is she really intending to stay in Kesterly, or does she have another motive for being here?'

His eyes were cold as he said, 'You're the one who had lunch with her, so why didn't you ask?'

'Probably because I knew I wouldn't get a straight answer, and I'm clearly not getting one now. So what's really going on, Richmond? Are you involved with her? Has she come to try and break us up?'

Dropping his head into his hands, he gave a growl of pure anger as he said, 'I'm not getting into this now.'

Her eyebrows arched. 'Getting into what?' she countered loftily.

'Your bloody paranoia,' he shouted, making her flinch as he banged a fist on the counter top.

Her eyes flashed with fury. 'Don't you dare belittle me in that way. You know that woman's not stable and there's no doubt in my mind that she's here to cause trouble ... '

'Then don't see her again.'

'Maybe I won't, but what I'd like to know is how often *you're* seeing her.'

His voice thickened with contempt as he said, 'Probably as often as you're seeing Sean Kenyon.'

She stared at him hard. What was there to say that would get them out of this horrible impasse; that would make them start trusting one another again, when she'd never really trusted him at all? In the end, determined not to let him make her non-relationship with Sean the issue, she said, 'If you're going to keep taking things out on Sasha and me, it might be better if you went to stay with your mother. Let her deal with you, because ... ' Suddenly remembering that this might not be such a brilliant suggestion given who else was staying there, she found herself swallowing air.

Clearly realising she'd walked herself into a tight spot, he gave a bitter laugh, and leaving her there he went off to his study and closed the door, apparently forgetting that he was supposed to be making up with his daughter.

When Richmond finally climbed the stairs to Sasha's room half an hour later, his head was hurting so badly he started to wonder if he'd make it all the way. He guessed this was about the best he was going to feel during the days and weeks to come so it might be a good idea to start easing off the alcohol, because if there was one thing he was going to need, it was a clear head.

Just before he'd left the office earlier, word had reached the Kesterly staff that several of their London colleagues had had their computers seized by the police. There had been tears and outrage and no small amount of confusion. He'd even detected fear in some, as though they truly believed they might be off to jail when they'd done nothing wrong. He'd tried to reassure them that there was nothing to worry about, that the investigation was only happening because of a false tip-off to the authorities, so it had to take its course. He had no idea if anyone had believed him, but he hadn't hung around to find out. He simply hadn't been able to deal with any more questions or speculation without Cooper there to back him up.

He was due to speak to Cooper again first thing in the morning. By then they might have a clearer idea of what this 'new direction' in the investigation was all about.

As if he didn't know.

As he reached Sasha's door he gave himself a moment before knocking and asking if he could come in.

'Go away. I hate you,' she called back.

'No you don't, you're just playing hard to get.'

He knew he'd made her laugh, or at least smile, so he turned the handle and let himself in. 'I owe you an apology,' he said from the door. 'I should have shown more understanding earlier and I really shouldn't have shouted at you in the car.'

She was staring at her iPad, but he could see that she didn't have her earpods in, so she'd obviously heard.

'And,' he added, 'I'm sorry I forgot to transfer your pocket money. I'll do it tonight, before I go to bed. Promise.'

'Are you sure you've got the money?' she muttered tightly.

He turned cold and would have pretended he hadn't heard, had she not said, 'Well?'

'Of course I have,' he responded, as if it had been a silly question.

She still didn't look up, but he heard her perfectly well. 'Everyone's saying you're bankrupt and that the people who trusted you are going to lose everything.' She turned to face him. 'Some of them are my friends' parents ... '

'Stop, stop.' Richmond managed to sound soothing, in spite of the turmoil inside him. 'There's a lot of gossip going round at the moment, and most of it is nonsense. I'm not bankrupt, far from it, and no one's going to lose anything.'

She eyed him warily, clearly wanting to believe him, but he could see she wasn't sure.

'I promise,' he added with a smile.

'So what's happening with the development?' she asked. 'When's it going to start again?'

'Soon. You have my word on that, so put it out of your head, and now let's talk about you. Why do you think Parker let you down tonight?'

She shrugged and turned back to her iPad. 'I don't know,' she replied, 'but I bet anything he's at Ruby's party.'

'So you don't think he's gone to Scotland?'

'No, not yet.'

'And Ruby's is where everyone else is tonight?'

She nodded.

Annoyed with himself for being so useless while wishing he wasn't having to give this any time at all, he went to put his arms around her.

'Don't,' she said, brushing him aside. 'I want to be on my own.'

He gazed down at her, wondering if she really meant that. Telling himself she did, he said, 'Shall I ask Mum to come up?'

'No! I don't need anyone.'

As he reached the door she said, 'By the way, did you know that Grandma and Grandpa have cancelled their holiday?'

He felt a dark thud hit his chest, although in the light of everything it shouldn't have been a surprise. 'Why did they do that?' he replied, certain he already knew the answer, but realising he had to ask.

She shrugged. 'They just decided that now wasn't a good time to go away.'

Knowing the decision had to be related to the news coming out of the London office, he closed the door quietly as he left and stood staring into space. His heart was hammering violently as he wondered how much Rena and David actually knew, how much Sean Kenyon had discovered and told them.

Maybe he should call to reassure them, tell them that he had everything under control and they could go off on holiday with easy minds. It was the sensible thing to do, and he'd have done it if he'd been able to face speaking to David, but right now he simply couldn't.

Chapter Eleven

SASHA. It was horrible the way my friends started to turn on me. I mean, it wasn't my fault the marina expansion had run into trouble. I don't know what they expected me to do. Actually, I think they just liked saying mean things about my dad, and posting lies about him online. You know how once that sort of thing gets started everyone seems to jump on it. They were blaming my mum too, and even saying they didn't know how any of us had the nerve to show our faces around town. Some of them even said they wanted to kill us, or burn our house down. They were the trolls, obviously, probably people we didn't even know, but I was still afraid someone might do it.

In the end I messaged my brother, Luke, and told him he had to come home because I couldn't cope on my own any more. He said that I should stop worrying and face down all the horrible people, because there was no way any of it was true. He didn't understand how bad it was; he only knew that later, when he eventually had to come home.

No, none of the trolls ever mentioned Dad's old girl-friend. I don't think they had any idea she even existed. I only met her a couple of times: once when she came to the house, which really pissed Mum off, and once when Dad and I bumped into her when we were out jogging. It didn't seem like a set-up arrangement, but what do I know? It never entered my head that they might be having an affair. I don't suppose you think of your parents that way, or I didn't anyway. Mine always seemed quite close really. Sure, they had rows and stuff, and sometimes Dad was way over the top in how mean he could be, but he always tried to make up for it after.

No, I'd never heard of Sean Kenyon then. I mean, I knew Mum had had a serious boyfriend before she got married, but she never told us anything about him. I only got to know he was in Kesterly when everything really kicked off ... It was terrible, horrible in ways you can't begin to imagine. Well, you know what happened in the end, so you know what I'm saying.

'I'm still in London,' Sean was telling Andee on the phone, 'but I'm about to email something for you to take a look at.'

'Great,' she replied. 'Did you get what I sent you?'

'Yep, but I haven't had a chance to open it yet. I'll do it now and we'll speak after.'

After ringing off Andee turned back to the email she'd forwarded to Sean just before his call. It had come in this morning from an ex-colleague at the Met and was confirming that officers from the Serious Fraud Office, after being contacted by the Financial Services Authority, were indeed looking into the affairs of Penn Financial. Apparently the investigation was in two parts, the first concerning the foreign bank that had helped get the project off the ground, and the second finding out where the second tranche of funding had come from after that bank had pulled out. There was a paragraph about commission arrangements versus wrap fees, which didn't mean much to her, but the faking of client's monthly statements and invented investment returns was clear enough. What the email hadn't told her was whether any evidence of this fraud had actually been found, simply that it was what they suspected had taken place.

If they were right it would mean that Richmond had fraudulently diverted funds from Penn's clients to try and keep the build going.

Unsure how shocked she was by this, though certainly perturbed, she clicked open Sean's email as it came through and read the accompanying message first. *Still don't know how or if Ana Petrov is involved in what's happening at PF, but this will give you a little interesting insight into things.*

Wondering how far Sean had got with her email by now, Andee clicked open the attachments he'd sent with his own, which turned out to be jpegs. The first shot was of an extremely elegant Regency house with a colonnaded entrance porch and tall sash windows. The second was of a street name in SW7, presumably where the house was located. The third was a close-up of the nameplates outside the house, apparently flats these days, with Ana Petrov listed at number six. It was only when she got to the last image showing title deeds that she understood the relevance of the first three shots.

Looking up as Graeme came into the room, she turned the computer so that he could view the photographs for himself.

'So it seems Richmond Benting is the owner of Ana Petrov's apartment,' she stated flatly as Graeme gave a sigh of dismay.

'Giving us evidence,' he said, 'of a relationship dating back to ... Actually, all it gives us is the date he bought the place, four years ago. There's nothing to tell us when she moved in. Or is there?'

Andee shook her head as she checked.

'And nor does it give us any clues,' he continued, 'as to what she's doing here in Kesterly.'

Andee was about to call Sean again when another email arrived, and seeing it was from her contact at the Met she immediately clicked on.

Thought these might be of interest. Taken by NCA surveillance team in Amsterdam April 2015. Chap to left of Ana Petrov is her father, Dmitri. Shadows in background: bodyguards.

As Andee scrutinised the shots, each of them showing Richmond and Ana enjoying a night out at a restaurant or nightclub with a large, bald-headed man and two others whose features were as robustly Slavic as Petrov's, she felt such a sinking dismay that she wanted to delete them all. If these men with their evident wealth and undoubtedly armed goons were being targeted by the National Crime Agency, it told her everything she didn't want to know.

'What the hell has he got himself involved in?' Graeme murmured.

Andee shook her head.

'Send it to Sean,' Graeme advised.

Minutes later Sean rang. 'Does this mean what I think it does?' he asked.

'I'm afraid so,' Andee replied, putting the call on speaker so Graeme could hear. 'We not only see how at ease Richmond is with known NCA targets, we're also seeing him with Ana Petrov over three years ago.'

Sean was quiet as he absorbed this. 'So I guess we're looking at the marina's initial investors?' he queried.

'Possibly, but I'm sure it would have been a lot bigger than just these three men. It'll be the kind of network that's got itself so tangled around cities, corporations and banks that's it's virtually impossible to trace.'

'But the NCA are on it?'

'It would seem so. These kinds of operations can take years, and they happen on more levels than we can even count, so who knows how long they've been watching Dmitri Petrov, or what they might already have on him. It could be they're waiting for him to lead them to someone else.' She took a breath. 'The question now is, should I tell Olivia about this?'

'Do you want to?' Sean asked.

'No, of course not.'

'It can't come from me, so maybe hold on to it for the moment. I'll confront Benting when I get back.' With a sigh he added, 'If this really is what it's looking like, the idiot has clearly got himself in way deeper than he can handle.'

'And he's tried to get out of it,' Graeme said, 'by cheating his clients and his firm in an effort to keep things going.'

Sean said, 'Frankly, I'm not seeing how the hell he's going to get out of it without ending up in jail. Or worse.'

With the 'or worse' echoing in her ears, Andee rang off and looked up at Graeme. Like most people, they were acutely aware of what could happen to anyone fool enough to get mixed up in organised crime; to think of anything like that happening to Richmond was as terrifying as it was sickeningly surreal.

Ana Petrov was sitting in the driver's seat of her VW Golf, shaded by the branches of a towering horse chestnut whose leaves were reflected over the windscreen and roof, so that she was blending almost chameleon-like amongst the foliage and other small dark vehicles parked around the garden square. From this particular vantage point, close to the gates of the Botanical Gardens, she could see the Folly quite clearly. She knew already that Richmond wasn't at home, and that Olivia was. She'd watched Richmond get into his Mercedes and drive away about half an hour ago. He hadn't looked happy, but that was hardly surprising considering the strain he was under.

She was feeling it too, but she was a lot better at hiding it.

She checked the time and gave a short, impatient sigh. She was eager for things to be over, to get on with her life, the new life she already had planned in the minutest of detail. However, she understood that to rush Richmond now could result in some serious mistakes. He needed careful and structured handling, but wasn't she an expert at that?

As she waited she let her thoughts drift back to the time he'd rejected her for Olivia, when he'd thought he could cast her aside as if she were of no more value than the dirt on his shoe. To punish him she'd gone out of her way to frighten Olivia, following her to lectures and coffee bars, and into parks when Olivia took her baby there. She recalled the satisfaction she'd got from striking her face so hard it had made her own hand sting. So much had happened since those dark and distant times, when her need for revenge had burned as hotly as her hate. She'd lost a sense of herself back then, had been governed by jealousy and rage and such a frenzied determination to win Richmond back that she might have carried out her death threats, if her parents hadn't whisked her out of harm's way.

She was a different person now. She understood people in a way that had eluded her when she was young. She'd learned from members of her own family how to master not only herself and her ambitions, but also the arts of distinction and patience, insinuation and timing. She'd become a skilled organiser and facilitator, a discreet and influential networker, a conduit for projects of a highly confidential nature. She'd run her gallery impeccably, free of scandal and debt, building its reputation quietly and effectively, making her father proud of the many ways she did business. She'd become rich in her own right, and as globally connected as her father, but all the while she'd been watching and waiting, judging carefully when to bring Richmond back into her world.

It hadn't been difficult. She'd learned over the years of observing him and having him observed that he was a faithless man who cheated on his wife regularly, so sleeping with a beautiful woman, for old times' sake, had come as easily to him as ordering dinner, or calling for a cab.

She'd never threatened to tell Olivia about their affair; she hadn't had to. He might not be whip-smart, but he was an intelligent man; he'd seen right away what a good idea it would be to buy a flat where they could meet. He understood how upset she'd be if he refused. After she'd moved in he'd visited more often than she'd expected, the underlying possibility of blackmail clearly not putting him off. Maybe it excited him, for he'd become a little more active in the bedroom over the months that followed.

It was a year into their new relationship that she'd reintroduced him to her father and a consortium of businessmen eager to invest in Britain. The marina expansion had been their idea, and when Richmond had discovered the sums they were prepared to put in it hadn't taken him long to understand what was happening – and that he had no choice but to go along with it. No one ever mentioned his family, or his business: his fears for them were no concern of theirs.

Now, seeing the front door of the Folly opening, Ana focused her gaze and tilted her head further into the shade. Olivia didn't even glance in her direction. She was too busy carrying a heavy bag and some boxes down to the car. The daughter came out, shut the front door and descended the steps to the forecourt. When she reached her mother, Olivia drew her into an embrace and pressed a kiss to her forehead. It was hard to be sure from this distance, but it looked as though Sasha might have been crying. She seemed flushed and her shoulders were drooping, but she helped load up the hatchback before getting into the passenger seat beside her mother.

Minutes after they'd driven away Ana picked up her snakeskin briefcase and an empty hold-all, walked across the street and let herself into the house. She knew the alarm code, but it seemed Sasha had forgotten to set it before leaving, so Ana stood for a moment listening to the silence.

This was her third visit to the house since arriving in Kesterly (not counting the night she'd come to dinner with Imogen), and she still didn't feel comfortable being here alone. It wasn't because she was afraid someone would come in, although it would certainly be awkward if they did, but because she felt, strangely, as though the house itself didn't want her there.

Reminding herself that the walls weren't going to start closing in on her or the ceiling come crashing down on her head, she set about her tasks quietly and efficiently, wanting to be gone in five minutes or less.

First she went to the TV room where she planted the snakeskin briefcase behind the furthest arm of the sofa, a place where it wouldn't be found right away. Then she ran up the stairs to Richmond and Olivia's room. On her previous visits she'd found the six-foot bed covered in expensive silver-grey linens and plush purple cushions meticulously arrayed, almost as if ready for a magazine shoot. This morning it was a mess, with the duvet half piled on to the floor and the pillows still showing where heads had lain. She wasted no time on it, turned instead to the wardrobes and took out one of Richmond's handmade suits. Next she went to the chest of drawers that she knew was his and removed more items, not so many that they'd be missed, but enough to half fill the holdall. She added some shoes, socks and underwear, selected a tie and then zipped up the bag. She was about to start back to the door when she spotted Olivia's hairbrush on the bed. Taking it with her, she descended the stairs and went to open the briefcase.

After adding the brush to an iPad, the pink lipstick and a compact she'd helped herself to on a previous visit, she refastened the clasps and put the briefcase back in place.

In the kitchen she looked around, not entirely certain of what she needed in there until her eyes alighted on a knife block beside the range. Yes, it was quite possible that one of those finely sharpened blades could come in very handy over the next few days or weeks. Taking the largest she slipped it into the holdall, and minutes later, without setting the alarm, she was driving out of the garden square heading towards the sea.

Sasha opened the car door almost before Olivia came to a stop outside her parents' home.

'Careful,' Olivia cautioned.

Sasha wasn't listening. She leapt out on to the pavement, ran down the garden path and disappeared into the house.

Following, Olivia felt weighed down by anxiety and guilt, and no small confusion. She was trying to tell herself she wasn't a bad mother and that she was doing the right thing, but it was hard to believe it when Sasha had asked to go and stay with her grandparents because she didn't want to be at home with her parents.

'You've got no idea what's going on, have you?' she'd yelled this morning. 'If you knew what people were saying about you ... '

'Then tell me,' Olivia shot back.

'Why should I? It's not up to me. Get Dad to tell you, but I'm not staying here any longer. I'm going to live with Grandma and Grandpa, and I'm not coming back until you and Dad sort things out, which might be never the way you're going.'

Now, digging out her phone as it rang, Olivia saw it was Richmond and gave a sigh of relief. 'At last,' she said. 'I've been trying you all morning ... '

'What's the problem?' he snapped.

'I need you to tell me what you said to Sasha last night. She's really upset this morning and wants to leave home. I'm outside my parents' place now and she's determined to stay here until we sort things out.'

He made a noise of irritation. 'You'll have to deal with her,' he retorted shortly, and the line went dead.

Incensed, Olivia clicked off at her end and walked into her father's embrace as he came out to meet her.

'Thanks for letting her stay,' she said. 'She's not in a very good place at the moment, so I hope she doesn't make life difficult for you.'

'She'll be fine with us,' he assured her. 'Are you rushing off now?'

'I'm afraid so, but I'll come back later to find out how she is.'

After they'd unloaded Sasha's things, Olivia drove away and half an hour later, outwardly calm, though knotted with dread and anger inside, she stood up as Richmond came into his office and closed the door behind him. During the wait she'd been busy on Facebook and Twitter, and felt sick to her stomach by all that she'd found.

Richmond Benting's a crook. Drive him out of town.

He's bankrupt. He's cheated everyone.

My gran's got her pension with him. Hope he hasn't stolen it.

We should burn his house down with his whole family in it.

Sasha swans about the place thinking she's God's gift, but who's paying for her to go to that fancy college? We are. Got to kill it.

My parents told me the police are involved. Lock him up.

That wasn't even the half of it, but it had been enough to make Olivia understand that things were a whole lot worse than she'd allowed herself to consider.

Richmond was behind his desk, looking at her as though she was someone taking up valuable time so she should make it quick.

'I want you to tell me what's really going on,' she said quietly. 'Please don't lie to me, or try to palm me off with excuses. I want the truth.'

He continued to stare at her, and she could see that in spite of her words he was working out how to spin the facts in a way that would minimise them, or perhaps even make her feel foolish.

'Is it true the police are involved?' she demanded.

His expression barely changed as he said, 'They've been asking questions.'

The admission was so matter-of-fact that it felt like a physical blow, happening at a dreamlike speed.

She hardly knew what to say next, as confusion and panic threatened to engulf her. Reminding herself that there would be time for emotion later, she managed to keep her voice steady as she said, 'How bad is it?'

His failure to answer was answer enough.

Swallowing drily, she said, 'And when were you going to tell me?'

In a tired, irritable way he said, 'People frighten easily where money is concerned, especially when it's theirs, and while the company's accounts are frozen there isn't much I can do to put their minds at rest.'

The company accounts were frozen. When had that happened?

'Yesterday,' he replied when she asked.

'And how – how much of this is connected to the marina expansion?'

'All of it. I've been trying to save the project.'

By using other people's money? Funds that were never meant to go in that direction? Since the answer was obvious, she said, 'How much are people owed?'

'I don't have the figures.'

He seemed so ... cold, so detached from it, as if he was discussing a random piece of lost property instead of people's life savings. 'Do – do you have any idea if you can get it back?'

He checked his phone as a text came through. After reading it he deleted it and said, 'I'm due to meet with the police in London the day after tomorrow. I'll be able to tell you more after that.'

OLIVIA. I drove away from Richmond's office that day in a state that I can hardly describe. It was as though I'd lost a sense of reality, was going along in a thickening haze of confusion where it was impossible to see anything clearly. Before I left he held me for a long time, seeming to tell me how important it was for him to know that come what may I would stand by him. I told him that I would, although I wasn't sure I meant it, because I really didn't know if I had the whole story. I was fairly certain I didn't.

He went to London later that day, promising to call as soon as he had some news. With Sasha at my parent's place I was alone in the house, so I started going through more social media postings and found them all to be as violent as they were cruel, and rigid in their belief that Richmond was a fraudster who needed locking up or worse. No one, it seemed, was prepared to give him the benefit of the doubt, because there didn't appear to be any doubt that the project had left him bankrupt and he'd tried to bail himself out by using funds from Penn Financial.

When I talked to my parents it was clear right away that this was what they believed too, and after some discussion we agreed that things were probably only going to get worse, so it would be for the best if they took Sasha to the villa they'd rented in France for a while. She really didn't need to be dealing with any more of it – in fact none of us did, but it was our duty to protect her as best we could. I texted Richmond to let him know she was going and he said he thought it was a good idea. I asked how his meeting had gone with the police and he texted back to say it still hadn't happened.

For the next two days I hardly left the house. I didn't want to see anyone. I was so aware of the abandoned building site on the other side of town that it was as though I couldn't move for it. I had no idea how bad things were going to get. I kept thinking about the children and how much they loved their father. The last thing you ever want as a mother is to see your children's belief in the father they've always been so proud of start to shatter. I guess it was already happening for Sasha ...

I needed so badly to hear Richmond say that Sean's company had decided to take over the project and that he was coming home to straighten things out, but I knew in my heart that I was fooling myself. His texts just kept telling me to be patient, and he'd stopped answering my calls.

In the end, knowing I was going to drive myself crazy if I didn't speak to someone, I called the only person I knew I could trust; the person I should probably have gone to right away.

Chapter Twelve

'Come in,' Andee said, holding the door wide open for Olivia to pass. 'How are you?'

Since it was likely Andee already had a fair idea of the answer to that, Olivia simply gave a sardonic smile.

Leading the way through to the kitchen, Andee said, 'It's just us. Graeme's up at Villa Tramonto inspecting some last-minute changes to the master suites.'

Remembering that the small, upscale hotel was due to open in less than a month, Olivia felt her heart twist with dismay. She was fairly certain Richmond had helped raise some of the finance for the project, and if she was right there was every chance the villa's owner was feeling as edgy these days as many other people in town.

'I made some coffee,' Andee said, going on through the open French windows into the garden, exotically colourful with its miniature pineapple palms, birds of paradise flowers and vibrant

hibiscus. There were bird-feeders and squirrel baf-
fles, and a lion's-head fountain sending a gentle
cascade of water into a stone trough below. It was a
peaceful, luxurious haven backing on to the Botanical Gardens, seeming a very long way from the
bustle of the nearby town.

As Andee filled two mugs from a cafetière, Olivia
sat into the comfortable sling of a director's chair
and said, 'Thanks for bearing with me this past
week. I'm sorry if I've let you down ... '

'You haven't,' Andee assured her gently, and passing her a coffee she sat down too.

After taking a sip, Olivia stared at her mug for a
while. Now she was here she wasn't quite sure how
to begin, until it suddenly seemed obvious. 'I guess
you're aware of the rumours,' she said.

Andee didn't deny it, nor did she spell out what
they were. She simply said, 'What does Richmond
say?'

Olivia took a breath and let it go slowly. 'Not very
much,' she admitted. 'He's in London. He promised
to call me as soon as there was some news, but that
was four days ago and I'm still none the wiser.'

'What has he told you so far?' Andee's tone was
gentle.

Olivia looked at her and away again. She knew it
was possible, given her connections, that Andee was
more informed about the situation than she was.

With members of her own family and Graeme's being clients of Penn Financial, it would naturally follow that Andee would look into things as soon as the rumours began. In part it was why Olivia was here, to find out what she knew. 'Actually, it's what he's not telling me that's worrying me the most,' she confessed.

Andee's eyes narrowed slightly. 'What do you think that is?' she asked carefully.

Olivia shook her head. 'He hasn't denied taking funds from the company,' she said. 'He claims he was trying to keep the marina project going.' She gave a shaky sigh. 'That alone puts him in serious trouble, but I guess what's worrying me the most is the bank that pulled out … I don't know if he still owes them money. I don't even know which bank it was, apart from the fact it was foreign.' She forced her eyes to Andee's. 'Even that doesn't sound good, does it?' she said, hating the truth of it.

Andee started to speak, but Olivia continued, half wretchedly, half angrily. 'I want to give him the benefit of the doubt,' she exclaimed. 'He's my husband, so I should, but how can I when he's already told me he used client funds to try and rescue the project? And now I don't even really know where he is, or what he's doing. He said he was going for a meeting with the police, but is that true?' She gave a heated growl of frustration. 'And there was me thinking that all I had to worry about was getting over cancer and Ana Petrov turning up on our doorstep.'

Andee regarded her closely, and allowed several moments to pass before she said, 'Have you seen Ana Petrov since you had lunch with her?'

Olivia shook her head.

'Is she still at Imogen's?'

'I guess so. You know, I'd rather think of him going off with her than I would of him cheating anyone, least of all people we know.' Her eyes closed in heartbreak and shame. 'I'm so sorry about your mother and Graeme's sisters,' she whispered brokenly, thinking of the fondness she had for those women, and knowing that she was never going to be able to look them in the face again. 'I wish I could tell you that there's a way to get their investments back, but at the moment I'm really not sure that there is.'

Clearly deciding not to make her feel any worse on that score, Andee said, 'Have you been in touch with anyone at the London office to see if they can tell you what's happening?'

Olivia shook her head. 'I don't really know any-one there, apart from Cooper Jarrett. I'm sure he's fully aware of everything. I wouldn't even be surprised if he's responsible for it all.'

Neither agreeing nor disagreeing, Andee eventually said, 'There's something I have to tell you.'

Olivia immediately tensed. It wasn't going to be good, she could tell by Andee's tone, and she could feel herself pulling back as even the potential of a new twist made her fearful.

'There's no easy way of doing it,' Andee said softly, 'so I'll come straight to the point. It's quite possible that Richmond allowed the marina expansion to be used as a channel for laundering money.'

Olivia's mouth turned dry, as the rest of her seemed to go numb. Though she hadn't voiced this to herself, she knew that deep down it was what she'd feared most. It made her head spin to think of her husband doing deals with people who were no more than gangsters, individuals he must surely have known would ruin him in the end. 'Why would he do it?' she asked hoarsely. 'He doesn't even know ... I mean, he's always been honest and ... ' She gave a humourless laugh. 'How can I say that when I apparently don't know him?'

'I've no idea why he got involved,' Andee replied, 'but I do have an idea of how it came about.'

Olivia looked at her, aware of a pounding tightness in her head, of a wall coming up again as though to keep Andee out. Pushing past it, she braced herself for more.

'I think ... It seems quite likely,' Andee said, 'that Ana Petrov's father introduced him to the initial investors.'

Olivia stopped breathing. She could feel the colour draining from her face, the rhythm changing in her heart. Though she understood the implications of what Andee had just said, each time they seemed to come clear they slipped away again, into a black gulf of denial. Ana Petrov had led him to this. Ana Petrov and her family were at the heart of it. She could get no further than that, didn't want to go any further.

In the end she managed to say, 'How – how do you know this?'

Nodding to show it was a reasonable question, Andee said, 'When I found out that due diligence on the marina had revealed a fraud investigation, I contacted an old colleague at the Met to see what more I could learn. He confirmed that an investigation was under way, and after digging a little deeper he sent me photographs … ' She paused, looked concernedly at Olivia and continued. 'They're of Richmond and Ana Petrov, dining with her father and two other men at a restaurant in Amsterdam. These men were, still are I'm told, under National Crime Agency surveillance.' After allowing that to register, she added, 'The photos were taken in April 2015.'

Olivia reeled, as the date hit her as hard as the link to organised crime. Her husband had been living a life she'd known nothing about, had deceived her on a level she could hardly begin to comprehend. He'd been sucked into the Petrov family's dark and murky world, a world that coiled itself through decent society like poisoned gas, invisible and deadly. He'd done a deal that he must surely have known would benefit them and ruin him ... She opened her mouth but no words came out.

Finally, she heard herself saying, in a voice that barely sounded like her own, 'Can I see these photos?'

As Andee went inside to fetch her laptop, Olivia pressed her hands to her face and tried to breathe steadily. She could deal with this, she told herself, she was going to find a way to get through it for the children's sake and for her own. But even as she tried to bolster herself she was faltering in the fear of where Richmond was now and what might be happening to him.

When Andee returned with her laptop she opened it, but before turning it so Olivia could see the screen, she said, 'Are you sure you want to do this?'

Olivia nodded, knowing she had to if she was ever going to make herself believe the nightmare was real.

She was bemused when the first shot came up; she'd expected people, but it was of a large Regency house with a colonnaded porch and black front door. Andee clicked the mouse and the next photo showed a street name and postcode. Another click revealed a title register, and as Olivia read

Richmond's name at the top she frowned in confusion. It was when she saw the shot of the nameplates showing who lived at Flat 6 that blood raced hotly through her veins.

She looked at Andee and the sorrow in her friend's dark eyes suddenly made her lash out, knocking the computer to the floor. She didn't need to see any more, whatever else there was hardly mattered. All that did was the rage burning inside her, the devastating sense of betrayal that was consuming her – and before Andee could do anything to stop her she ran back through the house and out of the door.

ANDEE. I told Olivia about the London flat first, because I thought she should know everything I knew, and I hoped that finding out through me would help her to prepare for whatever was going to come next. No one had any clear idea then what it would be; if we had, I guess we'd all have done things differently.

I presumed when she left my house that she'd gone home, just across the square. I checked regularly and her car was there, but she didn't return my messages or answer the door when I knocked.

In the end Graeme and I decided to use the key we kept for emergencies to let ourselves in. She wasn't there, and we could find nothing to tell us where she'd gone.

Richmond's face was pale, his expression impenetrable as he watched Crispin Blake react to what he'd just told him. Though the lawyer acting for Penn Financial had appeared shocked at first, and even vaguely disbelieving, he was now starting to look more puzzled, even anxious. In the end, after taking even longer to digest Richmond's proposal than Richmond had expected, he said, 'Does – do your former business associates know you're here?'

Richmond shook his head.

'Does Cooper Jarrett?'

'As far as I know,' Richmond replied, 'he's still with the investigators.' He didn't add that he suspected Jarrett was cutting himself some sort of deal. In Jarrett's shoes he'd be doing the same, but he didn't have the luxury of the swap, or of a deal.

Blake's gaze focused in hard on his client. 'You're wise not to name names,' he told him, 'but even so, I take it you understand what's likely to happen if I go to the police with what you've just told me?'

'I do,' Richmond replied.

'And that's what you want?'

'Of course it's not what I *want*.'

Blake nodded slowly, then turning to his computer screen he started to type.

As he waited, Richmond got to his feet and walked over to the window. Blake's office was on the fourth floor of a large, sixties building just off High Holborn, with a view down into the busy street below. In a derelict shop doorway opposite, a tramp was slouched up against a shopping trolley filled with his worldly goods, and surrounded by old papers and bottles. Richmond found himself wondering what could have happened to bring the old man so low. Had he ever known success, or love or happiness? Had he lost everything because of a crime he hadn't even meant to commit? This last question caused Richmond's insides to clench, for he was under no illusion of how it would be if he followed the path he'd just laid out to Blake.

Pushing his hands into his pockets, he turned his back on the tramp and looked across at his lawyer, who was taking two sheets of paper from the printer on his desk.

'Before we go any further,' Blake said, laying the two typed sheets out in front of him, 'I need you to look over this statement and make sure I've understood everything correctly. I will also require reassurance that you've given serious consideration to the consequences you'll face if you go ahead with ... '

'I have,' Richmond interrupted, coming to take the pen he was being offered. 'And I don't need to read it. I'm sure you understood me perfectly.' He added his signature to the foot of the second page and put the pen down. 'Now,' he said, picking up his keys, 'I need you to act,' and without another word he left.

An hour later Richmond was in the spacious third-floor flat that he owned and was home to Ana Petrov, on Pelham Crescent in South Kensington. He'd bought it for her because he'd known that if he didn't she'd make sure Olivia found out about their affair. Of course she hadn't threatened it, she was far too subtle for that, but he'd realised when she'd shown him the brochure for the flat that the choice was either buy it for her, or lose his marriage.

That should have been an end to it, any sane man would have walked away as soon as the keys were handed over, but he hadn't. He'd carried on seeing her, God only knew why, even now he couldn't rationalise it for himself. Maybe because she made it so easy, or because the risk excited him; more likely it was because he'd understood on an unspoken level that he'd be wise to do so. He was never going to deny that she fascinated him, as did her friends, until he'd begun to realise who they really were – and what they wanted from him.

People of that sort didn't take no for an answer. Like Ana, they didn't make threats, they simply let it be known through innuendo and metaphor what was likely to happen if he didn't come through with what they wanted.

So the marina expansion had gone ahead, promoted by him to the local authority, marina management company and even private investors, most of them dedicated believers in Brexit, as a way to prepare Kesterly for the great staycation boom. A lot of cash had changed hands to smooth the way, cash that, ironically, had made its way back into the project through private investment.

He paced up and down the sitting room, urging his phone to ring, ready to roar with frustration when it remained obstinately silent. He'd heard from one of the investigators that they'd finished talking to Cooper, but he'd heard nothing from the man himself yet, nor was he answering his phone. He needed to know what Cooper had told them, though the silence was giving him all the information he expected and dreaded.

Spotting the holdall Ana had brought in yesterday, he snatched it up and went to dump it with the others close to the door. She'd made three or four excursions into the Folly over the past weeks, using the key he'd given her to spirit away things for him to take into the future. It had been her idea to pack for him that way; it had pleased her, she'd said, to walk around Olivia's house, helping herself to Olivia's husband's belongings before she took the man himself. He hadn't refused her, because he'd known he couldn't.

It had also been her idea to start afresh some-where, and again he hadn't argued because he'd understood that he didn't have a say in the matter. If he stayed he wouldn't only have to face the disgrace of the financial scandal he'd brought on himself to try and save the marina project, there were also the reprisals her friends might inflict on his family.

Using her contacts, she'd arranged everything.

Starting as his mobile rang, he checked who it was, and sick with frustration he clicked on harshly. 'Olivia, I told you, I'll call when ... '

'I need to speak to you ... '

'Not now.'

'I want to know ... '

'Olivia, stop fucking calling me!' he shouted, and snapping off the line he sat down hard on the sofa and pressed his hands to his head.

Getting up again, he noticed Ana's keys on a side table at more or less the same instant as the downstairs buzzer sounded. He went to release the door to let her in, and continued to pace. She wanted to go now, today. Everything was ready ...

Feeling sick with the suspicion that Cooper Jarrett had revealed everything and it was already too late for him to carry through his own plans, he turned to open the front door of the flat. He needed to tell Ana that their future couldn't happen the way she was seeing it. They couldn't embark on the madness she'd set up for them. He was going to tell her that he'd already spoken to his lawyer who now knew everything but names, never names ... He stopped dead and a thundering shock tore through his head.

'Hello, Richmond,' Sean said affably.

Richmond's eyes almost burst from their sockets. 'What the hell are you doing here?' he snarled. 'You've got no damned right ... '

'Maybe not, but you, my friend, need to listen to ... '

'Don't you fucking ... '

Sean's tone lowered as he said, 'Are you determined to prove yourself the arsehole I think you are? The bastard who's planning to leave his wife and kids to live with the shame of what he's done, because ... '

'Get the fuck out of here!' Richmond raged.

Sean's expression tightened almost imperceptibly. 'Were you ever going to tell Olivia about your set-up here with Ana Petrov?' he demanded. 'Was it ever a part of your plan to admit that you were suckered into a deal that was never going to work, wasn't even meant to? Stupid questions, of course you weren't going to tell her. You were just going to fuck off into oblivion and let her find out ... '

'You don't know what you're talking about.'

'Oh, but I do. I think I probably know all of it, and I have to admit a part of me actually feels sorry for you. Or it would if you weren't so damned weak. If you'd found the balls to stand up to those bastards, if you'd had what it took to walk away from Ana Petrov.'

Sweat was beading on Richmond's neck; his jaw shook as he said, 'I'm not listening to your bullshit ... '

Sean nodded towards the bags. 'You're clearly planning a trip and I swear I don't want to be the one to stop you, but I'm afraid I must.'

'What the hell has any of this got to do with you?' Richmond growled. He wasn't a bad man, he was reminding himself; he was simply a victim of his own failings; of circumstances beyond his control. He was even trying to make good, goddammit, but this bastard Kenyon was clearly in no mood to cut him any slack.

Sean said, 'Olivia knows about this place, by the way. Your cosy little love nest here with Ana Petrov. Andee Lawrence told her. So she knows that you've betrayed her, cheated your clients, allowed yourself to be used. Tell me this, have you spared a thought for how it must be making her feel right now to know how she's wasted her life on a piece of scum who never deserved her in the first place?'

Richmond's guilt was turning him puce with fury. 'You haven't got a clue what ... '

'I can see your shame as if it were dripping from your eyes,' Sean told him savagely. 'You're so disgusted with yourself it surpasses even the disgust I feel for you. You fucking hate yourself, don't you, and boy, you've got some company there. But you don't care about all those people you've cheated, do you? All that matters to you is that you get yourself out of here before they come for you with handcuffs, and they're coming, you can be sure of that.'

'It's time for you to go,' Richmond growled, his eyes darting to the door.

Sean cocked an eyebrow. 'Oh no. I'm not going anywhere until I've done what I came here to do,' and his fists were already clenching as he moved forward to close the distance between them.

By the time Sean left the flat, he'd been inside for no more than ten minutes. As he opened the front door to the street he almost collided with a woman on her way in. He apologised briefly and continued to the pavement without looking back. He knew he'd just passed Ana Petrov, and from the feel of her eyes boring into his back it was possible she'd recognised him too.

It was early evening by the time Olivia arrived outside the address she'd memorised from the photographs Andee had shown her. It had been a long drive up the M4, and a dangerous one given her speed, but she was here now, still shaking with anger and so pumped with adrenalin that she felt she could tear the door off its hinges if no one answered.

Seeing Richmond's Mercedes parked further along the crescent she gave a growling sob of fury, but at least he was still here. She felt so outraged and violent that she had to hold on to a pillar to steady herself. Then she pressed the bell, and held it down, determined not to release it until someone let her in.

In the end a stranger came out of the front door, regarded her curiously, but didn't object when she slipped inside and ran up the stairs.

'Richmond!' she cried, hammering on the door of Flat 6 as though she might drive her fists right through it. 'I know you're in there, and I'm not leaving until you have the guts to face me.'

OLIVIA. It felt that day as though my life had stopped being my own. It was like I was heading for a slow-motion car crash that I couldn't avoid. I simply couldn't get my head around the deceit, and the fact that it had gone on for so long, and that he'd been able to look me in the face when he came home after being with her. What kind of man tells you he loves you only hours, maybe even minutes after he's said it to someone else? Was she the reason for his low sex drive with me? He was getting all he wanted from her, and I was simply the mother of his children, someone he didn't need anything more from than that?

I'd known, even before I set out for London, that there was a chance I was already too late. I'd checked his closets and study: things were missing, things he'd want to take with him, though his passport was still there. I took little heart from that – if he was planning to disappear he wouldn't need it. The fact that he was planning to abscond like a coward was bad enough, but what he was leaving me with, the scandal, the criminal investigation, the sheer devastation of my parents' lives, and mine, was enough to make me want to kill him. I even thought about asking Sean if he could arrange it, that's how crazed I was that day. I actually called him and left a message for him to ring back. He sent a text saying, 'Everything has been taken care of.'

I didn't understand what he meant. Had he read my mind? He couldn't have. I didn't question it any more than that. I was completely fixated on getting to Richmond before he left.

If she was there all the better.

So I kept on ringing the bell.

Chapter Thirteen

It was past midnight by the time Olivia returned to the Folly, exhausted from all the driving, but too hyped up even to think about sleep. In truth she barely knew what she was thinking. Her head was submerged in a dense, dark whirl of anger, confusion and dread. She kept retching, but there was nothing to bring up. She paced about the house, trying to calm down, but she was only making things worse. He'd gone. In spite of his car being outside the flat, he hadn't been there, nor had Ana Petrov. She'd been too late. They'd already fled, and now Olivia had somehow to make herself face the fact that she was probably never going to see him again.

The prospect of that panicked her. She wanted to scream and rage and claw at him with all the fear and hatred in her heart. He'd run out on her and the children, taken himself off to a new life somewhere she'd never be able to find him, leaving her to cope with the chaos and heartbreak he'd left behind.

Who was he? When had he turned into a stranger, a man of no compassion, no morals, no care for what he was doing to other people's lives? How was he going to live with himself in some distant land knowing he had children who loved him, children he'd never be able to see again? Didn't that matter to him? Was his fear of paying for his crimes so great that he'd sacrifice everything rather than face it?

She jumped violently as someone knocked at the door.

Was it him? He had keys. Maybe he'd lost them. It could be someone looking for him?

She stayed where she was, frozen in fear, and flinched as whoever it was knocked again. There was no logic, no proper connection to anything racing around her head as she went into the hall and called out to ask who was there.

'Olivia, it's Barry Britten,' came the reply. 'Can we come in please?'

She frowned in confusion. Why was her old schoolfriend here at this hour? A beat later she realised he couldn't be here as a friend. Barry was with the police.

Oh dear God, what was it about? What was she going to say if they asked where he was? Would they believe her when she said she didn't know?

Opening the door she looked into Barry's familiar, gentle eyes and felt herself starting to collapse inside. A woman stood beside him.

'The children are fine,' he assured her, misinterpreting her dread, and going to the first place any sane parent would go. The children were fine. That was all that mattered. How could she have lost sight of it?

'This is Detective Sergeant Anthea Ellis,' Barry said, introducing the woman, who was displaying her ID. She was small, slightly plump with an untidy bob and sharp, close-set eyes.

'Hello, Olivia,' she said, not unkindly. 'Could we come in please?'

Olivia stood back, fatigue and fear roughening her senses. She showed them through to the drawing room and turned on the lights. Alarm was dragging itself through the periphery of her mind, but it couldn't reach clarity. It was as though she was moving through a nightmare, a world that looked like the one she knew, but everyone in it had changed.

She sat down when she was asked to, and watched Barry come to sit beside her. There was something about his manner that was disturbing her, but she couldn't say what it was. Anthea Ellis took the sofa opposite them and quietly watched and listened as Barry came to the point of their visit.

'Olivia, I'm very sorry to have to tell you this,' he said softly, 'but Richmond has been found dead. He was beaten and stabbed to death ... '

Olivia felt the shock of his words as if it were physical. She stared at him, her eyes burning as she tried to process his meaning. It was as though some kind of craziness was throwing itself at a glass wall between her and reality, fierce and persistent, but it couldn't get through. Then she felt herself starting to shake, so hard that Anthea Ellis picked up a chenille throw and came to wrap it around her.

'Is anyone else in the house?' Barry asked.

Olivia managed to say no.

'Do you want to call your parents?'

'They're in France, with Sasha,' and a horrible, wrenching panic engulfed her as she thought of her children ... Were they safe? Richmond had been stabbed to death. Their father, the man they trusted and loved, and who'd always been there for them, was a liar and a cheat, and he was never going to be there for them again.

She fought for control, knew she should be asking questions, but right now she hardly knew what they should be. In the end, she said, 'Who – who did it?'

Taking her hand, Barry said, 'That's what we need to find out.'

Ellis said, 'Can you tell us where you were earlier this evening, Olivia?'

Olivia stared at her, trying to comprehend her words. She needed to account for her movements … Did that mean? Were they thinking … ? Dear God, did they seriously think she'd done it?

Richmond was dead. Someone had beaten and stabbed him to death. The words struck a terrible tattoo in her head. She gulped for air as the shock of it stole over her again and again. She put out a hand as though to reach for something, but she had no idea what.

'Olivia,' Barry prompted gently.

She turned to him, and suddenly realising she couldn't handle this alone, she said, 'I'd like to call Andee.'

Receiving a nod from Ellis, Barry said, 'I'll do it,' and taking out his phone he went into the hall to make the call.

Andee arrived a few minutes later, still bleary-eyed from sleep, but looking as shaken as anyone would be after being woken with such news.

Barry introduced the detective who'd taken over Andee's position in CID a few years ago, and prepared himself for Andee's questions.

'Where and when did you find him?' she asked, holding on to Olivia's hands.

'He was at a flat in South Kensington,' Anthea Ellis replied. 'We were contacted by the Met an hour ago to ask us to inform his family.' *And to question his wife,* she didn't add, but Olivia heard it anyway.

'Do they know who did it?' Andee enquired.

'Not yet.' Ellis repeated her earlier question to Olivia. 'Can you tell us where you were earlier this evening?'

Since she'd taken her mother's car to London, leaving her own outside the Folly, Olivia wondered if she could say she'd been here all day. But why would she lie? She had nothing to hide. She needed to make herself think straight, to stop feeling she had to defend herself, or anyone else from being suspected of a crime she knew nothing about. 'I went to the flat in South Kensington,' she admitted, 'but he wasn't there.' Realising he might have been, but had been unable to answer, she felt herself starting to fall apart. She was picturing him, slumped on the floor, blood pooling beneath him, a knife plunged into his heart, or his back, his eyes wide open and lifeless, his ears deaf to her shouts on the other side of the door.

It couldn't be real. She was going to wake up any minute. Or maybe she was going to throw up.

Turning to Andee, she said, 'I think he was planning to leave. Some of his things have gone ... ' Her train of thought was suddenly derailed by another that mattered much more. 'I need to call my parents and get hold of Luke.' The very thought of these next steps was sending her into a whole new level of panic and resistance. How was she going to find the right words to break this to the children when she was still struggling to accept it herself?

Andee said, 'Why don't you let me do the calling, and at the same time I'll get Graeme to organise their flights back. Do you know where Luke is at the moment?'

'Not really, but he has his mobile with him. Oh God, he'll have to make the journey home on his own.' Somehow the thought of that seemed even more terrible than everything else. At least Sasha would have her grandparents, and suddenly she wanted them all so much that she gave a wrenching gasp of despair.

After hugging her, Andee left the room, speaking quietly to Barry on her way out. Olivia heard the mention of a lawyer, but Barry shook his head, saying, 'Not yet.'

Not yet! Did that mean she was going to need one?

A moment after the door closed behind Andee, Anthea Ellis said, 'So you went to the flat. Did you go inside?'

'No one answered the door, so no, I didn't go inside.'

'What did you do?'

'I sat down on the floor on the landing and waited. I thought one of them would come back ... ' *He'd been in there and she hadn't known. Was there a chance she could have saved him?*

'One of them?' Ellis repeated. 'Who else were you expecting?'

Olivia took a breath. 'Ana Petrov,' she replied shakily. 'She's ... She's his mistress.' As her head spun with the reality of that and all its implications she wished she could snatch back the words, but it was too late, Ellis's interest was already piqued.

'Go on,' the detective prompted smoothly. 'You thought one of them would come back.'

'But they didn't,' Olivia told her. 'I had no idea where they were. I thought they'd ... I mean, obviously if I'd known Richmond was ... Was he there then? On the other side of the door?' It was unthinkable, too horrifying to imagine. She shut it down again. 'What time did it happen?' she asked hoarsely.

Brushing past the questions, Ellis said, 'How long has your husband been having an affair?'

Olivia swallowed drily and turned painful eyes to Barry. 'I only found out about it today,' she told him. 'I didn't even know about the flat until Andee told me. She'll explain, I'm sure ... '

'So you didn't know about the mistress before today?' Ellis interrupted, apparently needing to be sure about this.

Olivia shook her head and nodded, not sure which was the right response. 'I mean, I know who she is, but I didn't know ... ' Her eyes returned to Barry.

'They always say the wife is the last to know, and it seems it's true.'

'Did you go to London,' Ellis continued, 'with the intention of having things out with your husband?'

How could she deny it, when that was exactly why she'd gone?

They all looked up as someone else knocked on the door. Barry went to find out who it was, and when he returned the expression on his face made Olivia's stomach clench with dread.

'They've come to search the house,' he told her gently, 'and we're also going to need the clothes you were wearing today.'

Olivia looked down at them as though they belonged to somebody else. A blousy white top and blue capri pants. She realised they were going to be examined for traces of blood, and the very idea that anyone could think she'd done this filled her with so much horror that she lost the power to move past it.

Deep breaths, she reminded herself. *You need to keep calm, to find your inner strength, and remember you have nothing to fear from these people.*

Andee came in with a tray of tea and set it down on the table. 'I've spoken to your parents,' she said softly. 'They're going to let Sasha sleep on till morning and then they'll bring her home.'

Feeling desperate for her parents and her daughter, Olivia said, 'And Luke?'

'He's booked on to a flight at midday our time, which should get him in around six in the evening. Graeme's offered to meet him at Heathrow.'

'I should go,' Olivia insisted. 'I should have spoken to him. What kind of mother am I?' She was trying to find her phone.

Andee said gently, 'He doesn't know yet how Richmond died. I thought it would be too much for him to try to cope with on the journey.'

Olivia nodded, agreeing that had been the right call. She looked at her phone as it rang. Seeing it was Luke she immediately clicked on.

'Mum!'

'Darling, I'm sorry I didn't call. The police are here … They have to … There are a lot of questions … '

'How did it happen?'

'We're … They're still trying to establish that. We'll know more by the time you get here.' Could she say she'd pick him up? Would the police let her? 'If I can't get to the airport myself, Graeme will come. OK?'

'OK. Are you all right, Mum? I wish I was there, but I will be soon. Just hang on. I'll get there as fast as I can.'

As she rang off, Olivia's throat was tight with emotion. His effort to be strong for her was breaking her heart, but once the truth of this, and the shock, really hit him she was the one who'd have to be strong for him.

Her children were all that mattered now. They were all that had ever mattered.

Anthea Ellis was reading something on her phone. Messages seemed to be coming in every few minutes, and as she finished the latest one, she said, 'Did you drive your own car to London today?'

Olivia shook her head. 'I took my mother's. It's parked here while she's away. I knew it had a full tank, and that mine didn't.'

'What kind of car does your mother drive?'

'A Renault Megane. It's outside.'

After checking her phone again, Ellis said, 'Did you meet Sean Kenyon at the flat in South Kensington?'

Olivia blinked in astonishment, and saw Andee had been taken by surprise too. 'No,' she replied.

'Why do you ask?' Andee prompted.

'I've just been informed that he was seen entering and leaving the flat earlier today. Who is Sean Kenyon?' she asked them.

Andee explained some of the background while Olivia listened and felt panicked by the text Sean had sent, telling her that everything had been taken care of. What on earth had that meant? Surely to God not what was in her head now. Why had he even gone there?

' ... a neighbour has claimed there was a woman in Kenyon's car,' Ellis was saying. 'Are you sure it wasn't you?'

'No, it wasn't,' Olivia replied firmly. 'I didn't see him. I didn't see anyone.' She looked imploringly at Andee, wanting her to shed some light on this new turn, but Andee was clearly as baffled as she was.

Ellis was consulting her phone again. 'I guess I already know the answer to this,' she said, 'but I've been instructed to ask if you have any idea where we might find Ana Petrov?'

Olivia started to shake her head, wondering if now was the time to mention Ana's business contacts, but then she was thinking of Imogen. Presumably she didn't know anything yet. It was going to devastate her, and in spite of detesting her Olivia felt a wrenching pity for her. She'd lost her only son, how could she feel anything but compassion for that? 'Have you spoken to Richmond's mother?' she asked Ellis, the horror of it all coming over her again.

Ellis looked puzzled. 'Are you saying she might be able to tell us where to find Ana Petrov?' she asked.

'No ... I ... I'm not sure what I'm saying, but she and Ana have always been close. Someone needs to tell Imogen about Richmond,' she said to Andee, 'if they haven't already.'

Andee looked to Barry for the answer. 'I don't think anyone has,' he said. 'I'll check. She lives here in Kesterly,' he informed Ellis.

Returning to Olivia, Ellis said, 'So you don't know yourself where we might find Ana Petrov?'

Olivia managed to say no. She was feeling dizzy now, disoriented, as though she was about to pass out. She struggled to hold on, digging her hands into the sofa and pressing her feet hard to the floor. She blinked slowly as Andee came to her, but she couldn't make out what anyone was saying. She was dimly aware of Ellis and Barry getting to their feet, of someone laying her down, and the last thing she registered before shock and exhaustion engulfed her was Andee saying, 'It's OK, I'll stay with her.'

Olivia was still in the drawing room when she woke around seven a.m. to the sound of birdsong and muted voices elsewhere in the house. For a moment she was confused, couldn't understand why she was on the sofa, or where the voices were coming from ... Then reality emerged from the shadows, and as it reached her she felt it might choke her. She almost cried out for Richmond, as though he might somehow defy all she'd been told and come to her. She bunched her hands at her mouth, pushing back the grief and dread and many more emotions she didn't even understand.

He was dead, the truth of that was devastating her, but he'd betrayed her, had planned to abandon her and the children ... She had no idea how to feel, or even how to think.

She realised the police must still be searching the house. Or maybe they'd gone away and come back again.

Her next thoughts were so rapid and tangled that it was like an onslaught of madness. She wondered where Luke and Sasha were, why Sean had been at the flat. Where was Richmond? Talking to the police? On his way back to Kesterly? No, he was on a table in a laboratory identified by Graeme who'd driven straight there, stark white and lifeless under dazzling lights as a pathologist examined him. How many wounds were there? How deep? Which of them had killed him? *Who* had killed him? She thought of Ana, of the men he'd done business with ... She felt suddenly queasy and sat up too fast.

As her head cleared she knew she wouldn't be able to believe he was really gone unless she saw him, but she didn't want to see him, not the way he was now. She wanted him to come back, to be who she'd always believed him to be. Not perfect, but her husband, the man she loved, the man she'd lived with for over twenty years and thought she knew as well as she knew herself.

Grabbing her phone as it rang, she saw it was Sasha and clicked on clumsily.

'Oh, Mum,' Sasha gasped. 'I wanted to call, but they said you might be sleeping. I can't ... I don't want it to be true ... '

'I know, sweetheart, I don't either, but we'll get through it, I promise. Where are you now?'

'We're on our way to the airport. What exactly happened? Do you know who did it?'

'No,' Olivia said gently, thinking of how much else there was to tell. The mistress, the fraud, the planned escape ... She knew she'd never understand how he could have done what he had. Why hadn't he considered his children, even if he couldn't have considered anyone else? 'It might be clearer by the time you get here,' she said. 'How are Grandma and Grandpa?'

'I think they're OK. I mean, they're shocked and upset, obviously ... Grandma wants to speak to you.'

As her mother's familiar honey-soft voice came down the line, Olivia almost started to sob. 'I don't want you to worry about us,' Rena said. 'We'll be there as soon as we can. Just know we love you and as a family we are going to get through this.'

Olivia said, 'I love you too.' Then before her mother could ring off, 'Mum, I need to tell you that Richmond has been having an affair with Ana Petrov for the last few years. The stabbing happened at a flat in London that he owned and was where she lived. As far as I know they're still looking for her.'

Rena stayed silent, and understanding she didn't want to respond in front of Sasha, Olivia said, 'If you could break it to the others before you get here … The affair, I mean. I'm sorry to land it on you, but I think it's best Sasha hears it from you, now, before she finds out another way.'

'Of course,' Rena replied soberly. 'And the fraud investigation?'

'No one's mentioned it yet, but I'm sure they will.'

After she rang off she went to the kitchen and found Andee making tea and toast. 'The police are still here,' Olivia stated, her voice sounding flat and scratchy as it came through her swollen throat.

Andee nodded. 'You should eat something,' she said, pushing a plate towards her.

Obediently Olivia took a few bites, then unable to face any more she said, 'Has anything else happened?'

'Not that I know of,' Andee replied. 'Barry and Anthea Ellis have gone, but I expect at least one of them will be back again.'

Olivia got up from the table. 'I need to shower.'

'They want your clothes,' Andee reminded her, holding out a clear blue plastic bag.

Telling herself again that she had nothing to fear, Olivia took the bag and went upstairs. Unable to face her and Richmond's room, she used the guest suite instead.

Half an hour later, wearing a T-shirt and jeans she'd found in the laundry room, she brought the evidence bag down with her and handed it to one of the forensic team. She wasn't sure how many of them were in the house, but she couldn't think it really mattered when there was surely nothing here to find.

Her head spun again with the shock of it all, and she sat down hard on the bottom stair. She was aware of the family photos looking at her, eyes from a past that seemed as alien now as though it had been lived by somebody else. Betrayal poured over her memories like acid, staining them, changing them ... How was she going to explain this to her children? What could she say that would help them to understand what their father had done? Or what had been done to him at the end?

Coming out of the kitchen, Andee passed her a coffee. 'Terence Gould should be here any minute,' she said, sitting down next to her.

Knowing that this was the detective inspector who'd been Andee's boss during her time with Kesterly CID, Olivia felt her heart skip a horrible beat. 'Is he as fierce as he looks?' she asked, trying to make light of it. She'd seen him around often enough, and frequently in the media, and he had no problem coming across as someone you really didn't want to antagonise.

'Not always,' Andee replied. 'Anthea Ellis will be with him, and I should let you know that I've alerted Helen Hall to what's going on.'

Since Helen Hall was one of the most prominent lawyers in town, Olivia felt another clenching of unease.

'She doesn't see any need for her to be here yet,' Andee continued, 'but if that changes she's promised to come right away.'

Catching her breath, Olivia said, 'I hope you realise I haven't done anything wrong. It wasn't me who ... '

'Of course I know it wasn't you, but murder investigations are almost never straightforward, so it can do no harm to have a good lawyer on standby. That's probably Gould and Ellis now,' she said as someone knocked on the door.

As Andee went to answer it Olivia stood up and stared after her, still not able to move past the words *murder investigation*. Of course she understood that was what she was involved in, but she was having trouble making herself grasp the fact that this was her new reality. Her world had been turned inside out and upside down; everything was so shaken up, so different to yesterday that she could get no perspective on it. It was the sort of thing that happened to other people, strangers she read about in the papers, or pitied, maybe even judged when she saw them on TV. She thought about her friends and neighbours all over town, and realised that many of them must know by now that Richmond was dead. The gossip would spread so fast that speculation would have a hard time keeping up with it, but by the end of the day, maybe even sooner than that, everyone would have a theory, an opinion, and she wondered how many would say that he'd got what he deserved.

Though she was in wretched turmoil, she showed no sign of it as she went to meet DI Gould. The scrutiny of his piercing eyes was unsettling, but she calmed herself with the reminder that all she had to do was speak the truth. She couldn't save Richmond's reputation now. She could save nothing, so she had no reason to be anything but open and honest.

They returned to the drawing room, accompanied by Anthea Ellis, who was carrying a large blue plastic bag similar to the one Olivia had filled with her clothes. Trying not to feel anxious about what might be inside, Olivia sat down with Andee while Gould and Ellis took the opposite sofa. If Ellis minded about Andee, her predecessor, sitting in on the questioning now a superior officer was here, she wasn't showing it. She wasn't showing much at all as she opened the blue bag and drew out a briefcase that sent a bolt of shock through Olivia.

'Do you recognise this?' Ellis asked her.

'Yes. Yes, it belongs to Ana Petrov.'

'Can you explain why it was found here in your house?'

Olivia's jaw dropped. 'I ... No. She must have left it here. Where did you find it?'

Ignoring the question, Ellis said, 'Are you sure you didn't take it from the flat when you went there yesterday?'

'No! I mean, yes, of course I'm sure. I told you, I didn't go in.'

Ellis looked at Gould as he said, 'Do you have any idea what's inside?'

'No, how could I, when I've never seen it out of Ana's possession?'

Ellis snapped the clasps and laid the briefcase open on the coffee table. The contents comprised a handful of evidence bags and to Olivia's horror she saw that the items inside were her own lipstick, hairbrush, iPad and mirror compact.

She swallowed drily, looked at Gould, then at Andee, and couldn't think what to say.

'Do you recognise any of these items?' Gould asked.

'Yes ... I ... I think they're mine.'

As Ellis closed the briefcase and returned it to the bag, Gould took out his phone and passed it to Olivia. On the screen was the photograph of a knife beside a transparent evidence bag.

She reeled violently, understanding that this must have been the knife used to ... Then she realised that she recognised it, and felt unable to breathe.

'There's a knife block in your kitchen,' Gould stated, 'and one of the slots is empty. Can you tell us where the missing item might be?'

Olivia was stiff with horror and confusion. 'I've no idea. I mean ... I presumed it had been put in one of the drawers by mistake. We often do that.'

'It doesn't appear to be anywhere in the kitchen,' Ellis told her, 'and as you can see, the design on the handles of those knives in your block matches the one on the murder weapon.'

As Olivia's bile rose, Andee put a steadying hand on her arm and said, 'You're coming close to making some very serious allegations, so perhaps we need to call a lawyer.'

'We're simply trying to establish,' Gould said, 'how a knife that belongs in this house got to the flat in South Kensington.'

'Richmond could have taken it,' Andee pointed out.

'Yes, but why would he?'

Since it was impossible for anyone to answer that, Ellis said, 'Have either Sean Kenyon or Ana Petrov visited you here at any time?'

Stunned that the question included Sean, Olivia looked at Andee while replying. 'Yes, they both have, but if you're asking if they could have taken the knife then I ... I was with Sean the whole time, so I'm sure he didn't. He couldn't have without me noticing.'

Ellis said, 'I believe you and Sean Kenyon go back a long way.'

Olivia nodded.

'You were involved once? In a romantic relationship.'

Again Olivia nodded.

'Are you now?'

'No,' Olivia responded incredulously. 'He was in Kesterly to assess the marina project, not because I was here.'

'Do you still have feelings for him?'

Olivia opened her mouth but nothing came out.

'When were you last in touch with him?' Ellis asked.

Olivia cried, 'For God's sake, if I was going to plot something like this with an old boyfriend I'd hardly have used a knife from my own kitchen.'

'Did you plot something like this with an old boy-friend?' Ellis asked calmly.

Olivia glared at her, but fear was getting the better of her. *Why had Sean gone to the flat? What was all taken care of? It wasn't making any sense.* 'Where's Sean now?' she asked, turning back to Andee.

Ellis said, 'He's being interviewed at the station, here in Kesterly.'

Andee's eyes widened. 'He's here?'

'He is,' Gould confirmed.

'What about Ana!' Olivia cried. 'That's who did this, I'm certain of it. Or she'll know who did ... '

Andee said, 'Is Sean under arrest?'

'Not at this time,' Gould replied. His eyes were fixed on Olivia.

'Have you spoken to Ana yet?' she demanded.

'The last I heard,' he replied, 'they still haven't managed to locate her.'

'What about Richmond's mother? Ana was staying with her ... '

'She says Ana left her house on Tuesday and she hasn't heard from her since.'

'I take it you've alerted all airports and ports,' Andee said.

'I think we can take that as read,' he replied, 'but it's being handled by the Met.' He glanced at his phone as it rang, and excusing himself he went into the hall to take the call, signalling to Ellis to join him.

Feeling as though a terrible, suffocating darkness had briefly left the room, Olivia took several deep breaths. 'I'm finding it hard to grasp it all,' she told Andee. 'Am I right in thinking that Ana's tried to set me up for Richmond's murder?'

'She's certainly tried to confuse things,' Andee admitted. 'I take it the iPad isn't yours?'

Olivia shook her head.

'Then it'll be interesting to find out its relevance.'

Dreading to think what might be on it, Olivia said, 'Do the police know about the marina's backers? The connections to organised crime?'

'Yes, apparently they do, but as far as I'm aware CCTV of the area outside the flat is showing only three people, apart from residents, going into and coming out of the building. That's you, Sean and Ana Petrov.'

Olivia shook her head in bemusement. 'It can't have been Sean,' she stated distractedly. 'It makes no sense. It has to have been her. But why would she kill him?'

'There are obviously still a lot of questions needing answers,' Andee replied, 'but what I'd really like to know right now is what on earth Sean was doing there.'

SEAN. I had a pretty full picture of what had been going on in Benting's world of fraud and corruption by the time I went to confront him. In other words, I knew by then that there was no rescuing the situation. At least not as far as he was concerned. He was in far too deep.

When I got there it was obvious right away that he was in no state to listen to anything I had to say. He was seriously worked up over something, most likely the fact that he knew his time was running out. The police were coming for him, and for all I knew his dubious business associates were too, although according to an officer attached to the investigation, the main players in that little venture hadn't been seen in London for over a year. Did that make any difference? People like that have a long reach and a lot of connections. Nevertheless, it seemed more likely he was waiting for Ana Petrov so they could get the hell out of England before the hand-cuffs turned up.

I wouldn't say we had a chat, exactly. It was more of an exchange, sometimes heated, especially on his part. Of course I wanted him to know what I thought of him, I wasn't going to put forward any sort of salvage proposal without that satisfaction, and I managed to get some of it in. The rest, that the Kenyon board had turned the marina project down, but I was prepared to try and sort something out to help turn the eyesore of an abandoned build site into something more aesthetic and productive, went unsaid, because he wasn't listening. And frankly, I kind of lost heart when I got there. He pissed me off with his ranting, and the way he didn't even seem to be considering anyone but himself.

Obviously I didn't know then that he'd given his lawyer a full confession and was preparing to do his time. If I had I probably wouldn't have done what I did. Then again I might have, because for what he'd done to his family and to his clients he damned well deserved it.

I saw the girlfriend as I let myself out downstairs, we passed at the door, but we didn't speak. I had nothing to say. I just wanted to get away from there.

Chapter Fourteen

It was past ten o'clock by the time Luke arrived home that night, and the moment she saw him Olivia felt herself starting to fragment, as if she'd lost all power to hold herself together. Somehow, she managed. She didn't even cry, because what was happening to them, the way their lives were being turned inside out never to be the same again, was so far beyond tears that it felt pointless to shed a single one. However, seeing her darling son, her precious, special boy grown into a man during this short time gone, brought her very close to the edge. He might resemble her in looks more than his father, but he was so like Richmond in the way he held and expressed himself, even in the tenor of his voice, that it almost felled her.

'Graeme told me everything,' he said, hugging her tight, 'and I want you to know that I'm here for you, OK?' He looked determinedly, fiercely into her eyes, then hugged her again. He didn't mention Ana Petrov, but she could sense his anger, his outrage that his father had allowed anyone to breach the sanctity of their family. The rest of it, for the moment, had been pushed into second place. Seeing Sasha hovering close by, he pulled her into the embrace. 'I'm sorry I didn't listen when you messaged me,' he said, pressing a kiss to her head. 'I'm such a dumb fuck, sorry, Mum, didn't mean to swear. Shit, this is doing my head in. I'm so spaced out, I hardly know what to say.'

'You don't need to say anything,' Olivia told him. 'You being here is enough, but I'm sorry it has to be like this.'

'Not your fault,' he said gruffly, and she could see how protective he was feeling towards her. *You hurt my mother and you hurt me, even if you are my father.* 'I feel totally weirded out by it all,' he said, dashing a hand through his hair, then seeing his grandparents waiting their turn to greet him, he went to wrap his arms tightly around them. 'I get that this isn't anywhere near over,' he told them, 'but we're going to pull together as a family, right?'

'Of course we are,' Rena assured him, her eyes glistening with tears.

'We should go,' Andee said softly to Olivia as she reached for Graeme's hand.

'No, please don't,' Olivia objected. Then realising they'd probably had enough of the Bentings for one day, she added, 'Unless you want to, of course.'

'You've got a lot of catching up to do,' Graeme reminded her, 'and everyone's tired. We're just across the square if you need us.'

'Thank you,' Olivia murmured, putting her arms around him. 'Thank you so much, both of you, for everything.'

After they'd gone, she turned back to the others and waved them through to the kitchen. While waiting for Graeme and Luke to arrive she and her mother had prepared some tapas dishes, aware that no one had eaten that day, and knowing that if anyone's appetite would need feeding it would be Luke's.

It turned out that they were all able to eat at last, and because they were so tired, or too emotionally drained to discuss anything else, it seemed easier to ask Luke to tell them about Thailand and why he'd broken up with his girlfriend.

Over the next two days, as they continued to talk to the police, and tried to piece together the consequences they were likely to face as the days and weeks unfolded, they didn't venture from the house unless they had to. Nor did they watch the news or log in to social media. Andee had warned them not to; the last thing they needed to deal with right now was the outside world's conjectures and opinions on what had happened. Luke was all for confronting everyone, including the press, but his grandfather had stern words with him and took him off to a quiet place where they could talk some more.

Meanwhile, Olivia and her mother listened for hours, almost without interruption, to Sasha and how she felt about her father's betrayal and the 'totally fucked-up fraud' that was going to leave a lot of people she knew with a deep hatred towards the Bentings.

'It's not like we stole their money,' she cried furiously. 'It's not our fault he did what he did ... '

'We don't know that anyone is blaming us,' her grandmother said gently.

'They're bound to be. I know I would if I was them.'

It was so hard for the children, too hard, but to Olivia's relief no one came from the Met police to interview her further, so at least they didn't have to deal with the horror of their mother being a suspect in the murder of their father.

Whatever Ana's intentions had been on that score clearly hadn't borne fruit. At least not yet.

Richmond had been dead for three days when Andee rang with the news that none of them had expected to hear, ever – Ana Petrov had been arrested at Charles de Gaulle airport. Olivia had been so certain that they'd never see the woman again, that she'd been swallowed into the darkness of the world she'd come from, that hearing she was in police hands made her feel almost elated. It was as though she'd managed to score one small victory.

'Apparently,' Andee said, 'she was travelling under a false passport, and was trying to board a plane for Ankara.'

Ankara?

What did it matter where she was heading? It only mattered that they'd found her.

'Someone's gone over there to bring her back,' Andee continued. 'As far as I'm aware no one was with her, but I expect she'll have a lawyer all lined up by the time she's back on British soil.'

Not doubting that, Olivia said, 'Please tell me they'll keep her in custody.'

'As she's already proven herself to be a flight risk there'll be no chance of bail.'

Wanting to believe that, Olivia said, 'Do you know if she's confessed to anything?' She might be delusional for even asking the question, but if there was anything to know she wanted to hear it.

'From what I hear she's claiming that Richmond was already dead when she returned to the flat.'

Stiffening with shock and incomprehension, Olivia said, 'So why did she run?'

'I'm afraid I don't know what answer she's giving to that, but what I can tell you is that Sean has been returned to London for further questioning.'

OLIVIA. We didn't hear anything from Sean, or about him, over the next few days, but what I did find out was that people who'd once been our friends were no longer. Of course that wasn't surprising, who could blame them, but it hurt nevertheless. They were sure they knew what had happened because other friends, PF staff, newspapers and online postings had told them. They weren't all investors in the marina project or contractors whose businesses had been badly affected, even ruined, but it didn't stop them taking umbrage on other people's behalf.

We weren't allowed to respond, everything was sub judice, but we probably wouldn't have anyway. We were all still in shock, and it wouldn't have helped anyone, least of all us, to try to address the situation. No one ever seemed to consider the fact that we were victims too, both in a financial and familial sense. My parents were likely to lose the dance studio and part of their pension; and it turned out that the Folly had been mortgaged for more than it was worth. So the children were going to lose their home as well as already having lost their father.

I thank God for Andee during that time. She was the strong and rational mind we all needed. She kept us in touch with the investigation and told us when Ana Petrov's application for bail failed.

To me that felt like another small victory.

'I don't know how to feel,' Luke stated angrily one evening, when they were all sitting together. 'I keep thinking of what he did, to you, Mum, and to everyone else, but I still can't seem to make it fit with my dad.'

'That's how I feel too,' Sasha told him.

'It's like I want to cry,' Luke explained, 'because I definitely loved him and I'm going to miss him, but then all the terrible stuff comes up and I just want to kill him.'

'You should try to forget the bad things,' Olivia advised gently, 'because for you it's not about what he did, it's about who he was as a father. And he was a good father; you know that.'

'Except he was going to leave us,' Sasha pointed out with a sob. 'They found his fake passport, the ticket, his clothes, everything ... So how can you say he was good?'

Unable to explain what he'd done, much less what he'd been thinking, Olivia gathered them to her and cried for them in a way she couldn't cry for herself. It was tearing her apart to watch them trying to cope with so many confused and terrible feelings towards the father they'd always loved and trusted, but it was impossible to know how to restore their faith in him.

'*Adem Bekker*,' Ana Petrov had said that day at lunch. '*We're making things work very well ...* ' Bekker was the name on the passport that had been found at the South Ken flat, showing Richmond's photo. How Ana must have enjoyed herself that day, flaunting the truth of her relationship with Richmond in Olivia's face.

Looking up as her mother came into the room, she smiled shakily and rested her head on Sasha's.

Rena said, 'Imogen's coming to the funeral.'

As Olivia's heart turned over she tightened her hold on the children. None of them had seen Imogen since it had happened; she'd gone to London to stay with friends and had sent Olivia an email saying she'd be in touch soon. The shortness of it, the unspoken, but unmistakable hostility that might even have been blame had convinced Olivia not to try and force any more communication. She had enough to be dealing with, and Imogen clearly wanted to handle her grief in her own way.

'So how many will we be?' Olivia asked.

'Us five,' Rena answered, 'Andee and Graeme, and I've just heard from Gina at The Salon that she and Gil would like to come and show support for you and the children.'

Deeply touched by that, Olivia felt a lump form in her throat.

Andee arrived a few minutes later, her expression grave and faintly uncomprehending as she said, 'Sean's just been charged with Richmond's murder.'

Olivia felt her head start to spin as Rena gasped and David protested loudly.

'What about Ana?' Luke demanded. 'Has she been charged too?'

'Yes, she has,' Andee confirmed.

'So they did it together?' Sasha asked, clearly bemused.

Andee's eyes met Olivia's. Neither of them had an answer to that question, much less an understanding of what had happened.

Rena leapt to her feet. 'I don't care what anyone says,' she declared in an almost evangelical tone. 'I cannot and will not make myself believe that Sean had anything to do with it.'

Olivia swallowed hard and squeezed Luke's hand as he said, 'Let's just focus on the funeral now. It's not going to be easy for any of us, we already know that, but as long as we're with people we know we can trust, that's all that matters.'

LUKE. The day of the cremation was cold and mizzly, the kind of weather that seems about right for that sort of occasion. We bumped around the house like ghosts that morning, hardly seeing one another, then stopping to hug or to offer words of reassurance. None of us had gone to see the body. I'm not sure whether that was a right or a wrong decision, it was just that none of us could face it. There was so much we needed to say to him, to ask him, I don't think we could have coped with the impossibility of it.

The funeral car didn't bring the coffin to the house either. A number of our neighbours had lost money as a result of the fraud, so Grandpa decided it would be best for the hearse to go straight to the crematorium.

Mum and Grandma chose the music, going for movie themes that Sasha and I had loved as kids and had sung along with Dad while we were driving, or in the bath, or just because we felt like it. That was hard, I have to admit. I nearly lost it when we got to 'You've Got a Friend in Me' from *Toy Story 2*, but I understand that Mum and Grandma had decided to try and focus us on happy times, and honestly there had been a lot of them. That was what made everything so weird and difficult, it was like he was two people, but we kept reminding ourselves that we weren't there to say goodbye to the man we didn't know, we were there to honour the father we loved.

Sasha and I sat either side of Mum, holding her icy hands and fixing our eyes on the celebrant, who did an amazing job of presenting Dad in the light we needed to see him. She must have been aware of who he was and what he'd done, and of how he'd died, but she didn't refer to any of it. Even though we're not a religious family we closed our eyes as she prayed for him and for us, and I think we all got some comfort from it. Grandpa read a poem by Emily Matthews, but no one gave an eulogy, and no one was aware of exactly when Grandma Imogen arrived at the back of the chapel. We just realised she was there as we got up to leave. Two people were with her, friends from London we presumed, but neither of them came to offer condolences and so we didn't attempt to speak to them either.

Grandma and Grandpa had requested family flowers only, and when we got outside there was the single arrangement that Mum had organised from us five, and another large spray that we guessed was from Grandma Imogen.

Mum and Sasha were talking quietly with Gina and Gil while Grandma and Grandpa thanked the celebrant, when Grandma Imogen suddenly called out in a weirdly shrill voice, 'There are some flowers missing. There should be another bouquet. I organised it myself.' She was staring at Mum, like she was accusing her of stealing the flowers.

Grandma Rena quickly stepped between me and Grandma Imogen and said, in a low voice, 'Those particular flowers weren't welcome, Imogen. When I saw them, I asked for them to be removed.'

'You had no right to do that,' she snapped, sounding like she was about to crack up. 'She asked me to send them. I promised I would ... '

'Then you shouldn't have,' Grandpa cut in fiercely.

Realising who we were talking about, I said, 'Grandma, you couldn't have been thinking straight. If you were you'd have known it wasn't the right thing to do.'

Her eyes went all strange and I could tell she was going to say something none of us wanted to hear, so I quickly held up my hands and said, 'OK, let's stop there. This isn't the right occasion for anyone to fall out.'

Her chalky face turned even whiter as she looked at me. I could see how much she was suffering, but I have to be honest, it was hard to feel sorry for her. 'Your mother …' she said.

Grandpa didn't let her get any further. 'If you love your grandchildren, Imogen, and I know you do, then think about them. They've lost their father, and you've lost your son. That should be bringing you together, not tearing you apart.'

Grandma Imogen looked at me, her face trembling like she couldn't keep her emotions in any longer. 'Ana isn't to blame …'

'I don't want to hear about her,' I cut in savagely. 'You know what she did, what she's been charged with, so I don't understand how you can stand there talking about her …'

'It was Sean Kenyon …'

Mum was suddenly there and so was Andee. 'I'm very sorry for your loss, Imogen,' Mum said with a dignity I know I'd never have found in her shoes. 'You're welcome to join us at the house if you're not rushing off.'

I looked at Grandma and reached for her hand. 'Do it for Dad,' I told her, hoping it was the right thing to say.

'But what about Ana?' she asked me, as if she really believed I cared.

'What about her?' I cried.

Mum's hand gripped my shoulder, cautioning me not to say any more.

'If it weren't for your mother getting pregnant with you,' Grandma Imogen said, 'your father would have married Ana.'

Talk about flooring me. Can you imagine how it feels to have your grandmother say something like that, not only to me, but to my mother? I'm not sure if she even knew how hurtful it was, and even if she did, maybe she didn't care.

My mother held on to me again as Andee said quietly, 'I don't think we're going to resolve anything here today, and the next family are about to come in.'

We went back to the house then and I guess Grandma Imogen's friends took her somewhere, maybe back to London. We knew she'd been staying with Ana's parents at their massive house in Kensington – can you believe the fucked-upness of that – but like Mum said, she'd never understood the dynamics between those two families and she wasn't gong to start trying now.

What was concerning us a lot more that day, and all the following days, was where we were going to live. The fact that Mum had lost most of her money too meant that my sister had to give up the dream of going to college in London – and I had to abandon my place at uni. Sure, I could have got a student loan, but we needed income, not debt, so I realised I'd have to focus on getting a job.

In so many ways it felt as though our lives were disintegrating around us. It was totally mind-blowing, really scary, because without any proper money or somewhere to live what chance did we have of being able to start again?

Chapter Fifteen

Realising there was no point pretending that somehow they'd be able to keep hold of the house, Olivia set about packing the day after the funeral. The children did too, understanding that a lot would have to go, not only because they wouldn't have room for it at Grandma and Grandpa's where they were going to stay for a while, but because much of it had belonged to their father.

Letting go of his possessions brought home like nothing else that he was really gone. As Olivia sorted through them she was assailed by so many emotions and memories that it was impossible to concentrate on her task, as each one brought more questions, grief, anger and the increasing cruelty of knowing that she'd never be able to confront him, to ask him *why*, to hear from his lips how he'd really felt about leaving them. In many ways the inability to reach him made her feel more cheated than ever. She had nowhere to focus her anger, no one to punish for what he'd done to her and her family, no one to reassure her that it wasn't as bad as it seemed. It was, of course, and it was only going to get worse as reality dawned clearer each day, proving in a stark, brutal way that there would never be any going back. This couldn't be repaired, nothing could change what he'd done, and he was never going to explain himself.

It sickened and enraged her to think of his affair, and of how each time he'd gone to London he'd entered into a completely different world. She wondered how much he'd thought about the children while he was with Ana, or doing his deals; how often he'd spoken to them when he was in the company of men who were no more than villains.

It was the planned desertion that was the deepest wound of all. It could eat her up and even destroy her if she thought about it too much. No letters or emails or anything at all from him had come to light saying goodbye, or asking them to understand, as if they ever could, or even saying he might see them again one day. In one of her darker moments she threw out their wedding and honeymoon albums, along with the letters and cards he'd sent her over the years. The photographs of him that didn't include the children were in a box marked for the tip that would go as soon as it was full. It felt like a purge, a shedding of the sham their lives had become. It would take a lot more than that to make her feel free of it when a deeper, less biddable part of her heart was so deeply attached to all that had been good about him, but at least it was a start.

Her parents filled bags with his clothes and took them to a charity shop in a nearby town – it didn't feel right to donate them to the needy of Kesterly – and the police still had his computer so Olivia didn't have to concern herself with that. She rang Imogen to ask if there was anything she might want, but Imogen said she already had everything she required, thank you. Olivia had no idea what her mother-in-law had meant by that, but she didn't try to find out. There was a chance, she knew, that the children were going to lose touch with their grandmother over this, and she didn't feel inclined to try and remedy the situation right now. After all, Imogen had apparently chosen Ana over them, and the worst pain of all for Olivia was knowing that Richmond had done the same.

Would you really have left them, she asked silently. She was in her bedroom staring at a photograph of him with Sasha and Luke, laughing uproariously at something beyond the frame. He looked so happy there, relaxed and thrilled to be a dad. This was the Richmond she'd loved, the man she felt she'd known, the father the children had adored. Surely that man was real? She knew he was, but so too was the man who'd brought all this chaos and uncertainty into their lives.

Feeling the breaks in her heart deepening and tearing, she ripped the photograph into pieces and reached for her mobile as it rang. Seeing it was Andee, she clicked on right away.

'Hi, are you OK?' Andee asked gently.

Olivia said wryly, 'Trying to be. Any news about Sean?'

'I'm waiting to hear back from one of the directors at his firm, but apparently his lawyers are saying he should be released later today.'

Experiencing a rush of relief that told her just how concerned she'd been about Sean subconsciously, Olivia glanced at her phone as someone else tried to get through. 'It's Anthea Ellis,' she told Andee. 'I'll call you back,' and going through to the detective she said, 'Please let this be good news. I feel due.'

With the sound of a rueful smile in her voice, Ellis said, 'We've just heard from one of our colleagues in London so I thought I should contact you right away. Apparently a bag of blood-stained clothes was found in a skip near St Pancras a couple of days ago. It turns out they belong to Ana, and the blood is Richmond's.'

The blood is Richmond's.

Sinking down on the bed, Olivia tried to think of something to say, but she had no words. There was only the horror of what had happened, and the relief

– was it really relief? – of finally knowing for certain that Ana was guilty.

'Why?' she asked in a whisper. 'Why did she do it when she was about to get him all to herself?'

Ellis had no answer for that, so she rang off, and forgetting to call Andee back, Olivia zipped up the suitcase she'd just filled and began picking her way through boxes and bedding to get to the stairs. The descent wasn't easy, for Sasha and Luke had littered the way with their belongings and the hall was filled with packing cases, as were most of the downstairs rooms apart from the kitchen, which they'd decided to leave until last.

Spotting her mother putting the kettle on, she went to lay her head on her shoulder and swallowed hard as Rena's arms went around her.

'You know I wouldn't be able to get through this without you and Dad,' Olivia whispered. 'None of us would, but I promise we won't fill your house up for too long. As soon as I know what funds are available to me, if any, I'll try to find somewhere for us to rent.'

'You can stay with us for as long as you like,' her mother reassured her. 'We'll love having you.'

Olivia gazed into her mother's beautiful sad eyes. This experience was ageing her, and the loss of her dance studio was probably feeling like the loss of a child. It had been locked up before the funeral, and all future classes cancelled. By now, Olivia suspected, a for sale sign was attached to the wall outside.

As Rena put a hand to Olivia's face neither of them mentioned the fact that her parents' house might soon have to go on the market too. There was no point. Saying it wouldn't change it, so they just had to keep reminding themselves that at least they had one another, and they'd get through it all somehow.

'Hi, I'm sorry, I forgot to ring you back.'

'Don't worry,' Andee responded. 'I've just spoken to Gould, so I know what Anthea Ellis was calling you about. Are you OK?'

With something like a smile, Olivia said, 'Please add that to the list of questions I don't know the answer to, but at least I'm still standing.'

'Have you told the children yet?'

'No, but of course I will. There's so much to process, we hardly get through one thing before there's something else to deal with.'

'I know, but now they have the results from those clothes at least some of the pressure should start to lift.'

'I hope so. Have they let Sean go now?'

'I wish I could say yes, but I'm afraid not.'

'What? I don't understand.'

'According to the lawyer, he's admitted that while he was in the flat that afternoon, he thumped Richmond, more than once.'

Olivia froze. *Sean had hit Richmond – on the day Richmond had been murdered.* She remembered being told that he'd been beaten and stabbed to death.

Andee was saying, 'This led the investigators to suspect Sean of being complicit in the murder. Apparently there were traces of blood on his clothes too, which would have happened when he hit him.'

'But why did he hit him?' Olivia wanted to know.

'The lawyer didn't tell me that, but I'm guessing he felt the need to teach Richmond some sort of lesson for what he'd done to you and your family.'

Olivia could feel herself turning hot with shame. That this was happening at all was appalling enough, that Sean had got caught up in it, that he'd felt the need to punish Richmond on their behalf, that he even *knew* what kind of a man Richmond really was ... It was so mortifying, so beyond anywhere she'd imagined herself to be at this stage of her life, in the post-cancer period she was trying to deal with, that she couldn't even grasp how low this was bringing her.

'What can I do?' she asked Andee. 'There must be something I can say to get him released.'

Andee said, 'Don't do anything yet. I had a call just now that I think might make the difference without you having to become involved.'

ELISE. I wasn't in the country when Sean was arrested, so I had no idea it had happened until a journalist friend called to ask if I knew what was going on. I managed to put her off, then got in touch with Andee Lawrence to find out if she could throw some light on things.

She gave me the number of a DC Morrison who was a part of the murder investigation team based in Kensington. He listened to what I had to say, then asked if I'd be prepared to fly to London to give a full statement. So that's what I did. It didn't take me long to find out, once I got there, that Sean had told the detectives about me, so naturally I asked why they hadn't contacted me and I was told that they'd tried, but hadn't been successful.

I'm not difficult to get hold of, so you must draw your own conclusions from that. Mine were that the need to wrap a case up fast might have been greater than the need to complicate the conclusions they'd already reached.

I was with Sean the day he went to the flat in South Kensington. He was taking me to Heathrow so I could catch a flight to Geneva, and he said he wanted to stop off on the way. I didn't know who lived in the building he went into in South Kensington until later, but obviously

I was asked what time he went in and how long he'd stayed. I was also asked if there was any blood on his clothes when he came out – there was none that I could see – and then they wanted to know why I'd left London in such a hurry afterwards.

I can tell you, it wasn't a particularly edifying experience, but I was willing to go through it because I was in absolutely no doubt at all that Sean had had nothing to do with the murder. It was absurd to me that he was even being accused of it. However, it seemed Ana Petrov kept insisting that Richmond was already dead when she went into the flat, and that she'd passed Sean on his way out. That much was true, she had passed him, because I saw it happen. I even asked Sean when he got into the car if it was her and he confirmed that it was. However, I don't think I was completely believed until Ana's blood-stained clothes were discovered in a skip near St Pancras. This is presumably where she boarded the Eurostar for Paris, and no doubt she'd expected to be many thousands of miles away by the time the incriminating evidence was found.

No, I didn't stay in London after I'd given my evidence to see Sean when they finally released him. Of course I was tempted, I still had feelings for him, but I already knew our relationship would never work, different hemispheres simply don't allow it for long. And he's far too close to his family in Oz to consider relocating back to Europe.

Olivia sat back from her laptop, needing to put a distance for a moment between herself and the email she'd just read. It was from the lawyer who was acting for Penn Financial in the matter of the fraud investigation. When she'd first realised this, in one wildly optimistic moment she wondered if he was going to tell her it had all been a terrible mistake that he'd now managed to clear up; or maybe there was some money somewhere that would help to ease the pressure that was increasing by the day.

It turned out to be neither of those things.

Dear Mrs Benting,

Please accept my deepest condolences on the death of your husband.

I would have been in touch before now, but I have only today received clearance from the police to share with you the statement Richmond made to me on the day the tragic events took place.

I have no reason to believe that he spoke anything but the truth.

I am attaching a copy of the statement to this email. When you have read it please feel free to call me at my office, or on my personal mobile, both numbers below, if there is anything you would like to discuss.

Sincerely yours,

Crispin Blake

Olivia swallowed hard as she stared at the screen. Blake's message had given no clue as to what she should expect from the statement, but her imagination was doing a fine job all on its own. Realising that the only way to stop the dread, to shut down the fear of more treachery, more loss even, was to open the attachment and then deal with whatever it contained, she clicked on the link.

She watched a Word document fill the screen, and only then did she fully realise that she was connecting to Richmond. The shock of it, the surreal immediacy, made her want to draw back, or to try speaking to him, but stronger, far stronger was the need to know what some of his final words had been.

She read the two pages quickly, too quickly, her heart pounding in her ears, in her throat, in her chest, as her breath shortened and hot, bitter tears stung her eyes. By the time she reached the end she was shaking, but she knew she needed to read it again, more carefully, to make sure that she'd understood everything he'd said and what it meant.

Someone knocked on the door, and seeing it was Andee she beckoned her to come in.

'Sean's been released,' Andee told her.

Olivia nodded, unsurprised but no less relieved. It was something she'd think about later, when she could make her mind function beyond this new turn in the drama that had become her life.

Positioning the laptop so Andee could read the statement with her, she returned to the top where all the legal wording was necessarily in place. It was below this that the statement began, dry, unemotional, and in places it didn't even seem like Richmond speaking, but there was no doubt in her mind that it was.

He came right to the point, no preamble, no explanation or excuse, just the facts as he saw them, intended for other eyes, not hers.

I started an affair with Ana Petrov in the summer of 2014. It continued for a period of ten or eleven months, at which point it was made clear to me that if I didn't purchase a property for us to continue our relationship my wife would be informed of my infidelity. This was the first instance of blackmail and I complied. The second instance came after Ana Petrov introduced me to a group of businessmen who were looking for an investment opportunity in the UK. It soon became evident that it would be in my own and my family's best interests if I made this investment possible. As I realised what kind of people they were I saw no alternative but to comply with their plans. I tried to persuade them that the marina expansion project, as they presented it, was unviable, but I soon realised that my only role was to make sure it happened. They provided funds to help facilitate the planning permission, but it is not the purpose of this statement to name those who accepted the bribes.

The bank that backed the project was selected by these businessmen; neither I, nor my financial director, Cooper Jarrett, were invited to explore potential investment elsewhere. When the bank pulled out we were given no explanation, we were only told that it would not be in our interests to pursue matters through the courts. This was when I began to use funds from Penn Financial and its clients to try and keep the build going. I admit that what I did was illegal.

I have had no contact with the businessmen since their withdrawal, but I have had contact with Ana Petrov. When the fraud investigation began she sought to organise a way out of it for me that would involve a new identity and a new life with her in Malaysia. My fear of prison persuaded me to go along with these plans in so far as I never tried to stop them, or her.

I am now at the point where it is expected of me to leave my family and my country. It is not my intention to do so. I fully understand that to stay will result in prosecution for my complicity in a scheme to launder money and for the fraudulent activities perpetrated on Penn Financial.

I am prepared to accept the consequences of this statement, which I have instructed my lawyer to deliver to the lead investigators in the case.

As Olivia's eyes travelled over his signature, almost seeing his hand inscribing it and even feeling some of the terrible emotions that must surely have been in his heart that day, she was aware of Andee's comforting hand on her shoulder.

'So,' she said shakily, 'now we know why she killed him.'

Andee nodded. 'He must have gone to the flat to tell her about the statement,' she said quietly. 'And she ... Well, we know what she did.'

Olivia was still staring at the screen, trying to imagine how he'd felt when he'd given the statement. 'There was nothing for me,' she murmured. 'No note, no explanation.'

'Because,' Andee said gently, 'he thought he would see you.'

Realising that was probably true, Olivia felt her breath catch in her throat. He hadn't known Ana was going to do what she did, hadn't prepared for it, presumably hadn't even considered it. But he should have. Of all people, he had known that she was capable of almost unimaginable iniquity.

Finally connecting with what really mattered about the statement, what mattered more than anything, she whispered, 'The children meant more. He wasn't going to leave them.' She said it again, and again, and as relief began to unravel all the painful torment inside her she found herself sobbing so hard in Andee's arms that she could barely catch her breath.

Chapter Sixteen

LUKE. It really meant something to find out that we'd mattered enough to Dad in the end for him to do the right thing and stay to face the music. Definitely that worked for us – for me, anyway. It restored some of his integrity, and allowed me to think of him in a way that didn't keep filling me up with this crazy rage that made me want to yell at him, even hit him if only I could. That's the trouble with someone dying, you can't get to them for the things they did wrong and let them know what you think, how much it's affected you. The frustration totally does your head in.

When we heard about his statement it calmed me down a bit. Of course I was never going to feel good about the things he'd done, and definitely not about the way he'd cheated on Mum. It was his affair with a psycho that had led to everything, so maybe that's a lesson to me for the future.

Sasha went on having a hard time with it all, but at least she agreed to some counselling, which we hoped would get her through it. Don't get me wrong, I didn't brush any of it under the carpet, I just didn't feel the need to talk about it. What was there to say? Have you got any idea what it feels like to be the person whose Dad bilked innocent people out of what was rightfully theirs? It totally sucks, let me tell you. Who's that going to help? No one, that's who.

Moving out of the Folly and over to Grandma and Grandpa's kind of wasted me for a while. I totally loved that house. We all did. It was our home, you know. All our memories were there, it felt like a part of us, but then I kept reminding myself that our memories were a bit like a stage where a great performance was happening for everyone to see while all sorts of bad stuff was going on behind the scenes.

'Are you scared, Luke?' Sasha asked me the night before we left the house.

I told her I wasn't, but I was. I didn't know what of, exactly, it was just there, in me, and I honestly couldn't see that it would ever go away.

Finding DI Gould in his office, Andee tapped on the open door and went in.

Looking up from his computer, he nodded a greeting and gestured for her to sit down. 'Thanks for coming,' he said, going to close the door. 'There's something I want to run past you before I do anything about it.'

Intrigued, Andee watched as he reached beneath his desk to produce the snakeskin briefcase that had been found at the Folly.

'I received it from the Met police this morning,' he explained. 'Now that Ana Petrov has changed her plea to guilty ... '

'She has?' Andee said, surprised.

Gould nodded. 'I got a call last night.'

Stunned that the woman had given up the fight, Andee said, 'What about her family?'

Gould shrugged. 'What about them? They might be involved in a whole lot of other shit, but Benting's murder is all hers.'

'I thought they'd have lawyers all over it.'

'They did, but for reasons known only to them, they've decided to back away.'

'Because of what a trial might bring to light,' Andee stated. 'Of course. We should have seen it coming. Have you seen her statement about what happened?'

'No, but we know Benting changed his mind about taking off with her, so it's pretty certain that's why she turned on him.'

Andee agreed, and her eyes went to the briefcase as Gould said, 'It's this that I want to talk to you about. I think we can agree that its discovery at the Benting house was intended to cast suspicion on Olivia Benting after her husband absconded.'

Andee nodded slowly, going through in her mind what was most likely to have been in Ana Petrov's. Her expensive briefcase in Olivia's possession, Olivia's personal items inside, a knife gone from Olivia's kitchen and two missing people known to be having an affair ... 'So it wasn't enough to take her husband,' she said quietly, 'she had to mess with her reputation and freedom too.' Her eyes went to Gould. 'I hope you're asking me what you should do with it all.'

'I am,' Gould replied.

'Trash it. There's absolutely no good reason in the world why Olivia should ever see that briefcase again, and she can live without the other things.'

'I guessed that would be your reaction, but I wanted to be sure. Leave it with me. It'll be pulped by the end of the day.'

OLIVIA. Naturally it was a relief to us all when we heard that Ana Petrov had changed her plea to guilty. The last thing any of us needed was to go through a trial after everything else we'd endured. Apparently she'd confessed to the murder, but that was as far as she'd gone. She'd said nothing about dragging Richmond into a dead-end deal with her father, or about any involvement she might have had in the fraud at Penn Financial. As far as I knew the police – the SFO and NCA – continued their investigations, but no one came to interview us. We learned from the lawyer, Crispin Blake, that Cooper Jarrett had admitted to his part in the fraud, and the courts might have gone easier on him had he been able to return at least some of the funds, but he hadn't. He was sentenced to five years in prison, and was also prohibited from operating as an accountant, or in any other capacity in the financial sector, for life.

I tried very hard not to think about Ana Petrov as she, and the rest of us, waited to hear what her sentence would be. I wanted to pretend that she was dead too, that she'd never even existed, but it was as though she had some nefarious energy about her that fizzed and slithered around the edges of my mind. She was always there, just out of sight, a darkness, a ghost, that wouldn't go away.

She wrote to let me know that she'd added me to her visitors' list. *I'm sure you'd like to talk about Richmond,* she said in her letter, *I can tell you everything you need to know.*

I admit I was tempted; in fact I came very close to going, but in the end I was persuaded not to.

'She'll lie and mess with your head,' Andee warned me. 'You won't be able to trust a single thing she says, so don't give her the satisfaction.'

Andee's advice was good. I knew this for certain when Ana wrote to me again and ranted on hysterically about winners and losers and how much Richmond had despised me. I tore the letter up, and did the same with each one that followed. As I did so I could almost feel her frustration, her helpless rage as she realised that she could no longer get to me. It was a small victory, but one that mattered.

Finally she received the mandatory life sentence we were all expecting but were afraid wouldn't happen, and soon after she was moved from Holloway prison in London to Drake Hall in Staffordshire. It's my hope that we will never hear from her again.

Chapter Seventeen

Over the following weeks life went from bad to worse as Olivia learned just how desperate her financial situation really was, while those also affected by the fraud at Penn Financial were made aware of the full scale of their losses too. At times it felt as though the entire town had been victims, which wasn't the case, of course, but whenever Olivia went out she only seemed to bump into those who, having been cheated of the person who'd wronged them, were holding her and her family responsible in his place.

Sean was in touch before flying back to Sydney, but he only spoke to David so Olivia didn't get the chance to apologise for the way he'd got caught up in events that he should never have been dragged into anyway. As she imagined how glad his children would be to have him back, she found herself wishing she could see them together. She came close to emailing a few times, but then she reminded herself that he'd probably be happy to forget about her and her family for a while.

More often she thought about Richmond, and how much she missed him in spite of it all. As time passed she was coming to see him more as a prideful fool than a villain, someone who'd done what he had to try to save his marriage and his family. She knew she wasn't necessarily wrong about that, but no one had forced him into the affair with Ana, and no one had prevented him from telling her the truth while he'd had the chance. Her feelings were so mixed about him that it was almost impossible to grieve without being overcome by a desperate and inescapable sense of betrayal and frustration.

It was about a week after Ana's move to Drake Hall that Sean made an unexpected return to England, and now here he was, all six foot two of him, as carelessly handsome and confident as ever, and as unwilling to listen to apologies as he was to elaborate on his time in police custody.

'Hey, it's over,' he replied dismissively when Rena asked about it. 'It was just a misunderstanding that could have happened to anyone.'

Olivia raised an eyebrow.

'OK, I admit,' he said, 'it should have been sorted out much quicker than it was, but like I said, it's over.' And he abruptly changed the subject to the reason why he'd come.

As Olivia registered what he was saying, his words apparently making perfect and profound sense to him, she could feel herself becoming more and more resistant. In the end she didn't allow him to finish before she said, 'You don't have to do this. I think our family has already presumed too much on your time and friendship ... '

Cutting her off, Sean asked David and Rena, 'For the record, do *you* have any objections?'

'For the record,' Rena declared, 'I'm not sure we've kept up with everything you're proposing.'

Knowing that her mother had understood the proposal perfectly, Olivia slanted her a look before returning her attention to Sean, ready to carry on her protest.

'The way I see it,' he said, before she could steal his thunder again, 'is the build site can either stay as it is for the next decade or more, a real eyesore on your landscape, a mecca for druggies and gangs, not to mention a constant reminder to those who lost money by investing in it. Or my company can take it over and turn it into a marina expansion that's more realistic and more affordable and will end up bene-fiting the local community as well as us as a group, and the financiers we bring on board.'

'But I thought your company had already turned it down,' David said.

'It's true, we weren't going to touch it in its current form, no one would, but you know how nature hates a vacuum ... We're in a position to fill it, provided we can have full control. That's what I went to tell Richmond the day he … Well, as we know I didn't make a good job of it, my temper got the better of me, so I never actually got round to explaining the real reason I was there. Anyway, our London-based construction team has been working with a firm of architects who have experience in this sort of project, and together they've come up with designs for an expansion on a much smaller scale. Ten moorings reduced from fifty, a low-rise apartment complex for thirty dwellings, an eight-room boutique hotel, a four-level multi-storey car park and half a dozen retail outlets.' His eyes returned to Olivia. 'It isn't a favour,' he told her gently. 'It's a business venture that could work for everyone, provided the local authority is willing to green-light it. We have no reason to think they wouldn't.'

'I imagine they'll snatch your hand off,' David commented.

Meeting his eyes, Sean said, 'As far as Penn Financial goes … '

'We're looking into ways of wrapping it up,' David admitted.

Sean nodded. 'I'll put you in touch with some firms who might be interested in absorbing it into their existing business once all the investigations are over, and we have a full picture of what's left.

They'll obviously want to put their own guys in to run it, and I imagine the name will go.'

David thanked him, his expression showing that he accepted this was the only way forward for his company and remaining clients now.

For the second time since arriving Sean glanced at his watch. 'I'm sorry, but I don't have a lot of time,' he said. 'I wanted to make you aware of the way we're looking at things before they start moving ahead. I'll have someone send you a copy of the plans, if you're interested. Now, I'm afraid I have a plane to catch.'

Olivia watched him embrace her parents, and smiled as he called out 'See you, guys,' to Luke and Sasha, who he'd clearly realised were listening outside. No doubt she'd find out soon enough what they thought of him and his idea for the marina. Meanwhile she followed him to the door and linked his arm as they walked out to his car.

'Are you going back to Sydney?' she asked softly.

'No, I have to be in Dubai for a few days, then it's London for a while as we get the ball rolling on this, and a couple of other projects we have in the pipeline.'

'So how hands-on are you with it all?' she wondered.

'Not very, to be honest, but I like to know what's going on, and I'm told it's good for morale to have me around.' He grinned roguishly, and she couldn't help but laugh.

'Listen,' she said, turning to him as they reached the car, 'I understand this isn't a favour, but if you didn't know us, if my father hadn't ... '

Putting a finger over her lips, he said, 'I promise, I wouldn't have been able to talk the board into anything if it wasn't good business.'

'But you did talk them into it?'

He grimaced. 'Let's just say I presented a way of looking at things that I thought might appeal to them.'

Rolling her eyes, she said, 'Will you be back in Kesterly when things get under way, presuming they do?'

'I won't be here for that,' he replied, 'there are others whose job it is to structure and manage the projects, but there are a couple more things I'd like to discuss with you. The first being your home. I can help you to buy it back ... '

'No, no,' she interrupted quickly. 'It's kind of you, it really is, but I ... I couldn't let you. It would feel wrong for many more reasons than it would ever feel right.'

'Mm, I guess I can understand that,' he admitted, 'but you're going to need somewhere to live.'

'We're OK here for now. It's helping us to cope, feeling one another close.'

'Sure.' He gazed into her eyes and, on the verge of being caught up in the magnetism of him, she made herself turn away.

'Your family must miss you when you're gone for so long,' she commented as he got into the car.

His eyes twinkled. 'Miss me? They don't go in for that sort of thing. They just FaceTime and text through the night like I was still in their time zone.'

Enjoying his charade of the put-upon dad, she said, 'They're lucky to have you.' Even as she spoke she realised it sounded like a criticism of Richmond, but there was no way to take it back.

'And yours are lucky to have you,' he told her, moving past the moment. 'We'll talk about them some more when I'm back. You take care of yourself now, and if you're worried about anything you know how to get hold of me.'

As he drove away, leaving her feeling oddly dejected, as if a light inside her had dimmed, she was aware of Luke coming up beside her.

'So you guys were an item once,' he commented, slipping an arm through hers.

'A very long time ago.'

'He seems cool. I like his ideas about the marina, don't you? I think Dad would have gone for them if he was still here.'

Olivia's smile was flat. 'Yes, he probably would have,' she agreed, thinking of how little say in it

Richmond would have had from a prison cell. Since there was nothing to be gained from pointing that out, she put it out of her mind and started back to the house.

Luke said, 'Grandma calls Sean an unstoppable force.'

With a laugh, Olivia said, 'He's certainly that.'

More quietly, he added, 'I get the impression it means a lot to them that he's across this. They seemed to be, I don't know, kind of stronger when he was here.'

Though she hadn't noticed it herself, Olivia didn't doubt it was true. She was aware of how much her parents had seemed to age over the past weeks. They weren't as resilient as they used to be, and she knew that their worries weren't even close to being over, for her father had recently learned that he had no pension at all to call on now. All they had was the eventual proceeds of the dance studio, which was proving hard to sell, and this house, which they would feel unable to put on the market while their daughter and grandchildren were living there.

Going to her father as she returned to the sitting room, she wrapped her arms around him and held him tight. 'You were right to call on Sean for help,' she told him, knowing he needed to hear it. 'I'm glad you felt you could trust him.'

'Oh, I think we can,' he replied warmly. 'And now we have to let him lead the way until we have a clearer idea of where we're going.'

'Of course,' she murmured, knowing that was something else he needed to hear. Without his company and clients, his friends and future, he was rudderless and frightened, so it was no wonder he was ready to cling to any lifeline Sean could throw him. There were plenty of others in town who would be ready to accept similar help, when the alternative was to leave in place a perpetual reminder of a scandal, a theft of their trust and investments, that had had such a negative impact on their lives.

For her part it wasn't that her loyalties lay with Richmond, for they really didn't; it was simply that the last thing she needed was to start depending on Sean when it was so important for her to find her own feet. It was the only way she could face the future with any hope of restoring her dignity, while protecting herself from ever being hurt, or betrayed, again.

Chapter Eighteen

In spite of her resolve to get back on her feet unaided, Olivia couldn't help feeling relieved when she heard a couple of weeks later that Sean was back in Kesterly. She hadn't realised until then just how anxious she'd been that he, or more likely, his board, would reconsider their decision on the new marina project and pull out. Such a loss of confidence could prove one blow too many for some in town; it certainly would for her and her parents.

She needn't have worried; apparently Sean hadn't come alone, and from the day of his arrival the abandoned site had turned into a hive of activity as Portakabin offices were transported in, meetings sprang up in every available space, and the main contractors prepared to move back.

The only curious, and worrying, part of his return, for Olivia, was that he didn't seem in any hurry to see her. Of course he was busy, she realised that, and understood perfectly that he had other priorities. Nevertheless, he'd invited her parents to his flat a couple of times to discuss the plans for the project and to meet the team from the Kenyon Group that was overseeing it. He'd even taken them to lunch on one occasion, but no one had called her to see if she'd like to join them.

'He said to tell you that he'll be in touch soon,' her mother had assured her on returning, still flushed from a glass of wine too many. 'Honestly, there are so many comings and goings over there it makes your head spin.'

As she waited for a call – though she wouldn't admit to herself that she was waiting – Olivia kept busy with the soul-numbing task of going through the rest of Richmond's paperwork. She was still in regular contact with the police and lawyers, and it needed all her attention to make sure she was getting things right. However, knowing that Sean was just across town trying to sort out the mess Richmond had created there wasn't helping her concentration at all. It wasn't so much that she wanted to see *him*, although she did, it was more that she was starting to feel excluded.

Going to answer the door as the bell rang, she saw with pleasure that it was Andee and stood back for her to come in. 'How did it go?' she asked, leading the way into the kitchen.

'OK,' Andee replied, and taking a medium-sized buff envelope from her bag she put it on the table. 'I think you'll be pleased.'

As she picked it up Olivia could feel an all-too familiar heaviness weighing her down. Earlier that morning Graeme had organised the auction of several items of the furniture and artwork he'd stored for her in his warehouse on the edge of town. This was the only way she was able to raise funds at the moment, and saying goodbye to the pieces she'd collected and cherished over the years was proving even harder than she'd feared. It was why Andee and Graeme had advised her not to come to the auctions when they happened.

'I think most of it went to good homes,' Andee said softly.

Olivia nodded and attempted a smile of gratitude.

Regarding her more closely, Andee said, 'Is there something else?'

'No, I'm fine,' Olivia assured her, and turning to put the kettle on she made herself sound chatty as she said, 'Have you seen Sean since he got here?'

'Yes, we had dinner with him and a couple of his colleagues last night,' Andee replied, sinking into a chair. 'It seems everything's going ahead at full speed. The upbeat mood around town is infecting everyone, whether they're involved in the new project or not. It's just what everyone needs, to feel a sense of optimism again, knowing that jobs and apprenticeships are back on the table.' She didn't mention anything about investment opportunities, and Olivia was grateful to her for it. 'Of course,' Andee was saying, 'they want to know who's behind it all, but as far as I can tell Sean's keeping a very low personal profile.'

Thinking that wasn't much like him, and yet maybe it was, Olivia swallowed hard on the dispiriting emotions inside her. She knew she wasn't dealing with things the way she should, that she was in danger of sinking into a horrible glut of despair, but she couldn't think how to climb out of it.

'What is it?' Andee prompted gently. 'I can tell there's something, and I don't think it's just the fall-out from everything.'

Sighing, Olivia brought her head up and decided to come clean. 'I seem to be the only one who hasn't seen Sean since he got here,' she said, feeling foolish even as she uttered the words.

Appearing perplexed and surprised by that, Andee asked, 'Have you tried calling him?'

'No, I haven't,' Olivia admitted, feeling even more foolish now, 'but I think I will.'

In the end, after leaving a message on his mobile and receiving a text saying *Will be great to see you, come over any time*, Olivia got into her car to drive to the marina. This would be the furthest she'd ventured from her parents' house in recent weeks, and aware of the rumours that had started up in the last week or two, it was an uneasy journey. Apparently, she'd sold the Folly for over two million, and was only staying with her parents until they'd sold their house and the studio. After that, the whole family was planning to escape to some island paradise so they were going to be all right, thank you very much. No losses for them.

Two million. What she wouldn't give for even a small fraction of that – at least then she might be able to scrape together a deposit for a rented flat somewhere on the edge of town, leaving her parents free to do what they needed to with their house. Actually, she felt quite strongly that she wouldn't mind starting afresh somewhere else, somewhere she wasn't known or surrounded by misunderstandings and memories. Once the children were properly sorted she might broach the subject with her parents. Perhaps they could pool their resources once the debts were settled and move further inland, where property prices were more affordable. Or they could go to another part of the country altogether.

Now, as she drove across town, she kept her eyes fixed on the road ahead, thinking with sadness of the times she'd hardly been able to go a hundred yards without waving to someone, or even pulling over for a quick chat. Certain that wasn't going to happen today she stayed focused on her destination, only allowing herself to be sidetracked for a moment as she passed the turning that led up through town to the Infirmary. Her next check-up at the breast clinic wasn't for several weeks, and with a horrible sinking feeling she couldn't help wondering how and even where she might be by then.

Was she really thinking that having cancer was easier than this?

Pulling up at the marina's security barrier, she felt her insides twisting as she spoke to a guard through an entryphone. Sean suddenly seemed so remote and inaccessible surrounded by this luxury and power, the head of a company so large and success-ful that it made her own world seem almost trivial by comparison.

'You're in luck,' the guard told her, 'he's in the apartment. Furthest block on the right, you'll see a visitor's space outside, feel free to use it.'

As she followed the directions she drove slowly, carefully, not wanting to collide with the workers in hard hats and business suits who were spilling off the pavements as they made their way to and from the site at the far end of the complex.

There was another security check before she was allowed through the door of the palm-fronted lime-stone building she'd been directed to, which seemed to take so long that for one bewildering moment she thought Sean was telling them to send her away. Her mouth turned dry as she tried to think of what she'd do or say if he did, but then a buzzer sounded, releasing the lock, and a friendly concierge was already summoning the lift.

Determined to assert some confidence before she faced him, she rode to the penthouse suites on the fifth floor and found herself in a deep green and ochre marble hallway with hidden spotlights in wall niches over feature water fountains. She'd been told to follow the sign for No. 1, and did so.

To her surprise she found the front door open, so half stepping inside she called out to let him know she was there.

No reply.

Venturing along a dark hallway lined with colourful pastels of seascapes and sunsets, she passed the closed doors either side of her and headed for the one at the end. Since it was partially open there was a triangle of sunlight to guide her, and as she stepped through it she almost gasped at the sheer beauty of the room she found herself in. Though it was large, with vast picture windows looking out on the marina and sun-dazzled swathe of estuary beyond, it felt far more welcoming, relaxing even, than she'd have expected in such a modern development. The three outsized sofas were in soft shades of caramel with ivory-coloured accents, their cushions luxuriously deep and inviting. There was an enormous bamboo coffee table in front of them with bowls of colourful stones at each end, and a shelf beneath full of papers and brochures. The rest of the glass surface was littered with used coffee cups, two empty cafetières, the remains of a large carrot cake, empty wrappers that must have contained an assortment of petits fours, and half a dozen or so crumb-covered plates.

She turned around and was drawn to the kitchen's dark-panelled walls and large frosted-glass cabinets. The appliances blended so well they were almost invisible, and the bar that separated the space from the sitting room was lit from above by fittings she couldn't even see.

'Ah, you're here,' Sean declared, coming into the room from a door opposite to the one she'd entered through.

She spun round and felt her heart contract so tightly that it stole her breath. His hair was still wet from the shower and mussed after a vigorous towel rub, and for a moment she was reminded of the young sailing instructor she'd fallen for all those years ago. The rest of him, dressed in a white linen shirt and navy chinos, was a different sort of look, casual but sophisticated, yet somehow still Sean.

'Sorry, I'm going from one meeting to the next here,' he said, 'and I felt it was time to freshen up before the day went any further. And please excuse the mess,' he added, indicating the coffee table. 'The caterers should be here soon to clear it away.' He glanced at his watch. 'I guess they'll start setting up for the next meeting before they leave, but we've got a few minutes before they arrive, and I can't tell you how good it is to see you.'

The pleasure that came into his eyes just about melted her, and she felt herself relaxing and finally able to smile. 'I thought you might be avoiding me,' she said, making the truth sound like a tease.

He grimaced, showing her that her suspicion might be justified. 'It's been crazy here,' he explained. 'Wall-to-wall meetings with more people than I ever knew even existed in Kesterly – though a lot are from London and various government departments. I can make coffee or tea, if you'd like some.'

She shook her head, and wandered to one of the sofas where she sat down, trying not to be over-whelmed by the realisation of just how successful, even powerful he was these days. She hadn't really taken enough time to consider it before, but now, confronted with it, even in this small way, she couldn't help being impressed, even slightly overawed.

Taking the other end of the same sofa, he turned towards her and made himself comfortable as he said, 'So how have things been?'

Just like him, straight to the point, and making it about her, not about him. But she wasn't ready to go there yet. 'Andee tells me there's a lot of excitement in town about your takeover of the project.'

He nodded slowly and took out his mobile as it rang. 'I'll get back to you,' he told the caller, and connecting to someone else, he said, 'Ryan, can you hold anyone who comes in until I'm ready to let them up?' After switching the phone off, he put it on the table and turned back to her. 'We need to talk,' he said, brushing past her comment about the town's excitement, 'so let's make it now before everything kicks off again.'

Feeling oddly unsettled by that, she made herself smile as she said, 'Talk? What about?'

He fixed her with his deep blue eyes and gave the impression he was deciding where to begin, although she suspected he knew exactly what he wanted to say. 'It's not my intention to take over your life,' he told her bluntly, 'but there are things I can do to try and make the foreseeable future easier than it's looking right now.'

As she tensed, ready to protest, he said, 'It's not a weakness to accept help when it's offered.'

'I realise that,' she countered, 'but it's not your responsibility ... '

'Why don't you let me decide what's my responsibility and what isn't?'

'But if it concerns me ... '

'It does, but more importantly it concerns your children. Luke had to abandon his gap year when all this blew up, so I think he should continue, if it's what he wants. If it isn't, we can rethink. Maybe he'll want to go straight to uni. Sasha's already at college here in Kesterly, I know, but if she still wants to study at the college in London we can make it happen. From what your parents tell me, I think both the kids will grab the opportunity to be anywhere but Kesterly for a while. However, if you tell me differently ... '

Realising he was giving her a moment to protest again she summoned breath to take it, then realised she couldn't when what he was offering the children wasn't only a way out, it was the way forward they both wanted.

Apparently reading her silence as acceptance, he moved on. 'I'll be talking to your parents again before I leave to carry on figuring things out with them – but now I'm talking to you. The rent on this apartment has been paid for the next twelve months; I want you to feel free to make it your home. There are three bedrooms, one each for you and the kids, although I don't anticipate them being here much. I know you have a job with Andee ... '

'Hang on, hang on,' she cried, putting up her hands to stop him, 'you're behaving as though the decisions have already been made ... '

'For my part they have,' he told her. 'The rest is up to you.'

She looked at him steadily, not wanting to take his charity, although she knew he didn't see it in that light. She did, however, and though she might not be able to afford her pride, it was all she had left.

'Think it over,' he said, breaking the stand-off.

'I don't need to,' she responded. 'I can't accept, but thank you ... '

As though she hadn't spoken, he went on, 'Andee's going to get the interior design contract for the new hotel. As you're working with her, you'll have an income to help pay the utilities and other upkeep on this flat.'

At that her eyes closed and she gave in to an exasperated smile. Clearly he'd read her mind and had addressed the issue before she could even raise it. 'Wouldn't it make more sense for one of your directors to use the place?' she asked.

'They're already sorted,' he assured her. 'Like I said, the rent's paid, no one else needs it, so if you don't take it up it's just going to sit empty for the next year.'

'Where are you going to be?'

'I'm leaving for Sydney on Monday night, and I don't see myself being back here any time in the foreseeable future.'

Aware of the heat suddenly burning her cheeks, as her heart tried to cope with this new feeling of loss, she said, 'Of course. It's where your real responsibilities lie.'

He didn't deny it. 'There's one last thing I want to run past you before you go,' he said. 'I don't know how much attention you've been giving to the media, or the gossip and rumours around town, I hope not a lot. But the inaccuracies are out there and I know that in some people's minds you're still cheating them, and that you were actually involved in the fraud. I'm sorry that those people are never going to get their money back, but you and your family shouldn't be the ones taking the blame for something you had no part in, or control over. I've already spoken to a couple of reporters I know and trust about coming to interview you and the family. Of course, you can say no to this if you want to, or you can tell them as much or as little as you feel comfortable with. Myself, I think it'll help you in more ways than one to get the truth of the story out there. You've been as badly affected as anyone in a financial sense, on a personal level ... Well, you don't need me to spell out what you've been through. As I said, it's your decision, but I think you should discuss it with your family and decide whether or not you want to go ahead with it. I hope you do.'

This was so unexpected, and on the face of it, so abhorrent a prospect that she could hardly think of the right way to respond. In the end all she said was, 'Are they interviewing you too? I mean, you are playing a part in it all.'

The lines round his eyes deepened with humour. 'Not unless it becomes relevant,' he replied. 'What matters in all this, to me, is that you and your family don't go on being wrongly judged and vilified by people who ought to know better, but are choosing not to.'

Getting to his feet, he came to her and pulled her up into his arms. 'You're going to be fine,' he told her softly. 'You'll survive this, I know you will, just don't be too proud to let me open a couple of doors.'

Loving the feel of his strength and kindness as it stole into her spirits, picking up her energy and seeming to make it a part of his own, she held on to him, not tightly, but closely enough to inhale the familiar male scent of him as she wished this moment could go on and on.

'Talk to the reporters,' he said, as he walked her to the door, and after touching a kiss gently to her lips, he waited for her to leave and went back inside.

SEAN. Believe me, it wasn't easy saying goodbye to Olivia that day, but it had to be done. The time wasn't right for us, not then, and to be honest I felt pretty certain that it never would be. She had a lot to get over, and it had only just begun. Richmond had left her in a hell of a mess; I was doing my best to make it easier, but getting into a relationship that would be fraught with problems from the start wasn't the way to go. Of course it was tempting, I could feel the bond between us as strongly as I'm sure she could, but my life was – is – on the other side of the world, and that was never going to change.

OLIVIA. I walked away from the apartment that day feeling more upset than I had any right to. I could hardly make my feet move forward, taking me away from him, but somehow they kept going, as if they had the sense of self-preservation that I lacked. I knew, of course, that my emotional chaos was skewing my thoughts and feelings in ways I couldn't even express, but knowing it didn't come close to breaking me out of it. I simply didn't seem capable of understanding what was the right thing to do.

I made myself focus on the children, and what he was prepared to do for them. Of course that made me more emotional than ever, kindness does that, don't you find? And Sean's always had a way with kindness that makes it seem far more impulsive, or casual than it really is. As if it's something that he's doing amongst many other things on his agenda that day, so you shouldn't make a big deal of it.

I drove home in a daze, my vision blurred by tears that didn't fall, they just burned and clogged up my throat and made me forget where I was going. My heart ached and ached, until I dry-sobbed my way to the front door where my father was waiting.

The days that followed were probably the most difficult in all the other difficult days, as grief and loss finally sucked me into the abyss I'd been struggling so hard to avoid. It seemed to make no sense that this should happen when Sean had already given me the light at the end of the tunnel. I guess there's just no fast way of getting there, everything else has to be gone through first, and there was certainly a lot to go through.

I didn't see Sean again before he left; I only knew he'd gone when my mother told me.

'You're kidding me,' Luke protested, when Olivia broke the news that he was able to resume his world travels. 'Who is this guy? I mean I get that he's an old friend of yours, and that he's going out of his way to sort things out at the marina, but why would he do something like this for me when I've hardly even met him?'

'Because that's who he is,' Rena stepped in proudly, 'he does things for other people, and he's happy for you to be in touch with him if you'd like to be, so you can ask him any questions yourself. We've got his email address and mobile number, and he says if you're in Australia or New Zealand at any time you should look him up. He moves between both countries.'

Luke seemed more amazed than ever as he turned back to his mother.

Aware of her mouth twisting as she tried to speak, Olivia said, 'He'll have all the best connections, and water sports are his thing, so ... ' She shrugged, unable to say any more. The fact that he was going away was breaking her heart, and that he could be going to Sean ... It was hard to put into words how that was making her feel, so instead she just tried to feel happy for him and relieved that he would be in safe hands.

Seeming to pick up on her thoughts, Luke's enthusiasm faded as he said, 'It's great what he's doing, and don't get me wrong, I'd love to take him up on it, but it's feeling kind of unfair to just leave you guys while everything's still up in the air ... '

'We can handle it,' his grandfather told him firmly, 'and in some ways it'll be easier for us if we know you're having a good time and not being dragged down by it.'

'Especially if you're with Sean,' Rena added. 'You will go to Australia, won't you?'

Luke shook his head, as though to make pieces fall into the right places. 'I still don't get why he'd do all this for me. I mean, I've got friends, but I can't see them ever doing anything like this, if they were ever in a position to and I doubt they will be. You get what I'm saying?'

Without looking at Olivia, Rena said, 'Sean's a bit more than a friend. Grandpa and I think of him as the son we never had.'

Luke turned to Olivia, his expression seeming to ask how she saw Sean, but he didn't speak the words, he simply came to wrap her in his arms as he said, 'I'll only go if you want me to.'

'Then you'll go,' she whispered.

LUKE. It was Sean who ended up telling me about his relationship with Mum all those years ago. We'd been surfing that day on Bondi Beach with his sons Tom and Noah, and after their mums came to collect them, Sean and I went back to his apartment overlooking Sydney Harbour for a couple of beers on the balcony. I already thought he was totally awesome, but when he started opening up about Mum and how they'd felt about one another back when they were young ... It was pretty mind-blowing, I can tell you. At first it was difficult to handle; I mean, you don't really think of your mum in that way, do you? OK, I get that she's attractive and all that, but seeing her through someone else's eyes, even if it was a long time ago ... To be honest I'd never really given any thought to what might have happened in her life before Dad came along, but she'd obviously had a big relationship, and I couldn't help feeling glad it had been with Sean. The thing I liked best about him while he was telling me about the places they'd been and the things they'd done, was that even though he hadn't married her back then when he probably could have, he sure as hell hadn't fucked up her life, the way Dad had.

I was still trying to get my head round all the Dad stuff, you can't just shrug off something that big, much as you tell yourself you can, and I was starting to realise that it was going to dog me for years. On the other hand, I found talking to Sean and being part of his three families – can you imagine having three! – helped me a lot. We'd go sailing, all of us, or sometimes it would be just me and Sean, or we'd go flying – he had his own plane – and though we rarely dwelt on things, it was really good to know that we could if I wanted to. Best of all was that Mum and my grandparents had someone like him in their corner, even though he was half a world away. I don't think he and Mum were ever in touch while I was there, and the only times Mum and I mentioned him during our FaceTime chats was when I told her what we'd done that day, or if she asked how he was.

It only occurred to me just before I left to go and join some mates in New Zealand that Mum might be wondering if Sean had someone else in his life.

'I'm pretty sure he's a totally free agent,' I told her during our next chat, 'so you ought to get yourself over here.'

'That's what we keep telling her,' Grandma said, coming into the frame and looking as pleased with me as she had the day I'd learned to ride a bike.

Mum said, 'I'm up to my eyes with this hotel project in case you'd forgotten, and before you go any further with your Cupid ambitions, I'm very happy as I am, thank you very much.'

She couldn't see Grandma shaking her head in the background, but it was good enough for me, so off I went to Sean and told him straight out that I thought he ought to invite Mum over. He just laughed and gave me one of the manly-type hugs he was so good at – and up came all the guilty feelings I had about liking him so much when my dad hadn't been dead all that long.

He really is totally awesome though; there's no point trying to deny that.

SASHA. I knew my brother was hero-worshipping Sean Kenyon, it was impossible not to, when he kept going on and on about him. Every time we FaceTimed it was Sean this, or Sean that, and I have to admit I felt a bit envious, because it sounded as though they were having a fantastic time – and I was definitely envious of the way he was starting to seem like part of Sean's family.

But I was having a fantastic time too. I totally loved my London college being a boarder and everything. I'd made so many friends, and I knew I had Sean to thank for it, which is why we were in regular email contact. I wrote first to let him know how much his generosity meant to me, like it had totally changed my life, and when he wrote back he said he wouldn't mind knowing how I was getting on with things from time to time. So I gave him the same updates that I gave Mum and my grandparents. I sent them to Grandma Imogen too, though separately, so she wouldn't see who else was in the loop. I went to hers for lunch or dinner sometimes, because it wasn't far from the college, and I felt I ought to, but I couldn't help feeling different about her after everything that had happened. As far as I could make out she was the only one of us who hadn't lost any money. I mean, I didn't want her to be poor or anything, but it turned out that Dad had seemed to think it was all right to cheat everyone else out of their capital, just not his mother. There might be some kind of honour in that, but I struggled to find it myself.

The phase of hating my dad and feeling glad he was dead lasted quite a long time for me. There were some really dark days during the first year when I felt scared and so creeped out that I kept having nightmares about him morphing into a Tywin Lannister sort of person. In case you don't know that's one of the villains from the first few series of *Game of Thrones* who ordered his son to die and enjoyed it.

I really missed Dad and I was desperate to talk to him, but only so he could tell me that everyone had got everything wrong. I didn't want to know that he was guilty; it just didn't fit with my dad, and I could never stand to think of him being stabbed to death, that just completely screwed me up every time I went near it. Luckily the pastoral carer at college knew about my background so she kept a close eye on me, and because the murder had happened in London my friends didn't connect it with me, and I never confided in anyone because I knew no one would be able to keep it to themselves.

I had proper counselling because Mum insisted, and I guess it helped in the end, because after about a year I realised I didn't feel quite so bitter or scared any more. I've never been able to see Dad in the same light again, though, who could given the circumstances, but Mum and the counsellor kept saying I should just focus on the good times, because in spite of what he'd done he'd really loved me and Luke. That was fine, I suppose in the end he proved it, but the Ana Petrov thing was something I knew I'd never get over, not only for my sake, but for Mum's.

Something I never told Mum, or anyone else, was that I applied for a visitor's order to go and see Ana Petrov.

She'd already received a life sentence by then and had been moved to a women's high security prison in Stafford. I don't know why I wanted to see her, exactly. I suppose I thought I could tell her what I thought of her, or spit in her face, or get her to tell me why she'd done what she had, but I never got the chance. She refused my visit, and the letter I sent expressing my disgust and hatred never received a reply.

It was during the Christmas break of my second year of college that I decided that instead of going home for the holiday I'd fly out to Sydney to join Luke. He'd gone back there after touring New Zealand with his mates, and had ended up staying. He was working for Sean's company at that time, but he was due to start uni in Melbourne in the new year. Can you believe that? He'd only given up his place at Edinburgh to go and study law Down Under. As you can imagine Mum was freaking out about him being so far away, so much so that she and my grandparents suddenly announced that they were going to join us in Sydney. That was the most fantastic Christmas present ever, I can tell you, especially because by then Luke and I were determined to get her and Sean together. We'd decided they were meant for one another, and if they couldn't see it we'd have to make them.

It was the coolest thing ever when Sean hugged Mum hello at the airport, straight out of a movie. I swear to God I've never seen anything so romantic in my life. It was like the rest of us weren't there any more, they just kept looking at one another and looking at one another until in the end Luke told them to go and get a room, which made everyone laugh, and we set off to Sean's amazing apartment on Sydney Harbour.

We had the most brilliant Christmas ever that year, on a private beach just outside Sydney with Sean's ex-wives and four kids, who were all amazing. After the new year he took us travelling around the country to see all the sights, and his daughter, Evie and son, Tom, came too. Evie's only fourteen, but she's already super cool. We got on really well, and her younger sister, Grace, is so naughty and funny, you just have to love her.

At the end of a fortnight we all flew to New Zealand, but I could only stay for a week because I had to fly back in time for college. This meant I didn't get to see the new leisure centre project Sean's company had just won a contract for somewhere near Lake Taupo, but to be honest I wasn't much interested in building sites so I didn't really mind.

Before I left Luke told me that he was going to do his best to persuade Mum to stay, or at least to think about moving over there, so I'd better prepare myself. Actually, I was totally OK with it, or I thought I was until I realised I really didn't like the idea of her being so far away from Grandma and Grandpa because I knew how much they'd miss her. Grandma hadn't really been the same since giving up her dance school, it was like she'd lost her sense of purpose, and although they hadn't been forced to sell their house after all – I think thanks to Sean – I knew Grandpa was still being affected by all the bad stuff Dad had caused. I was worried about how they'd manage if Mum wasn't around, not that they were invalids or anything, but they definitely weren't as on top of things as they'd been before their lives had gone into meltdown.

Anyway, it turned out that I needn't have worried about Mum staying in Oz, because they all, apart from Luke, came back to England at the beginning of February, as scheduled, and so Kesterly was where I went for my Easter break. Mum was still living in the marina apartment that Sean had rented while he was there, and she was really enjoying her job kitting out the new marina hotel with Andee. The thing is, we all knew she'd got close to Sean again while we were Down Under, and I could see that she was missing him, or at least thinking about him a lot. She even admitted it when we had one of our heart-to-hearts one night, and because I love her so much it made me cry. I knew by then that she'd already been torn between him and her parents once in her life, and now it was happening again. Hoping to make things better we opened a bottle of wine and tried FaceTiming Luke so he could cheer us up. As usual he wasn't around, and Mum couldn't be persuaded to try Sean, not while I was there, so we opened another bottle and missed Luke's FaceTime back because we were passed out on the bed.

The first we knew about Sean and Luke coming to Kesterly was when they suddenly turned up in the summer as though everyone was expecting them. Me and Mum definitely weren't – I got a kind of feeling my grandparents were – but it was totally amazing to see them, and the way it lit Mum up was like the best thing ever.

Chapter Nineteen

It was raining again and as the wind tore around the marina, rocking the boats and making the masts clatter and creak like an untuned orchestra, Olivia was picturing Sydney Harbour and how different it was there. Of course it was a busy terminal, unlike Kesterly, and she'd never been in winter, so perhaps their storms were even worse than the one going on outside at the moment. But here they were in the middle of an English summer and they'd had to cancel their plans to go sailing for the fourth day in a row.

Of course she didn't mind really, since it meant that she had Sean all to herself until the others turned up later for dinner. Right at that moment he was sleeping after they'd spent most of the afternoon making love, and as she lay there looking at him she felt her heart swelling with so much tenderness it was hard not to touch him. There was a slight frown between his eyes, and stubble around his jaw that she loved to scrape her fingers along.

His chest and abdomen were fully exposed, as were his thighs, and she wondered how the sheet had managed to catch around his hips to cover the most intimate part of him. She knew if she peeled it away he'd probably wake up, and to find her gazing at his nudity would arouse him all over again. She wanted to, and yet at the same time she felt mesmerised by how peaceful he looked, and by how close she felt to him even though he was lost somewhere inside a dream.

As disloyal as it still made her feel, she was ready to admit to herself now that she had never, not even in their best moments, known this sort of connection with Richmond. She'd even forgotten that it was possible, until she and Sean had discovered it again last Christmas. Everything about him felt right, the way he looked at her, touched her, spoke to her and made it seem so effortless to love her. When she heard his voice her heart swelled with emotion, and when she saw him smile she was so happy she overflowed with it.

It was true she'd felt self-conscious undressing in front of him the first time it had happened, no longer the young girl he'd once known, and being so different now since the mastectomy ... He'd been so tender and understanding and even ironic in the way he'd looked at her that she'd ended up laughing, even as she gasped with desire.

'I don't want you to change a thing,' he'd told her, 'unless you want to,' and she could tell by the way he'd held her and kissed her fading scars that he meant it.

'Mum, you've got to stop looking at him like that,' Sasha had scolded only yesterday, while they were having coffee at the Seafront Café on The Promenade. Sean had just left to go to a meeting over at the new marina, which was rapidly approaching completion, and Olivia was still watching him cross the street to his car.

'Like what?' Olivia cried, astonished.

'Like you're seeing him without any clothes on. It's so obvious and what's worse is he keeps looking at you the same way. It's mega-embarrassing.'

'Not for us it isn't,' Olivia retorted happily.

Laughing, Sasha squeezed her hand and said, 'It's so good to see you like this, and to be out somewhere so public. It's like we don't have to hide ourselves away any more, even though I suppose in some people's eyes we still do.'

Since it was clear that in some cases they were never going to be forgiven for being Bentings, Olivia had decided a while ago that they could no longer let their lives be governed by the few. They'd done everything in their power to make amends; they had no reason now to feel afraid of holding their heads up again. Luckily Fliss who owned the

Seafront Café hadn't invested with Penn Financial, so she'd been thrilled when Olivia had started coming again.

'Are you sure you don't mind about me and Sean?' Olivia asked, searching Sasha's eyes. She already knew the answer, she just wanted to hear it again from her daughter who'd seemed so much more grown up since going away to college.

Keeping hold of her mother's hand, Sasha said, 'You asked me that when we were in Oz last Christmas. I didn't have a problem with it then, and I really don't now.'

Smiling, Olivia said, 'I feel like our roles are reversing, you giving me your approval, me needing it.'

'Well you have it, and you know you have Luke's too. He's really bonded with Sean, in case you hadn't noticed.'

Of course Olivia had noticed, and like just about everything else right now, it made her feel ridiculously emotional when she saw them together. A part of her couldn't stop wishing that Luke was Sean's, but obviously she'd never admit that to Sasha, and much less to Luke. After all, their father was their father for all his sins, and the feelings they had for him, no matter how tortured and confusing, were always going to be bound up in the love that was rightfully his.

'Do you think about Dad very much?' she asked.

Sasha's eyes dimmed for a moment. 'I guess so, and I'm finding it easier to focus more on the good times than I used to. What I can't help wondering now is how you're going to feel when Sean leaves at the end of the month.'

Olivia's heart flipped and tightened with the dread of it. 'Devastated,' she admitted, 'but we're going to New Zealand for Christmas, remember? I'll see him again then.'

He had a home in Hawkes Bay and another on the Bay of Islands, so the plan was for both families, hers and his, to sail from one location to the other, stopping en route to celebrate Christmas with friends in Tauranga. They were going to be away for six entire weeks – four in Sasha's case – before they had to return to Australia and England. She was looking forward to it, of course, but the time in between was going to be hard, when she knew already how much she was going to miss him.

Still, she was determined to focus on the happiness they gave one another while they were together, and even if they were taking a long-distance relationship to extremes, it was theirs and they loved it.

'What about you?' she asked Sasha softly. 'How's your love life these days?'

Sasha shrugged. 'Pretty non-existent, but I'm OK with that.'

Surprised, considering what a beautiful young woman she was growing into, Olivia said, 'Are you sure there's no one?'

'Yes, perfectly sure. I promise if there was I'd tell you. I mean, it's not as though I never meet anyone, and sometimes they're kind of cute, but there's never been anyone I've wanted to get serious with.'

'So you're still ... a virgin?'

Sasha's eyes widened in mock astonishment. 'You're my mother, you're not supposed to ask questions like that.'

Olivia smiled as she waited.

'OK, yes I am,' Sasha finally admitted, 'but so are lots of my friends. They're not like the girls I knew here, who were always in such a hurry to give it away.'

More than pleased to hear that, Olivia said, 'Did you ever hear from Parker again?'

As Sasha's eyes closed she gave a groan of dismay. 'I came so close to making a fool of myself with him,' she sighed. 'Thank God it didn't happen is all I can say, because I never really liked him that much. I mean, I thought I did at the time, obviously, but now I know it was me not being able to get things straight in my head.'

Proud of how mature she was sounding, Olivia said, 'And they're straight now?'

Sasha's smile was mischievous. 'If I say I want to feel the same way about someone for my first time as you did for yours, does that make me sound straight?'

Holding her gaze, Olivia said, 'You do realise who that was, don't you?'

'Of course I do,' Sasha replied.

Now, watching Sean's eyes come slowly open, Olivia waited for them to find her, and smiled at the way they seemed to deepen in colour and humour as he registered where he was and who he was with. 'Hey you,' he said softly.

As his hand came to her face she turned her mouth to his palm and kissed it.

He watched her for a while, then pulled her closer so they could feel the full length of their bodies entwining. They began making love again slowly, almost sleepily, joining together in a way that was as fulfilling as it was erotic. She wondered if she could ever get enough of his body, the hardness of his limbs, the scent of maleness, the feel of his heart beating against hers. He seemed to know each part of her in a way she didn't even know it herself. He took all of her, holding her, kissing her, joining them as tightly as it was possible for two people to be as he gave every-thing of himself.

They weren't ready to let go when the entryphone buzzer sounded, alerting them to the others' arrival, and they groaned with disappointment as they reluctantly rolled apart.

'They're going to know what we've been doing,' Olivia stated as they got up from the bed. 'Sasha never misses a thing.'

He was checking the time. 'It's probably not them,' he told her. 'I've invited some other people over for drinks.'

Curious she waited for him to elaborate.

Coming to take her in his arms, he said, 'Would you agree that the reporters I suggested you talk to did a good job of getting your story across last year?'

Surprised that he was mentioning them now when they'd completed their interviews so long ago, she nodded. It was true, the centre-spread article in both a national and a local paper had made life a little easier for her and her parents; she'd even had apolo-gies from some friends and neighbours for having treated her so badly.

'Well, the reporters are here again,' he told her, 'because they want to talk to you about turning all the material they have into a full magazine feature, or even a book.'

Olivia's eyes widened in amazement. 'Would anyone really be interested in reading it?' she asked doubtfully.

'I guess that depends on how well they write it, but one thing's for certain, we really ought to have some clothes on by the time we let them in.'

Chapter Twenty

ANA. Welcome to my new dwelling. It's larger than any place I've lived before, but it has none of the elegance or comforts, and no access at all to the front door. The grounds are fenced – I'm used to that, my parents were always big on fences or walls, but theirs were swagged in foliage, flowering hedgerows and with gates that opened and closed at the touch of a button. My clothes are drab and ill-fitting; I have no phone of my own, and access to the shared device in the public area is limited and never private.

I take showers with other women, if you can call them that. For the most part they are a species of humanity that feels quite separate from the one I inhabit. Sagging, tattooed flesh that even goosebumps seem to shrink from. Greasy, sparse hair that clings to scabby scalps like seaweed to porous rocks; coarse voices that swear and cajole, threaten and screech in diabolical tirades of anger and grief. The smells are so sour, so utterly putrid and gut-wrenching that I can feel them staining my lungs like a disease. I remain as aloof as my privately paid warders and my centred mind will allow. I am not a part of this sad and repulsive community. I keep myself apart both mentally and spiritually, physically too as much as I can. I speak only when I have to and eat almost nothing. I will not serve my full sentence. This has already been decided by powers beyond those that run this godforsaken bedlam. A token punishment for a crime that was ... What was it? How shall I describe it to you when I really don't believe it to be anyone's business but mine?

Everyone wants to know what happened the day Richmond died, what single thing was said, or what action was taken to make me reach for the knife. It was the knife I'd taken from Olivia's kitchen. You see how I think of it as Olivia's, both the knife and the kitchen. Not Richmond's. It all belonged to her.

I understood almost from the start that he'd never find the backbone to leave her and his children in spite of what he said, and what it would cost him to stay. Not that we discussed it at the beginning; disappearing and starting a new life was a subject that didn't arise until much later. By then he'd come to realise just how ... committed? beholden? indebted? he was to me – and others – for introducing him to a select network of private capitalists with a stream of funds to invest. They could make him rich beyond his wildest dreams, and though we could see that he was nervous, he was excited, even electrified by the prospect.

You assume the object of the exercise was to legitimise the financial proceeds of crimes undisclosed, committed by individuals unnamed. You are welcome to your assumptions. I have no more to say about them.

Returning to the day Richmond died: you assume, still, that it was me who stabbed him. I find that amusing, and I want to leave you with that assumption, riddled as it is in doubt, because you will always wonder, was it me, or was someone else there that day?

He didn't have to tell me he'd changed his mind about going with me, as I've already intimated I was expecting it, and had even prepared for it. I knew exactly where to find Olivia's knife that day in the flat – did I tell you that I considered using one of her knives to kill her husband to be a rather ironic touch? I believe it even cast her under suspicion for a while. That was satisfying.

It was a great surprise to Richmond to realise that he wasn't going to leave the apartment alive that day, and I keep wondering why. He knew very well that he could assist in investigations far beyond those happening at Penn Financial; that if he disclosed details of events leading to the incrimination of much bigger fish he would earn himself a much lighter sentence. He gave fervent assurances that he never would, but no one was going to run the risk of him changing his mind. So this is why I say I don't understand why he was surprised when he realised he was going to be stopped. But putting that aside, he knew very well that I'd never let Olivia win. I might no longer have wanted him for myself, but I wasn't going to let her have him either.

There really was only one way out for him.

My arrest at Charles de Gaulle airport wouldn't have happened if someone hadn't alerted the authorities to the time of my flight and the name I was travelling under. I understood straight away that I had become the victim of a twist in the game that had grown even bigger and deadlier than I had realised. Overnight our friends had turned into enemies, and just as quickly our enemies were friends.

Our world isn't like yours. We don't think like you, we don't react like you and we certainly don't live like you. Don't try to understand us; we're on a different level, so you'll never succeed.

My only regret is that I haven't persuaded Olivia to visit me. I want to look into her eyes when I tell her about Richmond, how willingly he betrayed her, and how he died. She deserves the details. She should be clear about what kind of man he was, and I want her to know …

Jennifer Hadley stopped the tape and looked across the desk at her partner, Tom Walker. As journalists and now biographers, they'd already determined not to be used in the mind games Ana Petrov was trying to inflict on Olivia Benting. This was far enough. The rest of the interview with Ana Petrov, showing her to be as vindictive as she was vengeful and sad, would be destroyed. No one, least of all Olivia, needed to read the lies and perversions of truths that Ana had concocted to try and bond herself to a woman she clearly hated as much as she envied and admired. The time had come for Ana to realise she had no more power. The game was up; she had not won. She was a loser in so many more ways than one.

Chapter Twenty-One

Olivia sighed in a gentle, yet slightly turbulent way as she looked up from the book she was reading and let her head fall against the sofa back. Memories were swirling around her like a breeze drifting in from a far-off world, a breeze that sometimes gusted, and at other times strengthened, wrenching at all it touched as though to punish, or distort, or uproot it.

Reliving that time of her life hadn't been easy, or welcome. She wanted nothing more than to put it all behind her now, even to pretend that most of it hadn't happened, and yet she was aware that without it she wouldn't be where she was today. The stepping stones, obstacles, tragedies and triumphs of life came in so many different guises and presented so many unexpected challenges to the heart and to the character of a person that it was often impossible to know at the time what good, or ill, would come from them.

She thought of Richmond and Sean, her parents and her children, her friends and the single most powerful enemy she'd ever made without even trying. She knew this was how Ana Petrov continued to consider her, that the need to punish and to control, poison, the life of a woman she barely knew was what kept Ana Petrov going.

This was why Olivia had resolved never to engage with her. It was true she'd felt tempted at times – meeting Ana Petrov's eyes from the visitor's side of a prison meeting-room table was an experience she might enjoy. It could offer some small satisfaction to gloat at Ana's miscalculation, to take her down with a few well-chosen words, but she knew that Ana would view the very fact that she'd come as a victory.

Staying away was Olivia's victory. She wasn't going to afford Ana the chance to plant her lies and distortions; she'd give her no opportunity to turn Richmond into a man whose failings were as deliberately dark and destructive as Ana's own. Ana Petrov wasn't going to have the chance to create a single shred of doubt where there needed to be none. She could no longer even send letters; a court-issued restraining order meant that anything addressed to Olivia was destroyed before it even left the prison.

So Ana Petrov was left to her frustrations and impotence, to whatever raging delusions and bizarre senses of entitlement that controlled her, for it still didn't seem enough for her to know that she'd succeeded in ending Richmond's marriage.

In that respect, she had won.

Olivia knew that Ana would probably see this book and think she'd won again, until she read it.

Feeling herself becoming submerged by the past, Olivia looked down at the closing words, knowing that in them she would find her way back to the present . . .

The authors of this book, Jennifer Hadley and Tom Walker, would like to thank everyone involved for speaking to us so freely and frankly about the events that in some cases so tragically affected their lives. When we were first approached by Sean Kenyon to put the family's side of the story across we imagined it would achieve at least one centre spread, and maybe a few more associated articles as further events unfolded. Although we were right about that, we knew early on that there was so much more to tell, and that is why we returned to Kesterly to discuss putting everything into a book.

For the most part we have used the extensive interviews we conducted to inform the content and structure of events as they unfolded, occasionally calling upon dramatic licence to give voice to those who were unable or unwilling to speak to us. This device is employed, in particular, in the scenes where Richmond Benting is at his office receiving the news from Cooper Jarrett that Mace had turned down their appeal for a rescue package. It's followed by Ana Petrov's arrival when he hands over the key to his house. Much later at his lawyer's office we imagine what is in his mind during the moments before he signs his statement of guilt.

You will see that we have also, in places, used extracts from the interviews we were able to carry out to allow friends and family to speak for Richmond as well as for themselves.

We want to stress that, before going to print, everything was approved by Olivia Benting and her lawyers.

We had hoped that Ana Petrov could be persuaded to add to the two interviews we conducted with her, the first taking place before her sentence, some of which is to be found early in the book. The second was at the prison where she is serving her life sentence, but since then she's refused to see us again. The conclusions we draw from that are probably the same as the reader's – she was strongly advised to stop speaking about her involvement in certain events touched upon in these pages.

In spite of her suggestion that someone else was at the flat the day Richmond Benting was murdered, it is our firm belief that she killed him. All the evidence confirms this, and we're certain that her attempt to cast doubt on it was another attempt to engage with Olivia Benting. We are assured by the authorities that there is no arrangement for her to be released at any time prior to a parole board recommendation. This hearing is not set to take place until she has served ten years of her sentence, and at the time of going to press she remains incarcerated at HMP Drake Hall.

We invited Imogen Benting to tell us about her son, and to give us her version of events, but she repeatedly declined. Olivia's parents, Rena and David Penn, also chose not to be interviewed, but they were tireless in their assistance with the articles and the book, as were Andee Lawrence and Graeme Ogilvy.

Many lives have been changed since Richmond Benting was persuaded to embark upon the marina expansion project, either through lost jobs and investments, or because, like Olivia Benting and her family, they were caught up in a world they knew nothing about until it was too late. To some it might seem a small story, but we would say that many stories seem small unless they're involving you. We didn't feel that Olivia and her children deserved to become a mere footnote to a much larger NCA investigation that continues to this day

As Olivia closed the book she was aware of the past finally rolling back over a far horizon to settle in its rightful place, out of sight, if never entirely out of mind. She'd known before she started that the read would be difficult, for this was the second time she'd braved it, and though the memories it had stirred up of Ana were as unwelcome as they were unsettling, it was the ones of Richmond that were the hardest to bear, and the last to let go. The dramatic licence the authors had used to give him a voice had affected her deeply both times, but she hadn't taken issue with it in the first place and nor would she now.

Of course, no one would ever be able to say for certain what Richmond had thought about, or how he'd really felt during that terrible period of his life, but the way they'd portrayed him as conflicted, riddled with guilt and fear, and with a conscience that was absent as often as it was present, had rung as true to her as if they'd somehow managed to speak to him. They'd allowed the world at large to believe that though he was a man of many flaws who'd compounded his mistakes by making more, at heart he was someone who'd loved his family, and who, in his convoluted and yes, arrogant, way, had believed he could protect them from the kinds of influences that were too corrupt and far-reaching for any normal man to defeat.

Putting the book down, Olivia inhaled deeply as she felt the comfort of the present continuing to claim her. In spite of all that had happened during these past two years, how much her and the children's lives had changed, there were still times when she found it hard to accept that Richmond was really gone. It was as though he was somewhere else in the world living out another existence, just as he'd planned. It could be that he'd come back unexpectedly one day eager to see them, and ready to explain away his absence with some fantastical story that wouldn't make any sense. Of course she knew he wouldn't. She still missed him, and she was glad of it, because if she didn't it would feel as though he hadn't mattered, and for her and the children that would never be true.

Getting to her feet she walked across the apartment and went to stand on the balcony, gazing first at the crowded moorings below and then on out to sea, where small wisps of cloud were floating lazily across the horizon. For some reason, after reading the book, it seemed like a different Kesterly this evening, one that was distant in spite of being right there. She turned her head to take in the long crescent of the bay sweeping over to the opposite headland; the muddied stretch of sand, the jumble of Victorian hotels and guest houses. It was the same coastal town that she'd grown up in, where her parents had built their businesses, where she'd first met Sean and where she and Richmond had settled to begin a new phase of their lives.

As fragmented and lengthy as it might be, theirs was just one small story in amongst the thousands of others that had played out in every part of the town over the years. It was as impossible to guess at the number of those stories as it was to know all their details. The hundreds of windows she could see winking pale pink reflections in the early evening sunset had witnessed as much joy as sadness, had stood firm in the might of storms and basked benignly in summer suns. The rooms, the alleyways, inner courtyards and garden squares were as much a part of the place as the dramas they'd seen unfold. The whole town, as her father had once put it, was the keeper of more secrets than the waves that rolled on to the shore.

For a fleeting moment she found herself thinking of Gil and Gina, the owner of The Salon, and the mystery of why two people who loved each other had parted. She thought of Andee's younger sister, who'd disappeared at the age of fourteen and had never been found. And then she thought of Richmond's secrets, and what it had cost him to keep them.

A flurry of seagulls swooped away from the nearby cliffs like scraps of paper scattering in the wind, and as they resettled on the yacht masts and moorings below, she found her mind turning back to the book.

What she'd liked most about it, she decided, apart from her children's courage in speaking out so honestly, was the writers' insistence that she and her family should not become mere addenda to Ana's story. Instead they'd achieved the opposite, for which she'd always feel grateful, since she recognised how tempting it must have been to set the rich and spoiled, some would say sociopathic, daughter of a billionaire businessman with connections to organised crime at the centre of events.

She could say that it was time now for them all to move on, but Luke and Sasha had done that a while ago. Having completed his first year at Melbourne Law School in a headrush of glory – quite literally, for he'd taken part in the Americas Cup halfway through – Luke was now fully submerged in his second year of studies. Sasha had texted earlier that week from somewhere in Argentina, where she was currently enjoying her gap year with friends before taking up a place at Auckland University next February to study biomedical science. Olivia really hadn't seen that one coming, but if she'd learned anything these past few years it was never to assume she could see anything coming.

As for her parents, they were now in New Zealand, having sold their beloved house here in Kesterly and taken the architect's plans with them to recreate the very same homestead in Hawkes Bay. Their acre of hilltop with a view out to sea was adjacent to a much larger plot that Sean had bought a few years ago, with a vague intention of developing in some way. This mini estate comprised a small complex of neglected stables, a vineyard gone mostly to weed, and a sorry-looking mansion just waiting for Olivia to transform back to its turn-of-the-century magnificence. When she'd asked why he'd bought it in the first place, he'd said that although he might not know much about horses or wine apart from being able to ride the former and drink the latter, he'd just got a feeling for the place, and maybe now he understood why. 'And look at it this way,' he'd added with one of his irresistible twinkles, 'having a second home on the North Island of NZ is a damned sight easier than having one in Kesterly-on-Sea.'

Hearing the door of the apartment open and close, Olivia stayed where she was, waiting for him to come and join her. When he did she felt his arms go round her, and it was as though the entirety of everything that mattered most in her life now was enveloping her. His lips brushed her neck and she leaned back against him, inhaling the scent of sea air, and the musky maleness that was uniquely him. In some ways it was as though they were young again, picking up where they'd left off, starting the life they might have had if fate hadn't had other plans.

'Did everything go OK?' she asked, as they stood quietly gazing out at the rapidly changing colours of the sky.

'Everything's sorted,' he confirmed. 'The new marina's being signed off next week so the remainder of our guys will be heading back to London; all the apartments are sold subject to contract, and the hotel has just started taking bookings for the spring.'

There was so much she could have said about that, such as how proud she and Andee were of the quiet elegance and comfort they'd brought to their part in the project, how mixed her emotions were when she recalled how it had all begun, how attached she would probably always feel to it, no matter where she was in the world. In the end she let her feelings go unspoken, and asked if he'd seen Graeme while he was out.

'Yes,' he replied, drawing her in close, 'and he confirmed that he and Andee will drive us to the airport tomorrow. So now tell me, what did you think of the book after reading it again?'

'They did a great job,' she said.

He waited, clearly knowing there was more.

'I guess it's just made me feel sad and nostalgic, and very lucky to be where I am now.'

Turning her to him, he searched her eyes with his as though they could find answers she wasn't willing to speak. 'It's OK to talk about Richmond if you want to,' he said softly.

She tried to smile, loving that he read her so easily, and how willing he was to embrace the ghosts rather than pretend they didn't exist. 'I'm not sure that I do,' she replied, 'but I can't help thinking about him and wishing that we, you and I, had got to where we are now in a different way.'

'I know,' he murmured, pulling her to him. 'I wish it too, but I guess what's important is to accept that we can't change what happened, and to know that neither of us was responsible.'

She nodded slowly, knowing he was right, and thinking of how he'd gone to Richmond that day ready to help him when no one else would. It wouldn't have changed what happened after he'd left, but she still wished Richmond had realised Sean was far more of a friend than he was an enemy. From there she wondered where she'd be now if Richmond had lived. He would almost certainly be in prison, and knowing Sean he'd be in contact with him updating him on progress at the marina, trying to keep up his morale by including him. The big question in her mind was, would she and Sean have fallen for each other all over again? Right now it was hard to imagine it not happening, but if it had she knew her conscience would have found it very hard to cope with while Richmond was in such a low and disadvantaged state. Even now she could feel it wrenching at her happiness as if to remind her that it had come at the cost of her husband's life.

As she gazed up into Sean's knowing blue eyes and considered all that he'd done for her and her